W9-CCR-829

ALBATROSS

Also by Evelyn Anthony

VALENTINA
THE FRENCH BRIDE
CLANDARA
CHARLES THE KING
ALL THE QUEEN'S MEN
VICTORIA AND ALBERT
ANNE BOLEYN
FAR FLIES THE EAGLE
ROYAL INTRIGUE
REBEL PRINCESS
THE RENDEZVOUS
THE CARDINAL AND THE QUEEN
THE LEGEND
THE ASSASSIN
THE TAMARIND SEED
THE POELLENBERG INHERITANCE
STRANGER AT THE GATES
MISSION TO MALASPIGA
THE PERSIAN PRICE
THE SILVER FALCON
THE RETURN
THE JANUS IMPERATIVE
THE DEFECTOR
THE AVENUE OF THE DEAD

ALBATROSS

by

Evelyn Anthony

G. P. PUTNAM'S SONS   NEW YORK

First American Edition 1983

Library of Congress Cataloging in Publication Data

Anthony, Evelyn.
Albatross.

I. Title.
PR6069.T428A78 1983 823'.914 82-20456
ISBN 0-399-12773-9

Printed in the United States of America

To Isidore and Blanche
with fond love

CHAPTER 1

THE CORRIDOR on the upper floor was painted a cheerful yellow. One of the doors leading off it was half open and Davina saw bright curtains and a table with a house plant. But nothing could disguise the pervasive prison smell. It caught at the back of her throat as soon as she walked through the small private entrance, leading to the elevator and the governor's office. She recognized the acrid taint of human sweat and excrement and disinfectant. The smell of prisons all over the world. The smell of Lubyanka The smell of Wormwood Scrubs. The prison officer walking beside her paused before a door marked "Governor's Office," knocked, and waited. She heard a voice say "Come," and wondered as ever why people dropped the "in." It was no longer an invitation.

He was a man of medium height, graying hair, and a pair of heavy-rimmed spectacles with thick lenses that made it difficult to read his eyes. They shook hands; he pulled out one of his modern chairs for her, offered her a cigarette, suggested a cup of coffee. Davina refused both. For a moment or two they sized each other up across his desk. It was a hard face, narrow-jawed, with a surprisingly muscular neck above the neat regimental tie.

"Well, Miss Graham," he said. "You'll find quite a change in him, I expect."

"Yes," she said. "It's nearly six years."

"He was pretty flabby when he came to us. Gone to seed physically. He's slimmed down quite a bit and he takes plenty of exercise. Likes his handicrafts; he made a damned good cigar box for me for Christmas."

She looked into the smiling face and said nothing. Peter Harrington. Handicrafts. Jesus God, she said to herself. What am I going to find . . . ?

"It's difficult sometimes," the brisk voice went on, "to think of him as a traitor. We've had several of them here, as you know. Pleasant men, on the whole. Amenable to the rules, educated people you could make contact with."

"They would be," Davina said. "Peter's hallmark was charm. Does he still have it?"

There was a second's pause before the answer. "Yes. Yes, I suppose you could call it that. He's popular with the staff. Gets on well with the other occupants of the section. He was quite emotional when he heard about your visit."

She looked at him and asked quietly, "Tears?"

"Not quite." He hadn't liked that question or the tone of voice.

He would be emotional, Davina thought. He knows why I've come, the bastard. He's been waiting for this for six years.

"When can I see him?"

He pressed a button on his internal phone and spoke into the set. "Send Harrington up right away."

"I would like to emphasize that I don't approve of your seeing him alone, Miss Graham."

He was standing, and Davina got up. "I appreciate that, Governor. But I think my office cleared that up with you. There's no danger, I can promise you. And there's no way anybody can listen to what I have to say."

"There'll be a man on duty outside my door," he said. "It will be unlocked. He'll come in when you call."

"Thank you," she said. Peter Harrington; she wished the governor would go out, leave her alone for a moment before the encounter. She had a ghastly feeling that he would introduce them and she would have to shake hands.

Harrington, the old friend, the colleague who had sold out his country for a Swiss bank account. The easygoing joker who quipped half-seriously about being in love with her, and delivered her to the KGB.

He had changed so much that for a moment she really didn't recognize him. He had lost a lot of his hair; that was the first surprise. Balding, very gray, and certainly slimmed down. He looked twenty years older.

"Hello, Davy. Long time no see." The voice was the same. The whiskey-and-tobacco voice; and the eyes were watchful, mocking, with hatred gleaming like a stone under water.

"I'll leave you," the governor said. The door closed.

"Sit down, Peter. How are you?"

He crossed his long legs and his foot swung. He was back in focus now. Older, thinner, marked by the years of his sentence, but still Peter Harrington. It was a very long sentence indeed. There were twenty-four more years of it to run.

"I'm fine, thanks. Did you bring any cigarettes?"

She gave him a packet, took one, lit it for him and then her own. She put the silver lighter back in her bag.

"That's nice," he remarked. "Present?"

"Last Christmas."

"Not from Ivan the Terrible, then?"

She didn't flinch. She gave him a look like an icicle. "No. You know he's dead."

"I did hear something," he murmured. "New boyfriend, then? Married?"

"No."

"Engaged?"

She dropped her bag on the floor and said, "Shut up, Peter. Do you want to talk or do you want to go back downstairs? I haven't any time to waste on you."

"Then why are you here? You're not visiting an old friend, not after six bloody years."

"I'm here," she said, "to do a deal."

"Ah." He let the sound out slowly, and he smiled. "I wondered if it might be something like that. A parole, a pardon even?"

"That's the last thing we talk about," Davina answered.

"It's the first," he said softly. "Or we don't talk."

"All right." She got up, hooked her bag over her shoulder. He was on his feet at the same moment, his face twisted with alarm.

"For Christ's sake—give me a chance, Davy. . . ."

"The same chance as you gave me?" she asked him.

He gestured wildly, throwing his arms out. "You can't still hold that against me—all's fair in our bloody game, you know that!"

"Keep your voice down, or the warder will come in. Sit down and shut up and listen, if you want me to stay."

She saw the droop of his shoulders and the way his body sagged into the hard little chair.

"What's the deal?" he said flatly.

"I want information. I want you to search your memory and give me some answers."

"I was three weeks under interrogation," he said sullenly. "I told Kidson everything I knew. He promised a light sentence. Fat bloody good that did me."

"You didn't tell him everything," Davina countered. "Nobody ever does. You kept something back, didn't you, just in case? Just in case you needed it—like now?"

"I can't remember," he said. "It's a long time ago. Suppose you tell me what the problem is?"

The decision had been left to Davina. "This is your operation," Humphrey Grant had said. "You're on your own. No instructions, no backup. There can't be, once you start. . . ."

The decision was hers, and she made it then. There wasn't time to play games with Peter Harrington or anyone else.

"We've got a traitor in the office," she said. "And he's right at the top. What do you know about it?"

"You know, John, I'm rather looking forward to retirement."

John Kidson glanced at his chief and shook his head. "I don't believe it for a minute."

"Oh, but I am," Brigadier Sir James White protested. He raised a hand and one of the club waiters moved toward them.

"Coffee? Brandy? Ah, two Armagnacs and a pot of black coffee, and my guest would like a cigar."

Kidson didn't show his surprise. The brigadier was not known for his extravagance when entertaining members of his staff to lunch. As if his thoughts had been spoken, James White said, "I feel this is rather a red-letter day, my dear chap. It's exactly eighteen years to the day that I joined the Service. I was thinking about it this morning on my way to the office. What an exciting time it's been!"

"It certainly has," Kidson reflected. "We were in a real mess when you took on the job."

"A bit of a mess, perhaps. Morale was very low. So were the funds. The Service hadn't been doing too well, and when Osborn resigned, there was a lot of dust to sweep under the rug. I remember my wife saying, 'James, it won't suit you at all. You'll tread on the politicians' toes.' She knows me too well, that's the trouble." He laughed lightly. "You never knew Osborn, did you, John?"

"I was a very junior civil servant," Kidson said. "But I heard rumors about him, of course."

"Yes, there was a lot of talk. He had unfortunate connections at Cambridge. And then his marriage broke up. The real reason was covered up, but it didn't stop the talk. Especially when our friend Philby fled the coop and came up smiling in Moscow."

Kidson pierced and lit the cigar. "Do you think he was bent, Chief?"

"Sexually, yes, and that's always a danger. But politically . . ." James White paused, his head a little on one side. The Armagnac in the glass was cradled and warmed by his cupped hands. "I don't know, John. And we'll never know now. It's a long time ago, and these things are best left undisturbed. How's the cigar?"

"Fine, thank you."

"I've got another eight or nine months if I stick to the official retirement date," the brigadier said. He sipped a little brandy. "I've got to think about my successor, John."

"I don't see why," Kidson answered. "Frankly, Chief, there's no reason for you to step down. And besides, there's nobody good enough to take your place."

The brigadier rewarded him with his avuncular smile. "That's very flattering, but not strictly true. I shall be sixty-five and entitled to a little peace and quiet. Time to cultivate my garden, if you like."

"I'm afraid I don't see you as Candide. You'll perish of boredom."

"Humphrey thinks it'll be him," James White went on. "He's never said anything, but he knows the time is coming. He's been deputy for too many years. He wants to step into the spotlight." Again he chuckled. "Not a good way of describing my particular role—what do you think of him, John? Would he do the job?"

John Kidson didn't answer for some moments. James White waited while he considered, and under the thick white brows his pale eyes watched the younger man as if he were examining an insect under a microscope. If you want to find out about a man's ambitions, ask his opinion of another man's promotion. The brigadier loved making up and collecting dictums of human behavior. One day he might publish a little book. Handbook for a spy. He liked the title. It appealed to his sense of humor.

Kidson looked at him. "I don't think that's a fair question. I've worked too closely with Humphrey to be able to give an objective opinion."

Clever, James White observed. He's damned him without saying a word. "I can give one, though," he said aloud. "And I've been with him longer than anybody. He's a marvelous administrator, brilliantly intelligent, and apart from his unhappy resemblance to Robespierre, he *is* incorruptible. But has he that flair for leadership? I'm not boasting, my dear chap, when I say that this has been my real contribution to the job. Getting other people to do the work for me."

"I'd rate it higher than that, Chief." Kidson smiled.

James White poured them both coffee. "Black, no sugar? Then, of course, there's yourself, John."

John Kidson said quietly, "Yes, I suppose I'm in the running. But Humphrey won't take it. He'll resign, and I wouldn't blame him."

"I don't agree," the brigadier countered. "He'll sulk, and you could have a difficult year to settle in, but he's essentially loyal to the Service. He'd work with you. And then, of course, you'd work with him, wouldn't you?"

"You know I would," Kidson answered.

James White put down the brandy glass and leaned a little toward him. "There is one other alternative I've been considering for some time. It might be possible to tempt Davina back."

This time Kidson was caught unprepared. "To take over from you? Good God!"

"You don't like the idea?"

"I don't like or dislike it. It's just a shock, that's all. She's finished with the Service for good. She's set up in a flat with Colin Lomax, and she's got a job in an advertising agency. I think you can forget her, Chief."

"Pity," White murmured. "I can't see her wasting her time selling deodorants or dog food or whatever."

He saw Kidson stiffen. "It's a two-hundred-million-a-year business," he said. "American-owned. There's practically nothing we use that they don't help to promote."

"That's right," he answered amiably. "Arlington Agency, isn't it? I know the chairman, as a matter of fact. Very impressive chap. Tony Walden. I should think he keeps Davina pretty busy. But she must find it rather tame."

"If you knew all about it, Chief," John Kidson said quietly, "why didn't you say so at the start?"

"Because I thought you might have some fresh news about her. Amazing how Colin recovered, isn't it? Wonderful what the doctors can do these days. He was only expected to last for a few months."

"Apparently the operation's been a complete success." Kidson followed the change of direction. "It'll take time before he's completely back on his feet, though."

"I'm surprised he and Davina haven't got married," White remarked.

"So am I," Kidson said. "But Charlie says they're better as they are, and she's annoyingly good at summing up that sort of situation."

"She'd know her sister better than you or I in that context," James White said. "It would be a pity for Davina to get married and sink into some domestic role. A terrible waste. Rather like working in advertising. Good Lord, it's nearly three! I'll get the bill."

John Kidson walked back to his office, leaving the brigadier to set off in his car. It was a fine day, and St. James's Park was full of tourists and children wandering along beside the lake feeding the ducks. It was a walk that Kidson had loved since he was a child; like the children in their jeans and sneakers, he too had stood by the water's edge and proffered bits of stale bread. Then, as now, the bolder ducks had waddled forward and snatched the crusts, and a cohort of chirping sparrows had surrounded the park benches, where office workers ate their sandwiches during the lunch hour. They had gone back to their desks; weary tourists rested in their place; young couples, arms linked around each other, strolled along the paths, and in the distance the towers and roofline of Whitehall gleamed like a mirage through the trees.

James White was due to retire. Part of Kidson believed it, the part that wanted to succeed, that quickened in excitement at the chance of heading the Secret Intelligence Service. But his experience of James White enjoined caution. Not just caution but positive disbelief. Nothing was as it seemed with the man who had controlled British intelligence for nearly twenty years. At times, he played with his own people as if they were opponents; or "puppets" was a better word. He loved to manipulate, to jerk the string without warning and see a subordinate dance. He hadn't taken Kidson out to lunch to talk about his successor. The appointment would be made by the Prime Minister when the time came, and White's recommendation would decide it. He hadn't wanted Kidson's opinion of either his own or Humphrey Grant's ability for the role.

He wanted to find out something about Kidson's sister-in-law, Davina Graham. That was the purpose of the lunch at the Guards Club. Kidson crossed the bridge that spanned the lake. She had left the Service. She was living with Colin Lomax and working in a highly paid, demanding job. A waste, James White had said. He wanted her back; she had defied him and turned her face against her old profession and her old colleagues. She had avoided John, meeting her sister Charlie for an occasional lunch, deliberately putting up barriers between herself and anyone connected with her past. Kidson had been puzzled, a little resentful, and then shrugged his feelings aside. Davina was difficult. His parents-in-law had implied it, without actually saying anything critical about their eldest daughter. Unlike Charlie, his wife. She had never needed to assert herself, or resort to mild aggression even. Her beauty and her charm secured her everything she wanted, and always would. After nearly six years of marriage, Kidson was more passionately in love with her than ever. He crossed over Birdcage Walk and turned up the unobtrusive side street that led to his office.

* * *

"He was in place when I changed sides," Peter Harrington said. Davina had a portable tape recorder on the table between them. It made a tiny whir, like a butterfly beating against a windowpane.

"How do you know?"

"Because my contact in West Germany let something slip," he said. He stroked his thin hair with one hand, his eyes half-closed in concentration. "I was playing hard to get—putting the price up and talking about my conscience and all that crap—isn't it great to talk to someone like you, Davy, who understands what it's all about. There's a bloody person in here that keeps trying to get me to pray with him. Keeps saying he knows why I did it and I mustn't go on blaming myself. Jesus Christ, the only thing I blame myself for is getting caught!"

"Stick to the point," Davina said. "Get back to the contact in West Germany. What exactly did he say?"

"Let me think," he insisted. "Let me get it right. I said, 'I don't like your side'—that's it, I remember now. He was a big fat bastard, very persuasive. 'You don't know anything about it. You think you're being loyal to your country by living on a dirty little salary while others are selling out and getting rich. You talk about "sides" as if it were a football match. Grow up, Mr. Harrington.' That's what he said. 'Others are selling out and getting rich.' I picked him up on it, all indignant. I wanted to *know*, Davy, if he had someone in mind or if it was just a comment made to encourage me. I called him a liar. I said nobody in the Service would last five minutes if they were playing that game. I said I wouldn't either. I gave him a come-on, and he took it. 'Your Service is the best friend we have. That's why you've nothing to worry about. Just do what we want, and watch yourself get rich.' I was certain then that he meant SIS had been penetrated good and proper." He flattened his sparse hair again and shrugged. "I joined, as you know."

"And you didn't think about it again? You didn't try to find out whether it was one man or a general penetration on several levels?"

"I didn't want to know," he said flatly. "I got on with my end of it. But all the time I had the feeling that there was some kind of backup behind me."

Davina changed the tape. Harrington helped himself to another of her cigarettes and lit it with the lighter she had left on the table.

Lomax had given it to her. She hated seeing it in Harrington's hand.

"When was the first time you had that feeling?"

He puffed out smoke and inhaled again greedily. "Difficult to say. In the States mostly. I felt I was being moved around, like a bloody pawn on a chess board. But I wasn't sure by which side. I had two contacts, remember? One Rumanian, one East German."

Davina nodded. She remembered only too well. Meeting him in the corridor when she came up to make her weekly report on the most important defector to leave Russia since Penkovsky changed sides. Peter Harrington, back in London after a posting to America. Demoted, shunted into Personnel. Shabby and hangdog. She had felt sorry for him. They went out to the corner pub and had a drink. . . .

"Yes," she said. "Go on."

He hesitated and then said quietly, "You're not going to get anything for nothing, Davy. I want to see something in this for myself before I spill out any more."

She reached out and stopped the tape. "Fair enough. I'll go back and think this over. You can do some thinking too. You can work out exactly how long you'll be in here if you *don't* cooperate. I'll contact the governor when I'm coming up." She scooped up the lighter. "You can keep the cigarettes."

He mumbled a crude obscenity, which she ignored. Then he stuffed the packet into the breast pocket of his denim jacket. "Who gave you the lighter?"

She could see the malice in his face. He needed to hurt her if he could, to give himself some self-respect. She decided to let him do it. "A man friend," she said. "Why? What do you care what I got for Christmas?"

"Just curious." He had a little grin on his mouth. "You got over Ivan, then?"

"It's been some years now," Davina answered. She wore her calmness well; he couldn't sense the angry beating of her pulse.

"What's he like, then? Still go for the Russian-bear type, do you?"

"He's not like anyone you'd ever know," Davina said. She walked to the door and opened it. The guard stepped inside the room and closed it. She went down the corridor with its yellow paint and the creeping acrid smell; she went down in the elevator and signed herself out at the private entrance. In the open air she took a deep breath; the streets were busy with traffic and people, the shops bearing the ubiquitous and rather tattered "Sale" notices that were the flag of recession. She had parked her car on a meter some distance from the grim prison facade. A ticket was folded under the wiper, fining the driver for exceeding the two-hour limit. She got in, and on an impulse of senseless irritation, crumpled up the paper in its sliver of cellophane and threw it into the road. Let them bloody well find her if they wanted the money. Two hours was not time enough. Not time enough to peel back the dirty layers of treason and deceit that had been laid down over many, many years. She would be back to see Peter Harrington again, and Peter Harrington would tell her a little more.

When she came up in the elevator to her apartment in Marylebone, she couldn't find the key in her bag. Lomax would be in. Lomax would be waiting. Thank God. She pushed the bell, and the door opened.

"Hello, my darling," he said. "I've missed you."

"I've missed you too," she answered, and put her arms around his neck to kiss him.

"How did it go today?" They were sitting side by side on the small sofa, and Lomax's large body took up most of the space. He held her firmly inside his arm, and one hand played with a strand of the dark red hair that hung over her collar.

"Better than I expected," she said.

"It didn't upset you to see him again?"

"I felt rather sick to start with; I remember opening a cheese once and finding it crawling—it felt like that when he walked in. But he wants to get out, Colin. He wants it very, very badly. And he'll talk to me. Not like today, just tossing a few crumbs, but properly. He knows a lot more than he pretends."

"Do you want a drink? I'll get you one."

"Not yet. Later, when I've had a bath. That place smelled, I'm sure it's come out with me."

Lomax turned her face toward him. "It did shake you, didn't it?"

Reluctantly Davina nodded. "A little. How did you get on with the physio?"

"Very well. We did quite a lot of hard work. She says I'll be half fit in about six weeks. I'm to increase my walk to a mile at the end of the month. No jogging; just a steady strong exercise at walking pace. Plus all the rest."

"You're very patient, Colin. I never thought you would be."

"I never thought I'd have the option," he reminded her. "Besides, I'm not having you marry a crock. I don't mind you going round talking to people like Harrington, but you're not getting into anything serious till I'm ready to go along with you."

"I won't argue with that," Davina said gently. "Now I'll have my bath and you can get a nice whiskey and soda ready for me so I can have it while I'm cooking."

He had green eyes, almost too pale; they seemed washed clean in bright sunlight. There was a spark in them as he looked at her. "You're not cooking tonight, my love. I had a wee check from the Ministry this afternoon. We're going out."

He was a handsome man, she thought, noticing that several women stared at him as they went to their table. The bullets that ripped into him in Mexico and the long, agonizing struggle back to life and health had fined him down. He had lost the muscled neck and powerful shoulders of the super-fit soldier, and there was a softness in his expression and in the line of the thin, rather hard mouth that had come over the long months of convalescence and the final operation to repair his shattered lung. He wouldn't marry her when he believed he had less than a year to live. She couldn't marry him until she had completed what she was doing. But she couldn't tell him that. He was proud and sensitive and suffered sudden flares of jealousy when she was away from him.

Her greatest mistake had been to introduce him to Tony Walden. The antipathy had been instant. The high-powered authoritarian tycoon in his forties embodied most of what Colin Lomax despised in civilian life. It hadn't helped that Walden was a good-looking man who radiated energy and fitness.

And she had sensed immediately that the former major in the SAS with the George Cross after his name had put Tony Walden on the defensive. They had squared up to each other like two fighting cocks in the little sitting room. Only the presence of Humphrey Grant had prevented open rudeness. His gaunt face seemed more greenish-gray than usual and his voice had rustled over the three of them like dead leaves being raked off a path.

"It's essential that Davina has this job as a cover. She has to be seen to leave her old associates and everything connected with them and be firmly settled in civilian life. It's very good of you, Tony, to help us out."

And so it had been set up for her in the privacy of the Marylebone apartment. A job with Arlington Agency, a legitimate salary that would be quietly refunded to Walden direct by one of the Service's overseas accounts. A flat and a live-in lover recovering from a near-fatal encounter in Mexico. And an open break with her old chief, Brigadier Sir James White.

Lomax's voice disturbed the flashback. "You're a long way off, my darling. We're having dinner together, remember?"

"I'm sorry, Colin. I was just thinking how all this started. And you started it. You were the first person to see some connection between what happened in Mexico and what had happened over the last few years. You smelled the rat."

"I know I did. I didn't reckon on that old sod Grant setting you out to catch it. Or me being around to sit on the sidelines. I should've kept my big mouth shut!"

They laughed, and the moment of tension passed. He reached across the table for her hand. One of the Spanish waiters saw them, and grinning, said something to a companion.

"You get yourself fit and well," Davina told him. And looking at him over the candle flickering in its glass shade, she said quietly, "I love you very much, you know. When I got to the flat today, I said to myself, 'Thank God he'll be there'—I wouldn't know how to cope without you, Colin."

He blushed like a schoolboy. He had once killed a man with a single blow in front of her. He squeezed her hand so hard that it hurt. "You'll never get the chance," he said. "Now, let's order something to eat, woman, before I change my mind and take you home to bed."

Late that night, as Davina and Lomax lay in each other's arms and slept, and Peter Harrington turned over in his cot for the twentieth time seeking sleep, the rose-red light of breaking day filtered through the windows of a Moscow apartment and touched the naked bodies of a man and a woman. They lay silently and still while the sun came up and their skins turned the color of blood. When it was fully light, the man turned to the woman and said, as Davina had done to Lomax, "I love you very much. I couldn't do without you, Natalia."

She traced his mouth with a pointed nail and then inserted the tip of her finger for him to bite. "As I love you, Igor Igorovich. Our love grows, day by day. Isn't that wonderful?"

He held the soft body close to him; her large breasts escaped his hands, spilling over, and the desire she kindled in him roared like a flame through belly and thighs already stiff from making love. At the end he said as he had done for nights without number, "Never leave me, Natalia—I need you."

And she gave the same whispered answer. "How could I leave you? Where would I go? You're my life. . . ."

By eight o'clock the apartment was empty. The bed lay white and crumpled with the pillows on the floor. It would be made, the room tidied, all traces of their presence cleared away. The woman who kept the apartments carried the red shield with the crossed swords of the KGB in her passport. The flats belonged to the Service; they were for the use of members of the Service and their families. They were not the most exclusive or luxurious, and the people allotted them were in the middle echelon of the KGB in Moscow.

The man who left by a side entrance was picked up by a black Zim, its bodywork polished until it gleamed like a great beetle as it sped down the center lane of the highway reserved for the Politburo and the highest officials in the party. It turned into the Kremlin gate exactly at eight-fifteen, and by twenty-two minutes past eight Igor Borisov took his place behind the famous desk in the room overlooking Independence Square. At eight-thirty exactly, his secretary knocked on the door and came in with the priority files and telexes from the previous night. She was a pretty girl, with a generous, rounded figure. Her manner was deferential and she didn't speak until he took the papers and said, "Thank you, Natalia."

She lowered her eyelids and murmured, "Thank you, Comrade General. Shall I bring you some tea?"

"Yes, thank you," he answered, not looking up.

Outside, the bells of the Kremlin churches had begun chiming the half-hour. The official day of Igor Borisov, Director of State Security of the Supreme Soviet and head of the KGB, opened like any other day. His secretary came back with a glass of tea in a silver holder, a half-moon of lemon floating in it like a yellow eye. She set it on the desk on a heat-resistant saucer. He drank it carefully; it was steaming hot.

"I'll need you in an hour for dictation," he said. Neither of them glanced at the sophisticated battery of recording machines beside him.

"Yes, Comrade General."

"And there's a telex from London." He looked at her, frowning. "I want to show it to you."

She gave a shy nod. "Yes, Comrade General. I'd like to see it."

He bent over his desk, and she left the room in her usual quiet way, closing the door without letting the lock click, in case he was disturbed.

Humphrey Grant put his foot on the brake, and the car began to slow down, drawing into the side of the road. It was a quiet street off the busy Marylebone Road, bordered by elegant Georgian houses occupied by lawyers in select little offices. He sat in the car watching in his rearview mirror until he saw Davina turn the corner into Mansfield Street. Grant didn't have any sympathy with women; his determined neuterism covered a latent homosexual taste which he would die without admitting. He couldn't judge her as an attractive woman, but a solitary walker, complete with rolled umbrella and Horse Guards Parade stride, paused and looked after her as she passed. He opened the door of the passenger seat and she got into the car. They didn't speak while he set off and turned into the broad thoroughfare of Portland Place.

"We'll go to the park," Grant said.

"All right." Davina nodded. It was a bright morning and she looked out of the window as they drove into Regent's Park. Some of the finest houses in London were set on its perimeter like grandiose sentinels of its privacy. The great terraces built by Nash had housed only the very richest until the war came. Now the classical facades were restored and painted, but the great rooms were offices where the harsh glare of fluorescent lighting filled the windows when darkness came.

Davina had never liked either the park or the famous terraces. For some reason there was a gloom about them; it was spurious countryside set in the heart of a city. In the winter it seemed to her the most depressing place on earth, and now the mugger lurked along the shadowy paths, in the tradition of his forebear, the footpad of the eighteenth century.

"You're rather silent," Grant broke in. "Anything wrong?"

"No, nothing. I was just thinking how I'd hate to live here, that's all."

"There's not much chance, I'd say," Grant remarked sourly. "Unless you become a millionaire. Or a property company. Let's pull in here."

There were other cars parked along the side of the road. Solitary drivers waited for the strolling prostitutes and whispered invitations to them through the windows. Patrols of traffic wardens and police harried them at night, but even in the early morning there were a few stragglers.

Grant brought the car to a stop. He looked in his rearview mirror, pulled up the hand brake, switched off the engine, and checked he was in neutral. Everything he did was methodical and maddening and seemed to take longer than necessary. Davina didn't know why he irritated her more than usual that morning.

She opened her bag and took out a cigarette. Grant creased his nose and said, "Must you do that? It makes the car smell."

"It helps me think," she answered. "Try opening the window, Humphrey. Or get one of those little air fresheners."

He wound down the window a few inches, and coughed when she started smoking.

"I saw Harrington," she said.

Grant didn't waste time or words on inquiring after his health. "Were we right?"

"Dead right," she said. "He didn't bat an eyelid when I talked about a mole high up in the Service. He said he was already planted on us when Harrington himself went over to the Russians."

"That brings us to eleven years ago, if my memory's right," Grant interposed. "We were all there then. Kidson, the Chief, myself, and even you."

Davina gave him a little irritating smile. "It's not me," she said.

He didn't take it as a joke. He turned sharply in his seat and said, "It could be. It could be me. It could be any one of us. Eleven years ago . . . You believe him?"

"Yes, I do. He's still full of his old tricks, but they've lost some of the novelty. I can see through him, Humphrey. He does know there's a traitor, and he has a lot more clues to give us. But we're going to have to pay to get them."

"An exchange, I suppose. That's the most complicated nuisance of all. And the opposition haven't any comparable agent of ours."

"He doesn't know that," Davina answered.

"But if we can't exchange him, what can we offer him?"

"How long has he been at the Scrubs?"

"He was held at Brixton for a while, but he was certainly at the Scrubs by the time you and Sasanov went to Australia. It's a very secure prison."

"What are we going to do, then?" Davina asked.

"Very secure," Grant went on, ignoring her question. "But it didn't hold Blake. . . . I think we'll arrange a move for him anyway. Just to be on the safe side."

"Where to? Won't that be very difficult? Won't it cause comment at the office if Harrington suddenly gets shifted from a place like the Scrubs?"

"It can be managed. Leave that to me."

"Without John or the Chief knowing?" Frowning, she threw her cigarette butt out of the window.

"Certainly. I've done things without consulting either of them." Grant didn't say it as a boast.

"I didn't realize," Davina remarked quietly. "I didn't realize you were so powerful."

"John and the Chief could say the same," he answered. "We've all worked behind each other's backs at one time or another. You should remember that."

"I shall," Davina said. "I'll go back in a few days and see him again. Don't do anything about moving him till afterwards."

"There's no hurry," Grant said. "I'll wait till we see what he has to offer. Do you want me to drop you at Arlington Place?" He didn't sound enthusiastic.

"No, thanks, leave me at the intersection outside the park, there on the right. I'll go and get my car."

He went through the routine of starting up, and just before the car moved off he glanced at her and said casually, "Do you actually *do* any work for Tony Walden?"

Davina stared ahead and said with equal casualness, "Yes, as a matter of fact, Humphrey, I do."

CHAPTER 2

ARLINGTON PLACE was a narrow street in the most prestigious square mile radiating out from Marble Arch. The Arlington Agency was housed in a tall, stuccoed house built for a tea merchant in the mid 1700s. It retained its original railings, portico, and facade; a fine wrought-iron staircase swept up from the hall to the upper floors, and the elevator was tucked away unobtrusively in a corner. There was the minimum of furniture in the entrance hall itself; a receptionist sat behind an antique desk and inquired what visitors wanted with a practiced smile. The phones and intercoms were not obtrusive; the visitor's impression was of quaint old-fashioned courtesy, and the impression was maintained to the moment he walked out into the street. Anyone at Arlington who failed to charm was promptly sacked.

There was no sign of the company's American parentage. Even the central heating was pleasantly low. The chairman insisted on flowers in his office and in the reception rooms. He had hung pictures from his own collection at salient points up the stairs where clients could see them. He loved early Dutch seascapes, but the client important enough to go into his room for a private discussion of their account could feast his eyes upon a magnificent fiery Turner landscape over the fireplace. Davina's small office adjoined this room, and she could see the picture when the communicating door was open.

The first thing she said when she went to Tony Walden's private office for the first time and saw it was an exclamation of surprise. "Good Lord—that's so like *The Fighting Temeraire.* What a marvelous picture, Mr. Walden!"

And that had won him straightaway. He had been married twice; his second wife was so like his first that friends couldn't think why he'd bothered to change. He loved beauty in women, in his surroundings, and his possessions. He perceived the sales potential of every form of vulgarity in the commercial market, and exploited it; at the same time, he preserved the purity of his own values. He sold soap and hair remover and floor polish, cigarettes and toilet paper and diet margarines and Swedish cars. He used nudity and crude status symbols to sell products which had nothing to do with either. He had a genius for persuading people that they wanted what they saw on television or on the giant billboards in the cities. His knowledge of selling had been gained by knocking on doors and selling cheap makeup to housewives. His financial acumen came from a degree in mathematics taken in his spare time at the London Polytechnic.

His accent was classless, carefully cultivated to betray nothing of his original background. Neither of his wives or his two children knew that he had been born in Poland just before the war. Only Humphrey Grant knew that he had supplied valuable information to MI6 about escape routes from the Eastern bloc in the 1950s.

He heard Davina come into the adjoining office; he was at his own desk by eight-thirty every morning and he worked on Saturdays until lunchtime. The Waldens lived in princely style in Grosvenor Square, but he refused to buy a status symbol in the country. He had no interest in country pursuits, and in the winter the English climate depressed him. When he took a holiday, which was usually allied to business, he went to California.

"Davina?"

She came to the door. "Good morning, Mr. Walden. I'm a bit late, I'm afraid."

"Don't be silly." He had a very attractive smile. "You know you don't have to come in unless it's convenient. You're looking very nice this morning. Blue suits you."

"Thank you." She turned to go back into her office. There was a pile of correspondence laid out on her desk. It was Davina's insistence that turned the cover into some semblance of a job. She was too independent to take money without making some return. Allied to her appreciation of his Turner, this had impressed Walden even more. He didn't need a personal assistant; he had two highly competent secretaries, one of whom had been with him for ten years and counted herself indispensable. Her name was Frieda Armstrong, and her colleague, her junior in the company by six years, was Chris Collins. Both women were well aware that Davina's presence was superfluous, and it was accepted at Arlington that the chairman had personal reasons for introducing her into the office. Compared with the classic beauty of Mrs. Walden, she seemed an odd choice as a mistress. Walden was well aware of what was being said. In a way, it amused him to confuse his clever staff. It also helped to focus his attention on Davina Graham and to see her in a sexual context. She was not his type of woman. He didn't like red hair; he wasn't attracted by her very slim figure, apart from her magnificent legs. She had a remoteness that he found irritating, and a decisive manner that should have put his back up immediately. However, none of these disadvantages had stopped him from being powerfully attracted, and he couldn't understand why.

He gave her work to do at her behest; if she was absent or late, he made no comment. All that was understood. If she was in the office and he wanted something done, she showed herself to be prompt and efficient. She never got in his way or tried to establish a relationship beyond the minimum courtesy between strangers. He had the impression that she knew him as a name but would have been hard pressed to describe his face.

She had closed the communicating door, and he had forgotten about her in a few seconds as he concentrated on his own work. Frieda Armstrong came in and out of the office; she took a series of instructions, reminded him of his appointments, glanced malevolently at the private office which she had been moved out of, albeit with a salary increase, and went out again. There was the twice-weekly conference at eleven o'clock, held in the long room on the second floor; it was twelve-thirty when Walden came back upstairs.

His mind had been so preoccupied he had to check in his diary in case a luncheon engagement had been penciled in. The two hours allotted were free.

He didn't smoke and he never kept alcohol in the office. There was a jug of fresh orange juice and ice always at hand. He poured himself a drink and relaxed. The door opened.

"I'm free this afternoon, Mr. Walden," Davina said. "I could make myself useful."

He looked at her thoughtfully for a moment. "Yes, you could, as a matter of fact. You could save me having a sandwich in the office and giving myself indigestion. Come and have lunch with me."

"I don't think it's a very good idea," she answered.

"Why not?'

She shrugged. She was annoyed to feel her face flushing. Damn red hair and the skin that went with it.

"Well, why not? You've got nothing to do, and I'd like some company. Meet me at Harry's Bar at one o'clock." He didn't wait for an answer. He went out and left her standing in the doorway, feeling foolish and boorish and neatly outwitted.

In view of what he had done to help, she couldn't possibly not turn up. Harry's Bar was an offshoot of the long-established Marks Club—exclusive, expensive, and popular with the young rich.

Davina had never been there. It wasn't a place that retired majors, however highly decorated, could afford to patronize. Because there was nowhere to park, she was five minutes late, and in a mood of bloody-mindedness she left the car on a yellow line. She would set the fine against expenses; Humphrey screamed like a banshee over minor infractions of the law like motoring offenses. Two in two days. Wormwood Scrubs to Mayfair. She wondered what a clever analyst in the computer section would make of that. . . . She entered the restaurant and was shown to a privileged table by the window.

Walden got up. "I didn't think you'd come," he said.

"I'm not that late, surely?" Davina sat down and immediately regretted the retort. "I didn't mean to sound rude," she said. "This is lovely, and it's very kind of you to ask me."

"Then why did you make such a fuss about coming? It's a very respectable place. As you can see."

She glanced up, following the movement of his head, and a very sociable royal duchess swept past them to the special table at the top of the room. Davina laughed. "Good Lord, 'respectable' is the word! Do you always lunch here?"

"Only when I have someone important," he answered. He had very dark eyes, and when he smiled, his Eastern European blood showed in the broad cheekbones and the wide mouth.

The food was Italian and superb; he ordered wine, and she noticed that he drank very little. "This is nice," he said suddenly. "I haven't thought about business since you came in!"

"I hope that's a compliment," Davina said. "I don't usually take people's minds off their work."

"Perhaps that's because you're so dedicated to your own," he suggested. "How is it going, by the way? Or shouldn't I ask?"

"You can ask," she said calmly, "but I can't answer."

"No, of course you can't," he apologized. "You must find my business very dull."

"As a matter of fact, I don't. It's very interesting indeed. Your marketing analysis is brilliant." She smiled and added, "Now I know why I buy all sorts of things I don't need!"

"And that's the secret." Walden leaned toward her. "Consumer goods—whoever thought of that description helped to make my fortune. We eat more than we need, we smoke and drink and dose ourselves with chemicals and inhale pollution every time we take a breath. The world is consuming itself, eating its environment alive. I grow fat on the cupidity and stupidity of my fellow human beings."

"Then why do you do it?"

"Because I love it," he said simply. "And if I didn't take advantage, someone else would. Don't you ever question what you do?"

Davina lit a cigarette. "Not very often. Not yet, anyway."

"I said you were dedicated. You wouldn't like it if I said 'fanatic,' would you?"

"I don't think I'd mind. I don't work because I'm ambitious or greedy for money; I work because I believe in my job. I believe it has to be done."

"And what about Major Lomax?" The question caught her unprepared. "Where does he fit in?"

"Into my personal life," Davina answered.

"I see," Walden said. "It must be difficult to have a personal life."

"Not if the other partner understands what you're doing," Davina answered. "And Colin knows the score."

"Then you're very lucky," he said. "I have been married twice; my first wife wanted a husband with slippers by the fire and my present one wants to go to nightclubs every night. The stupid thing is, they look so like each other, but the only thing they have in common is being disappointed with me."

"That sounds terribly sad," Davina said. "And just a little bit corny, if you don't mind my saying so. You've got children, haven't you—I've seen photographs on your desk."

"Two boys, both very nice, upright kids. One is at school still and the elder is at Kiev University. Both working hard, no drugs, no problems. I can't complain about them."

"You sound as if you are," she challenged him.

"You're very quick, Davina, aren't you—they bore me, that's the trouble. I can see you don't approve."

"Well, you've spent the last part of lunch running down both your wives and your children, so how can I? And your business, indirectly. Isn't anything right for you?"

"Yes," he said coolly. "The challenge of tomorrow. Getting the distillers' account away from my biggest rivals in the States. That makes everything else unimportant. I live for a challenge; it keeps the adrenaline going and the heart young. It's time to get the bill; I've an appointment at two-forty-five, and that old harridan Frieda will be clicking her tongue in the office. I've enjoyed our lunch. I hope you have?"

"Very much," Davina said, and realized that she meant it.

Twelve days. It seemed like years to Peter Harrington. He tried to dismiss his fears by remembering how much red tape was involved in an investigation. Of course Davina wouldn't come back to him quickly. He imagined the conferences taking place, the consultation with the Home Secretary to get the permission to visit him regularly, maybe to bring Kidson with her; that old death's-head Grant muttering away to the brigadier, wanting everything cleared and filed in triplicate. He made all the excuses he could think of, and none of them satisfied his clamoring nerves. Which was what the bitch wanted, he said to himself savagely. She was sweating him, and he had fallen into the trap.

He began pacing up and down his cell, something he hadn't done for the last four years of his imprisonment. He felt caged again, restless, unable to sleep; his mind ranged around the possibilities, and came up against her damnable silence. He tortured himself with the idea that the investigation itself had been shelved, and he would never hear from Davina again. The twenty-four years stretched ahead of him, and he came close to hysteria one night. He stood in the middle of the cell, sweat drenching his body, and shook his clenched fists at the wall. He had reached a stage of acceptance, a kind of weary limbo where his spirit stayed torpid, waiting but not hoping. Davina had given him hope, woken him to the possibility of freedom. The agony was unbearable when nothing more happened; the routine of waking up, working, reading, watching television during the recreation period, became a nerve-racking ordeal. Every time his cell door opened, he started up, thinking it might be a summons to the governor's office. Also, there was a prison visitor, who hadn't been to see Peter either.

By the thirteenth day he couldn't stop his hands from shaking. It was five o'clock in the afternoon, an hour before dinner, when the key scraped in the lock and the officer on duty said, "You're wanted upstairs." There were tears in Peter Harrington's eyes when he came into the governor's office and saw Davina sitting there. He blinked them away and assumed a little swagger as he settled into the chair opposite. His relief was so intense that he could have laughed out loud. But whatever happened, she mustn't see how near the breaking point he'd come.

"Cigarette?" she offered. He resisted the urge to grab one and inhale down to his feet. He couldn't trust his trembling hands. Not for a little while.

Davina didn't waste time. "I've got news for you," she said. "Not very good news, I'm afraid."

He couldn't control his color; it turned a sickly gray. "Oh . . . come to deliver the body blow in person, have you, Davy? Nice of you."

"This whole investigation is hanging by a thread," she said baldly.

"I believe in it, so does someone else in the office. I believe we've got a top-level traitor, and so do they. But there's a strong move to shut the whole case up."

"There would be," he spat out. "There bloody well would be, if the mole knows you're onto something! Who wants it shelved—that'll be a pointer!"

"The Foreign Office," she said. "They don't want any scandal leaking out. Who's behind it is anybody's guess. Nobody's owning up, but there's been heavy pressure on us to drop the whole thing."

He sank his head into his hands. "That's it, then. I know what heavy pressure means. I worked in the bloody place for twenty years. They'll have their way."

"Not necessarily," Davina said quietly. "I'm not going to give up without a fight."

"You nevcr did." Thc rcply came through in a mumble. "But you won't win against the Mandarins. Nobody does."

She hadn't heard the nickname for the power figures in the Establishment for a long time. It dated Harrington to the early postwar days.

"I can win," she said, "if I can show something that *can't* be brushed aside."

He raised his head and narrowed his eyes to focus on her face. He was growing shortsighted, and outlines weren't clear anymore. Clever bitch, he thought, giving me a heart attack first. My Christ, I've lost my touch, falling for that bad-news trick. There's no official cover-up. She's trying to force the pace, that's all, get me to give something for nothing.

"You don't have to believe me," Davina said. "It's up to you. I can walk out of here, and that'll be the end of it. And you'll serve out your sentence. Not twenty-four years, because you'll get remission. But long enough."

"Blackmailing?" he hissed at her.

She shook her head. "No. I stand to lose as much as you, in a way. The Service even more so. I need you, Peter, or I wouldn't be here. And you need me. That's not blackmail, that's fact."

"Give me a cigarette," he said. "All right . . . now. Let me ask you a few questions first. Where did you get the tip-off?"

Davina put the recorder on the desk, snapped the switch down, and it began recording. "It came from outside. We had an operative with military training. He joined me on a mission last year. And he noticed some funny coincidences. He began compiling a report, noting things that didn't add up, and which, frankly, none of us would have seen. It needed a fresh eye, Peter. At the end, what he'd done was put a lot of pieces of jigsaw together with one big missing piece. But it made a picture all the same."

"Made up of coincidences, though," Harrington objected. "No hard facts."

"No," Davina admitted. "But you know yourself that facts can be misleading. This was a sequence of events. Starting with Sasanov and you and me."

He sucked on the cigarette; he had regained his composure. The habit and training of his whole life reasserted itself and his mind started running ahead of Davina's voice. Himself and her and Sasanov. The Russian intelligence disaster of the decade. So nearly reversed and neutralized. Except for Davina Graham—that was the obvious reason. And yet there was a shading, a gray area that tantalized his instincts.

"I'd like to look at this report," he said. He could see by her expression that the suggestion was dismissed. "Listen to me, Davy," he said. "I'm not up to anything. I don't give a fuck about who wins the intelligence war. All I want is to get out of here; live out my life in some nice neutral place like Switzerland. I'm fifty-four, and I feel a fucking hundred. Let me see that report."

"Why?"

"Because all I know is the code name: Albatross." His voice rose. "If I knew who he was, I'd tell you, in exchange for a pardon. Or a deal with Moscow, like Lonsdale. I *wouldn't* hold out—I wouldn't drag this on for week after week for my own sake. I'm starting to go mad in here, now that you've stirred things up!"

She believed him. She believed the pitch of desperation in his voice, and the twitching hands fumbling with the packet of cigarettes. He had lost a lot of weight since she had seen him a fortnight ago. He was telling the truth. He knew there was someone, but he didn't know who it was. They would need his brain working in cooperation with hers if the missing piece of Colin's jigsaw was to be found and fitted into place.

"I'll get a copy of the report for you," she said. "I'll be back the day after tomorrow. And by the way, don't be surprised if you're moved."

He gaped at her for a moment, and then a sly smirk passed over his mouth.

"Moved? To an open prison?"

"I don't know," Davina answered. "But it's a bit too tight in here. Day after tomorrow, Peter."

"I'll be here"—he managed a joke.

"Good-bye," she said, and opened the door to let the prison officer take charge of him.

Frieda Armstrong was drinking tea with her colleague Miss Collins.

"If there's one thing that really annoys me, it's the way Miss Graham comes and goes and never lets me know! I had three personal calls for her this morning and I couldn't tell any of them where she was or whether she would be in the office at all today."

"Doesn't she keep an engagement diary?" Miss Collins suggested. She helped herself to a chocolate cookie. She loved sweet things. Frieda was very careful of her figure; she dressed well, and Miss Collins envied her style.

"No, she doesn't," the older woman snapped slightly. "And that's very unprofessional. I think I'll mention it to her."

"Mr. Walden said she was meeting a client," Miss Collins said, pleased to know something Frieda didn't.

"Very likely, but she didn't leave a note of it. I don't know why Mr. Walden engaged her in the first place. She's not really necessary."

Miss Collins sipped her tea and didn't say anything. She thought exactly the same as Frieda Armstrong, but she didn't dare say so. "She's got rather a curt manner," she remarked instead. "I've noticed it even with Mr. Walden."

There was a little spark in Frieda's eye. "Well, I was fairly short with her callers. One of them said she was her sister; she asked me where she was and when she'd be in and could she reach her, as if I was her secretary or something. I said I really had no idea and hung up."

"Quite right, too," Miss Collins said. "There's Mr. Walden's buzzer. Shall I go while you finish your tea?"

"No," Frieda said firmly. "I'll see what he wants." She hurried out, and the younger woman looked after her for a moment and then took another cookie. Poor Frieda, she said to herself. She's been in love with him for years, and he's never even looked at her legs. He's given mine a glance or two. She smiled to herself. She wasn't going to fall into the older woman's fantasy: waiting on the boss hand and foot, shielding him from every little worry and inconvenience when she could, and letting her own life slip away. Miss Collins had a man friend and a definite objective which included a nice little flat in Fulham and a change from single status. He liked her plumpness, too.

The phone rang in the Marylebone apartment. Lomax could hear it ringing as he unlocked the front door. He reached it just in time.

"Colin? Hello, it's Charlie. How are you?"

How he had disliked her on first meeting, he remembered. The self-confident voice still irritated him. Davina's beautiful spoiled sister, married to John Kidson after two divorces. The hell of it was that he had grown to like her very much indeed over the last six months. "I'm fine. Just back from a brisk mile walk—no, I'm not joking. Yes, I'll be one of those fellows you see running round Hyde Park soon." Her infectious laugh gurgled over the phone; she had a jolly, rather loud laugh. "No, Davina's not here. Try her office."

At the other end Charlie Kidson said, "I did. A very disagreeable person answered me. Snapped my head off and said she'd no idea where she was or when she'd be back. Tell her to ring me when she comes in. I want to make a date for dinner, Colin. Just the four of us. We haven't seen you for far too long. 'Bye."

Lomax put the phone down. Somebody had better sort out the Arlington Agency end. Even Charlie had sounded surprised, and in Colin's opinion she wasn't bright enough to be suspicious. He decided to have a word with Humphrey Grant. No point in worrying Davina. He said that privately about a lot of things. It was the nearest he could get to protecting her and assuming his natural role in their relationship. He had come close to dying for her once. He loved her so much he wouldn't have minded doing it again. Except that he wanted to live with her instead. He wanted to bind her to him, tether her with a couple of children, build a life for both of them in which the world of secrets and violence was only a memory.

But he had helped to put the net into her hands, and they were both too dedicated and professional to hand it back. First catch the traitor, the Russian implant that had grown in the body of the SIS like a silent cancer. Men and women had been betrayed to death and the labor camps. Davina herself had suffered torture; an innocent woman had been tormented and killed in Mexico, and the same sly hand had helped to guide her to her fate.

The man had to be caught. Then it would be time for Colin to lay claim once and for all to Davina Graham. In the meantime, something had to be done to tighten up the situation at Arlington Street. It wouldn't do if Kidson himself or the brigadier tried to contact her and the response was similar to Charlie's—they would quickly scent something was amiss. He called Grant's private number; it was nearly seven and Davina must be caught in the East End traffic to be so late.

"Hello?" Grant's voice was brittle and staccato. He never gave his number or identified himself until he knew who was calling.

"Lomax." Colin was equally laconic on the phone.

"What's wrong?" Typical of Humphrey to assume the worst.

"Nothing, except your cover. The agency doesn't deal with inquiries very well. It needs tightening up that end."

"I'll speak to Walden," Humphrey promised. "Is Davina back yet? No, no, I don't want her telephoning me. I'll meet her in the usual place tomorrow if she's any news. You ring me if she has. Just confirm the appointment for tomorrow."

"Right." Colin hung up. He poured himself a whiskey, shrugged aside the still-recurring urge to smoke a cigarette, and switched on the TV. He didn't watch the program, he looked at the flickering figures on the screen and dimly heard the sound of voices, while his thoughts ranged far away from the small sitting room. The first clue had appeared when he was studying the dossier on Davina Graham, long before he met her and they went to America together.

He had been trained to pick up details, however insignificant or irrelevant they seemed. The Special Air Service had trained his body and conditioned his mind to fight the enemy; but from there he had gone into the secret world of army undercover agents who penetrated the IRA in Northern Ireland. He was operating in that section when he won his George Cross. London knew the caliber of the man when they recruited him. A rare combination of brute strength and skill, with a considerable flair for intelligence work. It was a tiny piece of grit that lodged in his mental eye and worried him.

Six years ago Colonel Ivan Sasanov of the KGB had defected to the West. Davina Graham had been selected as his "minder," a job that required tact and patience and had always been allotted to a man. He remembered the comments made about her at the time. Dedicated, highly intelligent, efficient. Reserved. No men friends and no intimates in the Service. No friends to tempt her into indiscretion. He had read further back, right to the beginning of her recruitment and training, and found one brief reference to a colleague who had been friendly to her soon after she joined. Peter Harrington. Taken the new girl out to lunch once or twice, and to the local pub for a drink. No follow-up. Harrington was posted to Washington. The contact was so superficial it hardly merited a mention. Two, three years passed, and then the grit flew into Lomax's eye. When Davina was given the job of looking after the most important Russian to defect to the West, Peter Harrington was recalled in disgrace from his job and posted to Personnel in London.

And the consequences of that move were Service history now, and Harrington would be close to seventy before he saw the outside world. That was the start of Lomax's uneasy feelings, and they intensified as he had read on. He heard the front door open and sprang up to greet her.

He was out in the little hall and Davina was in his arms exchanging the long kisses that were more eloquent than any words of love. Sasanov had swept away her inhibitions; Lomax had taught her tenderness and subtlety in their sex life. There had been a long abstinence when he was little better than an invalid after Mexico. Now, nearly back to full health, he was an ardent and demanding lover, needing reassurance that nothing had changed.

They didn't eat till late that evening; she slept in his arms and he woke her with food on a tray. Davina sat up and smiled sleepily at him. "Darling, you spoil me. Do you know, you're a much better cook than I am?"

"Of course I am." Lomax grinned at her, climbing back into bed with his own supper plate. "Men are always better than women—even at so-called women's work. All the great chefs are men."

"Shut up and eat your omelet, you beastly chauvinist. It's delicious!"

When they had finished, he reached up and gently pinched the lobe of her ear. "You can make the coffee."

"Charlie phoned today," he said later. "She wants us to have dinner; just the four of us, she said."

"I suppose we'd better go." Davina frowned slightly. "I haven't seen John for ages."

"Don't you want to?" Colin asked.

"Not particularly. I don't want to pick up with anyone from the office at the moment. He'll start asking questions about Arlington and how do I like the job, that sort of thing."

"You'll cope perfectly well," he insisted.

She shook her head a little. "You don't know John. Seeing through people when they're lying is his stock in trade. And he mustn't suspect anything, Colin. You know that."

"It isn't him," Lomax said slowly. "It can't be."

"Why not?" She turned toward him. "The Chief, Humphrey, John. They're the only three important enough to qualify. One of them is a Soviet spy."

"Hardly Humphrey, who put you onto the investigation," he retorted. "That's straining credibility too far."

"What better way of stopping me from finding him?" Davina countered. "You gave him the report, Colin. He had to do something about it."

"I gave it to him because he recruited me and I trusted him. I still do. You know whom I suspect, and always have."

"I know," Davina answered. "James White. I'd like it to be him, Colin. Nothing would give me greater satisfaction than to nail him. But I don't believe it. It's too obvious, too easy. It could be John. That's what I'm scared of finding out."

"Charlie wanted you to ring back," he said. "I forgot to mention it. Stop worrying. I'll make an excuse if you don't want to go."

Davina hesitated. "No," she said after a moment. "We'll go. It would look odd if we didn't. I'll ring tomorrow."

"Do you have anything to report to Humphrey? He'll meet at Mansfield Street tomorrow if you want to see him."

Again she hesitated. "No, I don't think so. I don't think I'll tell him any more at this stage. I want to show Harrington your report. And I've made up my mind, Colin love; I'm not going to say anything to Humphrey about *that*."

"Why not?" He was surprised by her vehemence.

"Because he doesn't know I have a copy," she said quietly. "I've made up my mind to something else."

"God help us," he said. "What is it now?"

"If I'm going to do this properly, I've got to do it alone. I won't be making any more reports to Humphrey. From now on, he's a prime suspect. No less than John or the brigadier himself."

"Humphrey?"

Grant looked up from his paperwork. "Yes, John? What can I do for you?"

John Kidson ignored the unwelcoming expression on the bony face. Christ, he said to himself, advancing into the office, he looks more like bloody Robespierre every minute . . . and then he tried to remember who noticed the resemblance and pinned the nickname to Grant that followed him everywhere in other men's laughter. SGI. The Sea-Green Incorruptible. The whey-faced fanatic who slaughtered thousands during the French Revolution. . . . He couldn't remember who the originator was, but it was a cruel and accurate piece of mockery. And Humphrey Grant would know about it. He knew everything that went on in the building. Kidson settled into a chair. "I know you're busy, but so am I, Humphrey. I'm not taking any hints; I want to talk to you."

The pen was lowered and the papers set aside; Grant made a little humph of irritation. "What about? I *am* very busy, as it happens."

"The Chief took me out to lunch a couple of weeks ago."

"That's unlike him," Grant said. "He never spends money on any of us. What was behind it?"

"That's exactly what I've been asking myself ever since," Kidson answered. "He said he was due for retirement this year."

Grant nodded slightly. "So he is. That doesn't mean anything."

"He talked about a successor," Kidson said. There wasn't a flicker on the face of the man opposite him, but imperceptibly his body hunched and leaned a little forward in anticipation. "He mentioned you, Humphrey. He asked me what I thought about it."

"That was very underhand," Grant said suddenly. "How could you possibly give an unbiased answer? You could be in line yourself, John. Age isn't exactly on my side, compared to you."

"It wasn't a genuine inquiry," Kidson said quietly. "It was followed up by a suggestion that rocked me on my heels, I don't mind telling you! He said he was thinking of Davina."

Grant's head shot up. "A woman? What absolute nonsense! She'd never be appointed." Two spots of color flared on his cheekbones. He didn't like women; his ambition to succeed James White was acknowledged but never discussed. Now he exposed it in a burst of real fury. Kidson had never seen him so angry in all the years they had worked together. He actually got up from his desk and paced up and down. "Davina? For the top job? My God, what a bloody cheek that man has even to mention such a possibility! I've worked for most of my life in the Service, I've given up everything for it. If I'm passed over now, John, for Davina Graham or anyone else, I'm resigning the same day!"

"Hold on a minute," John Kidson said. "I don't think he was serious. I think it was a ploy, to test my reaction."

Humphrey glared down at him. "I hope he doesn't try to use it on me," he said.

"He wanted to pump me about Davina," Kidson went on. "Then it turned out he knew everything about her himself—where she was working, who her boss was. He was trying to prize something out of me, but I'm damned if I know what. . . . He kept saying what a waste it was for her to be in advertising. Said the same thing about marrying Colin Lomax. Such a pity, such a waste."

"He is thinking of her, then." Humphrey had sat down again. "He meant what he said in the first place."

"She's left for good," Kidson reminded him. "He knows that. He was hoping to pick up something from me about her that he didn't know. The more I think about it, the more it bothers me. That's why I thought I'd talk it over with you. You haven't been approached, have you?"

Grant shook his head. "No. No, far from it. The subject of his retirement is never mentioned. I don't let myself speculate because I know he'll never give up till he actually has to."

"I didn't mean about the job," Kidson reminded him. "I meant has he asked you about Davina at all."

"Why should he? We had no contact outside the office. You're her brother-in-law. It's quite different."

"You haven't seen her at all since she left?"

"She left when she and Lomax got back from Mexico," Grant snapped. "I went down to the parents' house to try to talk her into coming back. She refused point-blank. Lomax was given a few months to live; all she wanted was to look after him. Of course I haven't seen her since." His angular shoulders went up and down in an impatient shrug. "I can't get over the Chief going behind my back and talking to you," he muttered. "I wouldn't have believed he'd do a thing like that."

"There's something fishy about her job," Kidson said quietly. There was silence for a moment; he thought Grant hadn't heard what he said. "Charlie rang up once or twice, and yesterday she phoned again. She got the same answer. Davina wasn't there. Nobody knew where she was. I tried myself late yesterday. She wasn't in the office, and I got the impression the woman on the line wasn't expecting her to be."

Slowly Humphrey focused on him. Lomax was right. He would have to speak to Tony Walden that morning. Whoever took Davina's calls had to be pulled into line. "I don't see that matters," he said flatly. "What she does is her own business. You're her brother-in-law," he repeated. "Why don't you ask her yourself?"

"They're having dinner with us next week," Kidson said. "I think I'll do just that, Humphrey."

Grant permitted himself a thin smile. "Don't tell me your famous antennae are up, John—not about Davina, surely?"

"As a matter of fact," Kidson answered slowly, "they are. And so are the Chief's. He made a very important point at that lunch. Of all the jobs in the world, advertising is the one she'd like least. He said she'd find it tame. And so she would. But she'd also find it phony. No amount of money would make her stick that. That's what's wrong with it. She just wouldn't choose that sort of job. . . ."

"When people turn their backs on the Service, they change," Grant said. "We've both seen it happen. They lose their ethics; money becomes important. You may find that's what's happened to your sister-in-law."

"If she's turned into that sort of person," Kidson said as he got up, "she wouldn't be living with Colin Lomax. Don't forget him."

"Oh, I don't," Humphrey murmured. "Maybe you have a point, John. Let me know if you find out anything interesting, won't you?"

"Of course," Kidson said at the door. "That's why I came to see you."

Grant sat still for some minutes after he had left. Then he picked up his pen and twirled it around between his finger and thumb. It wasn't going well. Kidson and the Chief were asking questions. It was damnable luck that she and John should be related; it gave him the chance to keep her in view. Davina as White's successor. He had to swallow, because the bile of rage rose up into his throat. Rage and betrayal. Kidson hadn't taken it seriously. But Grant did. The job was his when it came vacant. It had to be his. He could head off Kidson; he could and would beat off any other contender, though there were a number in the Ministry of Defense and the Home Office who could qualify. But never in a nightmare could he have imagined that the post would be offered to a woman. And to a woman who might appeal to another woman in the top political position. He felt hot with anger. And he had set Davina on the hunt for the biggest quarry since Philby and his protector Blunt. If she succeeded, her stature would match that of any man in the running. He would never ever be able to go to James White's office and see Davina Graham behind that desk.

Stephen Wood had been a prison visitor for seven years. He started visiting at Pentonville, the recidivist prison in the East End of London, after taking a degree in sociology at Exeter University. He had a well-paid job in the Department of the Environment; his wife was a primary-school teacher and they had an eight-year-old son. Wood was a cheerful, extrovert personality, apt to crack hearty jokes with the prison staff, and unshockable where the inmates were concerned. He was practical and kind, but quite without sentiment. He had applied to join the visitors to Wormwood Scrubs when he and his family moved nearby. He was allotted to Peter Harrington after two years; the governor and staff considered Wood an admirable type, and Harrington was ready to welcome anyone who linked him with the outside world.

The two men seemed to get on well. Stephen lent Harrington books on carpentry, which was his own hobby, and he had a beneficial effect on Harrington, who started taking an interest in prison facilities and joined the handicrafts class.

It was nearly a month since Wood had come to see him. A note to the authorities explained that he had been on sick leave with a virus infection. When he came, he was welcomed by the guard on duty like an old friend.

"Hello, sir! Nice to see you again—heard you weren't too well."

"I'm fine." Wood grinned at him. "Sorry I've missed out. How are my two chaps?" There was a second man he visited in the top-security section. He had been convicted of armed robbery and murder. His mentality was that of a nine-year-old delinquent.

"They're well enough," the officer replied. "Who do you want to see first?"

"Harrington, I think," Wood answered. "I've brought him a couple of books," he added.

"That's all right, sir." The officer unlocked the door and Wood went in. Peter Harrington got up and they shook hands. "I'm sorry I haven't been to see you. Did you get my message?"

"Yes. Are you better now? A virus is a bloody nuisance; you can't treat them, can you?"

"No," Wood said, sitting down. "Antibiotics don't make a blind bit of difference. You just have to sweat it out. Literally." He laughed, and Harrington joined in. Outside, the prison officer heard the voices and didn't linger. He wondered what the visitors found to say to some of the men in his wing. With the exception of the traitor Harrington, they were all violent, dangerous criminals, and two of the most infamous gangsters known in London for twenty years were held here against attempted rescue. He went down the long corridor, his footsteps echoing, and reflected that it was only ten minutes before he went off duty.

After an hour, Stephen looked at his watch and got up. "I can leave you a packet," he said, and Harrington thanked him for the cigarettes. "Hope you like the books." Harrington picked them up and opened the first one. "It won the Booker prize," Stephen explained. "It's a marvelous novel."

"It's certainly long enough," Peter murmured. "But I've got plenty of time."

"That's no way to talk," the younger man chided him. "Look on the bright side. The other one's just a nonsense—one of those thrillers you race through in an evening."

Harrington opened the paperback and turned a few pages. "I've read it, thanks."

"Never mind; I'll bring you something else when I come next week. Good-bye, and see you on Tuesday." There was a bell to call the prison officer. After a couple of minutes the cell door was opened and he went out.

It was the relief officer. They chatted for a moment. "I'd better go and see Fredericks now," Stephen Wood said. "How's he been behaving?"

"Not too bad," the officer answered. "He'll be glad to see you; still doesn't mix much at recreation. He's a withdrawn type. You'd never know what's brewing inside him. I'll hang about outside for a bit, if you don't mind. Just to be sure he's not in one of his moods."

It was seven-thirty when Stephen Wood left the prison. He took the Underground home, and on the short two-stop journey, he opened the rejected paperback and read the message scribbled on a scrap of paper hidden inside. It was brief. "I've been approached. Request instructions." He got off at his station and walked briskly home to his supper with his wife and son.

"Davina? Come in a minute, will you?" Tony Walden buzzed through to the communicating office. She opened the door and he welcomed her with his big smile. "I haven't seen you for a couple of days," he said. "Not since our lunch."

"I meant to say thank you," she said. "It was very nice, I enjoyed it. I've been running around the last day or two, and when I was here, you weren't in your office."

"Sit down for a minute," Walden said. "I've had a flea in the ear from our friend Humphrey."

"Oh? Why?" She didn't looked pleased, he noticed. A very independent lady; did not welcome interference.

"Apparently people have called you here, and Frieda's given them rather short answers. Humphrey didn't like it. I've had a word with her about it, so I thought I'd let you know." The dark eyes considered her closely.

"When you say 'short answers,' " Davina asked, "what does that mean?"

"Apparently she gave the impression that you weren't a serious employee. That's what Humphrey was annoyed about. She didn't know where you were or when you'd be in, that sort of bloody nonsense. I've put her straight, anyway."

"I'm glad," Davina said. "It seems an unnecessary way to behave."

"She's jealous," Walden remarked. "She thinks we're sleeping together."

"For God's sake!" Davina snapped out. She felt her face flame with embarrassment. "What on earth gave the stupid woman an idea like that? I sincerely hope you put *that* right!"

To her annoyance, he laughed out loud. "How could I?" he protested. "What would you expect me to say? Look here, Frieda, don't think Miss Graham and I are having an affair, because we're not—she's a secret agent working for the government. Don't get so angry about nothing. She's jealous of anyone who might take her place. And after all, you're a very attractive woman. So she thinks we're lovers. What the hell does it matter what she thinks, as long as she gives the right answers when you're out of the office?"

"It matters to me," Davina said angrily. "I won't be put in a false situation."

"For someone in your profession," he said gently, "that's a funny thing to say."

"My profession is one thing," Davina answered, "my private life is another. I can't see what you find so amusing about it. Do you normally sleep with your personal assistants?"

"I've never had a personal assistant before you," he answered. She could see that for some reason he was enjoying himself, and that angered her even more.

"I have a private life too, my dear Davina. The trouble with Frieda is, she's never part of it. She wasn't bad-looking when she first came, but not my type. I like them blond and beautiful and absolutely brainless. So you don't have to worry. When will you have lunch with me again?"

"You can't be serious! After this conversation—certainly not!"

"What's the matter?" He spoke gently, teasing her. "Are you frightened your major would object? I'll invite him too, if you like."

"That," Davina said coldly, "I would like to see."

"You don't think we'd get on?" he challenged her. "The man of action versus the man of ideas. I think it could be very interesting. He didn't like me, did he?"

"No. You didn't like each other, that was obvious. Look, this is becoming silly. You called me to tell me about Frieda, and I'm very grateful to you for putting it right. I've actually got some marketing results to get ready for you, so if you don't mind, I'll go and do them."

"I do mind," Tony Walden said. "I can get those results from half a dozen people, and they'll produce them twice as fast as you."

"Thanks very much."

"Why don't you stop playacting? I'm feeding stuff to you because you took this bloody silly attitude about wanting to be useful and earn the salary. It was a nice gesture, a good conscientious attitude, and I admired you for it. But it's becoming a bore. Will you sit down for five minutes and let me explain something to you?"

Davina hesitated. She was on strange ground with this man; she didn't know the type, or quite how to cope with him. If she walked out of the office now, in some infuriating way Tony Walden would have won.

He made it a little easier for her. He said, "Please?"

As ungraciously as possible she said, "All right," and sat down again.

"You don't understand me, do you?"

It was an opening and she took it. "I haven't tried."

His slight grin denied her the point. "On the other hand, I took a lot of trouble to find out about you before I agreed to help Humphrey out. You're a remarkable woman; you have a brilliant record in the Service. I know about your major's medal, but I also know about your trip to Moscow. Yes, I made inquiries about you; not just from Humphrey. I wanted to know the sort of person I was giving a cover to before laying myself and my business on the line if anything went wrong. I'm a respectable tycoon now, but I wasn't always a fat teddy bear. That's why I agreed to take you in and provide cover for you. I hankered a little for the old days when there was a risk involved in living."

"I see," Davina said. "But what you don't understand is that this isn't some kind of postwar game. You said I didn't understand you. That doesn't mean to say I didn't make inquiries too before I came here. You got out of Poland and into the West when you were eighteen, and you made it alone from then on. You also helped people escape after the Wall went up. I know all this, and it's very admirable. But it doesn't give you the right to involve me on a personal basis, just because you've done Humphrey a favor."

"Why not? Why do I have to play some silly charade with you about marketing results, when what I want is to talk to you as a human being?"

"Because I can't," she said. She felt suddenly awkward, rather than annoyed. "I can't talk to you," she went on. "It's not the way things are done now."

"You're saying I'm old-fashioned because I expect to be trusted? Not with information," he leaped in before she could reply, "but with ordinary contact—an interval between clients, telephone calls—a lunch when I am not on duty being convincing or funny or selling the agency to someone. No, I don't understand why you can't afford that."

She didn't answer. There was an answer, Davina was certain, but at that moment she just couldn't think of one. "You make me feel rather mean and ungrateful," she said at last. "But you don't really need me for any of those things. You have a wife; probably girlfriends too. You should get what you want from them."

"I do," he said, and the smile was wide and mischievous. "What I lack is a little mental stimulation. And you're a stimulating person. You challenge me; that's what I like about you. I don't want to know what you're doing or what your work is. I want to talk to you sometimes, not behave like a dummy when you're sitting next door. Is that so impossible for you?"

"Mr. Walden," she said, "you are being bloody. What on earth can I say to all that sob stuff except, 'Yes, of course'? Well, I'm not going to. I'm going to go and spend twice as long as anybody else and get you the marketing results!" She didn't look behind her as she left the room, but she could hear him quietly laughing.

Harrington spent the Sunday rest day studying the duplicate of Colin Lomax's confidential report. He read it straight through once, absorbing an overall picture, refreshing a memory gone stale, with events in which he had played a major part. He didn't pause or bother about anything that seemed at variance with his experience. The details and the conflicts in the sheaf of typed papers could come later, and would take a long time to analyze. His mind darted along the pages like a ferret in pursuit of a wildly jinking rabbit. His early contact with Davina—the clever bugger was wrong there. He had just tried to pick her up, that was all. Nice-looking in a prim way, might be worth a quick screw—two lunches, a few drinks, a withdrawal when he realized she wasn't going to meet expenses, so to speak. Wise chap, he'd never tried it on. His Washington posting—he began to grin, remembering faster than he read. He'd begun blotting his copybook, soaking up the martinis and the Scotch at every official party, publicly lurching out into the night when everyone could see him. Those had been his orders. Get yourself recalled, and not to a foreign posting. He courted disgrace, and here the man who wrote the report had seen a glimmer through the murk of lies and counterlies. That recall and demotion to a humble backwater in the London office brought him right into Davina Graham's path.

His orders had been to make contact. He laid the papers down. He'd thought it was masterminded from Dzerzhinsky Square; he thought his own cunning act had brought him to Davina and through her near to the defector Sasanov. But now he realized it was two hands, not one, that had placed him in position. Who had ordered his recall, and who had sent him down to Personnel? His file would hold that answer. . . .

He went on reading, absorbed, and found the second question mark, and this was more suspicious than the first. Never discount coincidence, they taught in the Service. Never dismiss something because you can't explain it. There was no coincidence about this. The man who was appointed to Washington in his place was reassigned at the last minute. He could see the slick yellow hair and the sharp little eyes, hear the crisp diction with its register of contempt for lesser men like sleazy old Harrington, the drunk. Spencer-Barr. The Minister's nephew, the brilliant graduate from Cambridge and Harvard business school. A Mandarin in embryo, was young Jeremy. Destined for the top of the Establishment heap in due time. But the perfect specimen had a flaw. It ran through the bastard from the top of his spine to the tip of his tucked-up arse, Harrington mused. They hadn't found out about it till later, and by then Spencer-Barr was in Moscow, providing a vital liaison for the most dangerous and reckless SIS operation since the Cold War began. But someone had known. Someone had known what Spencer-Barr was really doing when they sent him to Moscow. Like the flutter of a magician's hand, the manipulator appeared and vanished. The KGB couldn't have engineered a better linchpin which would fail to hold. That too had been arranged in London.

Harrington was whistling; it was the same few bars of an old Beatles song. He had used it as a recognition signal in Washington when he met his contact in the airport lounge en route for New York. He traveled on the shuttle once a week. He met his fellow Russian agents every third week, and they used a rota. The only way he recognized them or they knew him was by the casual whistling of the old Beatles tune.

He hadn't thought about a traitor high up in the SIS until Davina came to see him—how long ago? Nearly three weeks. It seemed like an eternity. She had thrown a lifeline and he'd caught it, and, thank the Christ above, his memory had picked up the distress signal and registered an answer. He had always possessed a wonderful memory. There was a Soviet penetration. He hadn't lied, although he was going to if he hadn't been able to recall the truth. But he hadn't the faintest idea who it was, or whether it was more than one person.

He lit one of Stephen Wood's precious cigarettes. Funny how the truth was paying dividends. He'd spent the major part of his life telling lies and listening to them. Now, when what was left of that life depended on it, the more he told the truth, the better it was—he had decided not to try to con Davina. He made a wry grimace, mixed with hatred and self-pity. He'd learned to respect her intelligence the hard way. Thirty bloody years was quite a lesson.

He didn't know who or what or where the traitor was, and he said so. He asked for the report because without it he couldn't do a deal. Not that it would be the deal that she expected. Oh, no. Harrington had carried the red-shield badge with the crossed swords. The KGB punished betrayal, but not exposure. There was a Swiss account and a large sum of money waiting for him. The British would let him out, but only his Soviet masters would pay him. He must therefore deal with both. Stephen Wood had the message. That proved his loyalty. That would bring instructions, motivate a response on his behalf from the KGB. They had kept trust with him; it took a long time to get Stephen Wood into contact, but they were patient men. He couldn't stand Wood, with his hearty manner, like some games master exhorting the boys to play up and play the game. Who would think a man like that, reeking of middle-class morality and social consciousness, had dipped his hand into the muddied waters of subversion? He had passed only one message to Peter Harrington in two years. "You are not forgotten by your friends. Be patient." The months had passed and he had forgotten that message, as he believed he was forgotten. Until Davina Graham came.

The cigarette burned his fingers. He dropped it on the bed and cursed. The papers fell to the ground while he looked for it on the blanket, found it, stamped on it, sucking his sore finger like a child. He behaved childishly when he was ill or when anything happened to thwart his few pleasures. Once, when a simple box he was making in the carpentry shop split, he found himself crying. That was what prison did to a man; he indulged in bouts of wild self-pity now and again. Kinder to shoot a poor bugger than lock him away for the rest of his life and pretend it was humane. Better to give it to him in the back of the neck walking down the corridor, like they did in maligned old Soviet Russia, than keep him to eat himself alive with frustration and despair. Harrington picked up the papers, smoothed them; he'd trodden on the top one in his agitation. He made sure there was no spark in the bed; he'd become finicky and obsessive about tiny things. Satisfied, he lit another cigarette, positioning the tin ashtray by his side, and settled back to read and concentrate. For dear life. The old-fashioned phrase came to his mind, and he thought how apposite it was. Life, and any hope of enjoying it in freedom, depended on what he could get out of that report.

Igor Borisov swiveled his chair around and faced the window. He had a majestic view of the Lenin Monument at the end of Karl Marx Prospekt; he found it an aid to concentration. Behind him, Natalia waited in silence. He had a broad back; she knew every muscle in it, and had left little stinging scratches either side of his spine. They had been lovers for just barely a year. What had started as a sexual encounter had developed into a secret partnership. Natalia often looked at herself in the mirror and smiled at the face of the most powerful woman in Russia. There were women in public office in the Soviet Union; the Politburo was all male. But the mistress and confidante of the director of Russia's mighty security forces was more influential than some of the members of the Politburo.

Borisov commanded an internal army of a quarter of a million men. The soldiers of the KGB had the most modern weapons and sophisticated training, even at the expense of the regular armed forces. They were the instrument of the state and their function was to keep control of the Soviet people, and the Soviet generals. The powers her lover exercised outside Russia extended right across the world. Russian intelligence abroad was no less his responsibility than a quiescent population at home. Next to Zerkhov, General Secretary of the Party and President of the USSR, Igor Borisov was the most powerful man in the country.

She came up to him and slipped an arm around his shoulder. He placed his right hand over hers and stroked the back of her wrist with his thumb.

"What have you decided?" Natalia asked him.

"I don't want to decide, not yet," he said. "Albatross has served us well. Almost too well, because at last his existence is suspected."

"And the man Harrington?" There is no sound for H in Russian; Natalia pronounced it Garrington. Borisov turned back to his desk; she perched on the arm of his chair.

"He doesn't know who Albatross is," Igor said. "His last three messages confirm that. He is making time for himself until he hears from us."

"And this woman Graham is investigating," Natalia said quietly. "She's clever, Igor. After Mexico, I think she is the biggest danger you have in the British sector. Tell me, have you thought of getting rid of her?"

"Once or twice," Borisov admitted. "She wasn't intended to survive Mexico. I thought of sending someone in against her, then she retired and it seemed pointless. We kill one of theirs, they do the same to us. Nobody benefits from that kind of thing anymore. Only the savages in Bulgaria murder their opponents with poisoned umbrella tips."

"But the retirement was a feint," Natalia pointed out. "It was a cover so she could try to identify Albatross. If you don't want him exposed, Igor Igorovich, then surely the first thing you must do is neutralize her."

"Not if I can use her instead," he answered.

She started to argue that he had tried that once before, but quickly stopped herself. "How? How can she be used by us?"

"We are still controlling Peter Harrington. She doesn't know that. If he gives her what she wants, arrangements will be made to release him and we will be contacted in the usual way. But no one knows that he is in communication with us now. He can direct Davina in the way I want her to go, and in exchange he'll get his Swiss money. Don't underestimate him, Natalia. Our contact says he is a changed man from the one who made a mess of getting Ivan Sasanov back. Six years in prison has done him a lot of good. Run the fat off him, cut out the alcohol—he wants his freedom and he'll fight as hard as possible to get it now. He'll look for Albatross, don't mistake that. He'll try to find him because it's his only hope of getting out. Without telling us, of course. He'll play a little treason here and there, with both sides. But I have something in mind in which he can really be useful if Albatross is uncovered. And you can be sure that if Davina Graham doesn't find him, eventually someone else will. Suspicion is like dragon's teeth. The more you harvest, the more of the monsters spring out of the ground. Albatross is blown. I recognize that. It's a matter of time, that's all. I have to turn the reverse into an advantage."

"You will," she said softly. "You always do. Can you see how?"

He looked at her and smiled. "What would you do, Natalia? If you were in my place, what would you do next?"

He sometimes played this game with her; it used to frighten her at first. Too clever an answer might irritate; she had learned the first lesson of success with any man was never to compete unless you intended to fail. She mustn't appear stupid or naive. She had climbed up from the level of the mattress to confidante at the top level of his work. That hadn't been achieved without exquisite tact and timing. She knew very well what should be done, but the idea must come to him first.

"I would try to replace Albatross," she said after a pause. "But I don't know how."

"I have someone in mind," Borisov murmured. He saw the expectancy on her face and shook his head. He was a cultured man, extensively read and fond of classical and mythological allusions. It amused him to give his operators names with a double allusion. Albatross, the sacred bird that guaranteed the safety of the sailor. The man who killed the bird was condemned to wear its heavy corpse about his neck. . . . He had changed the code name when he succeeded the old director. His people in Western Europe were all called after birds, according to their characters or situations. Albatross had an old, mundane name allotted to him when he was recruited many years earlier. Borisov had christened him after the great bird of ill omen. His wings had overshadowed the SIS for a long time. Now the moment was approaching when he would be brought down. And whoever did it must carry the heavy corpse forever. . . .

"I'll tell you when I'm sure," he said to Natalia. "I want to let this germinate—you grew up on a farm, my love, you know that seeds mustn't be disturbed. This is something so original, so important, that I don't want to speak about it prematurely. I want to keep it inside and let it grow. Then I will tell you, and you'll be the first person in the world to know. You understand that?"

She bent and kissed him. "I understand," she answered softly. "You are a genius, Igor; that's all I need to understand about you. I wish sometimes we could make love here. . . ."

Borisov was tempted by the closeness and the pressure of her breasts against his arm to pull her down to the floor. But he had made the rule from the beginning. No intimacy inside the office. She was making his head swim with desire, and the whispered suggestion was repeated often now. Before, at first, they had never touched hands while they were in Dzerzhinsky Square. But gradually she managed to get near him, to rest a hand on his arm, to remind him of what they had done in private a few hours before. It would be easy to order a sofa for himself . . . easy—and a fatal mistake. He broke away from her and stood up.

"That's all, Comrade Natalia. I'll have my tea now."

Instantly she resumed her role. She wiped the sensuality off her face and stood before him in mute respect. From the sensuous lover she became the deferential secretary. He liked to show his power at times; she suspected that it stimulated his lust when they were in private together. "Yes, Comrade General. I'll bring it to you at once."

He watched her go and smiled. It was a smug little smile. He loved her; he was in helpless sexual thrall to her. He found her an extraordinary sounding board for his reflections, and capable of strange intuitive flashes that he had come to depend upon. She had established a hold over him he wouldn't have thought possible for any woman. He could revel in it only so long as he kept that ultimate authority which put her in her place. And made it all the more exciting to take her out of it when they were alone. Replace Albatross. How clever was she? he wondered sometimes. How much actual penetrating thought went into her simple statements—or was it just the feminine instinct developed above normal? Again, it didn't matter. He was the master as well as the lover. They interlocked in their relationship. He didn't doubt that she was deeply in love with him. And he admitted that he loved her with the heart, as the Russian saying went, not only with the loins. Replace Albatross. Withdraw the thorn from the enemy's flesh and slip another into the empty wound without their knowledge. It was indeed an original idea, and perhaps the most daring intelligence operation the KGB had undertaken in twenty years. He wouldn't talk to Natalia. He would wait and let the seed germinate. And when it was showing its first shoot, he would keep his promise to her. And afterward he would keep another promise, made to Zerkhov, the head of the Supreme Soviet and of the empire of Soviet Russia and its satellites in Eastern Europe. He would go with the plan and tell Zerkhov, and Zerkhov would keep the promise made to Borisov. To support him and work with him against the man they both distrusted. Yuri Rudzenko, the Foreign Minister, opponent of Borisov and hungry for Zerkhov's crown. The capitalist enemy was ever present, like the oxygen in the air he breathed. The dissidents and Jews were like the dust in that air; they irritated the nose and throat. But the threat of Yuri Rudzenko was like carbon monoxide. Once released, it meant death.

"You'rc not making a lot of progress," Grant said. They were parked by the curb in Regent's Park. That morning it was drizzling with rain and the place was deserted except for a few passing cars. "And please don't light that in here—I can't stand smoking in a confined place!"

Davina hesitated. She debated the choice of telling him they could get out and walk, or putting the cigarette away. She shut the packet and put it in her bag. "I'm dependent upon Harrington," she said. "If you want quick results, you've got to help."

He glanced at her suspiciously. "How do you mean, help? I can't risk being involved in anything like this, you know that perfectly well."

"You are involved in it," Davina pointed out crisply, rather pleased at the opening he had given her. "You're involved with me, Colin, and Tony Walden. You're wide open, Humphrey, if anyone started looking. So don't be damned silly. I want access to the filing room in the office."

"That's impossible." His traplike mouth snapped shut.

"Why? You've got a key. You could give me a pass to get into the building. The night staff would let me in."

"You've retired," he said. "Or had you forgotten? There is no way you can go back to the office and be seen."

"I've been away nearly a year," Davina retorted. "Don't tell me you haven't got some new people on at night. It was only a token anyway. Night watchman for outside, security guard for inside the building, emergency telephone and telex operators. Look at the duty roster, Humphrey, and pick a night when the new people are on. Then give me a pass and your key to the filing room. I'll do the rest, and nobody will think anything of it. That's if you're worried about time. Otherwise I'll go on sitting in Wormwood Scrubs picking over the same ground with Harrington. It's up to you."

He started the car and began to drive along the greasy road; the wipers hissed across the windshield. "Whose file do you want? It might be easier for me to get the details for you . . ." He was staring ahead, peering slightly.

Davina glanced quickly away from him. He didn't want her to have access to the filing room. For someone who worried about his involvement with the investigation, his suggestion that he might copy confidential information and give it to her was reckless past belief. "That's an offense under Section D," she reminded him. "You could go to jail for that. If you're anxious about your own position, let me take the risk. That's my job."

"Giving you a pass and the key is no better," he said.

They reached the intersection leading to Marylebone Road. She saw Lomax sitting in her car at a parking meter. "I'll get out here," she said. "I'll wait to hear from you. There's no point going back to Harrington till I've got more information." She banged the door shut and hurried away. He looked after her with naked dislike. Abrasive—it was an apt description of her. Unfeminine, he added, because it was pejorative, although a bosomy female filled him with revulsion. If only he hadn't needed her! If only he wasn't fighting for the brigadier's job, and seeing her as a potential rival. It made it difficult for him to speak to her without showing his hostility. She wanted a pass and a key. Very well, then, damn her, she would get them. And a part of him longed for her to get caught.

CHAPTER 3

"DARLING, WOULD you really be in line for the job?" The fire was low, and John Kidson sat with his wife and watched the logs glowing red, emitting sudden spurts of flame before they burned out. He loved the quiet evenings they spent together, and those were rare because Charlie loved going out and equally liked entertaining at home. John was often tired, but he couldn't deny her anything. She had cooked an excellent dinner—it still amazed him that she had any domestic skills at all—settled him in with coffee and brandy, and curled up like a beautiful red cat beside him. So beautiful, he thought as he did every time he looked at her. Beautiful awake and asleep, without a touch of artifice or makeup. God's perfect creation. And he, ordinary middle-aged John Francis Kidson, without any outstanding talents or money, had married her and made her happy.

They had a small son, growing up like his mother, to Kidson's delight, with the same golden-red hair and gray eyes. She was anxious for another baby; John had persuaded her to wait. There was plenty of time, he insisted. And he had mentioned the possibility, however remote, that he might take over from James White.

"You mustn't take it too seriously," he said. "I only mentioned it because . . . well, it'd make quite a difference to us."

"You mean money? I've got money, darling—we're quite all right."

"I know you have," he said gently. "And you know I won't live off it. So forget about that, my sweet."

Charlie laughed. An expensive apartment and a collection of very good modern pictures had been part of the settlement wrung from her second husband. She used the income to buy clothes and presents for John, and it was well invested for their son.

Typical of John to be proud about another man's settlement. He would never believe her when she said the departing husband had considered it cheap at the price.

"All right, we won't go into that again, darling. You like to be the big strong man of the family, and that suits me too." She bent over and kissed him on the mouth. "You'd like the job, wouldn't you?"

He hadn't admitted to himself just how much he ached to take over the running of the Service. For years he had accepted his secondary role as the finest interrogator and debriefer the SIS or its counterparts had ever had. He was proud of his record, and it was most impressive. There was always Grant between him and further promotion, and he had come to see that as inevitable. But since lunching with his Chief, the buried ambition had come to life, and with it a lot of uneasy self-examination. Should he take White seriously when he suggested that Grant was not automatically in line? Was this more than a device to prod him into talking, when James White threw Davina into the ring? Kidson hadn't believed him; Grant did. That made Kidson think again. They had all four dined together a few weeks before. He frowned, thinking about it. A jolly evening, Charlie called it. But she wouldn't notice the undertones. To Charlie every social gathering was a stage play in which she acted the star role and dazzled the other guests. Even her sister and the taciturn Colin Lomax were an audience to be won over.

Charlie thought it jolly, and a success. Kidson knew that Davina Graham was not relaxed and that Lomax was fending off questions for her. Outwardly it was a normal evening, with Charlie's gurgling laugh ringing over them, and Lomax telling Scottish jokes that got a little broader as the time passed. And Davina, whom he knew so well and had worked with for so many years, talking to him about everything but the work they shared. And not talking at all about the job she had taken in exchange. That had confirmed his earlier suspicion that her employment with Arlington was not what it seemed. He had watched her and Lomax, but there was no doubt about the state of that relationship. He was so much in love with her that his possessiveness was slightly comic. And how that independent woman loved it, Kidson decided, amazed at the inconsistencies of the female. They were a team in every sense of the word. Whatever was wrong, it wasn't between Davina and Lomax. He must look in other directions.

"You're not listening, John," Charlie reproached him. "I said, would you like the job?"

"Yes, I would." Kidson looked at her. "I'd give my eyeteeth to get it. And that's something I've never admitted to myself before. And I'd be bloody good in it, too. Better than Humphrey." He hadn't mentioned it to her before, because it stung his pride, but now he said, "And I didn't tell you, but the Chief actually said he'd been thinking of recommending Davina!"

"That's ridiculous." Charlie sat upright. "It's not a woman's job. What a stupid suggestion—anyway, she's left the Service—what's he talking about?"

"I don't know," Kidson admitted. "I thought it was just mischievous, or trying to get me to talk about her. Grant thinks he meant it."

"Why should James White want you to talk about Davina? And if he did, why not ask a question if he wanted to know—I don't see the sense in that."

"I didn't either," Kidson admitted. "I just felt there was something behind the lunch and the whole conversation. He knew all about her anyway. I had a word with Humphrey, and he hit the roof! My God, he means to get the job when the old man does retire—I didn't realize how much it meant to him."

"He wouldn't do it as well as you," his wife said quietly. "He hasn't got the personality or the vision. He's a natural second-in-command." John stared at her for a minute. Then he shook his head. Behind that lovely face there was a shrewd brain. She had slotted Humphrey Grant into place in a few words: a natural second-in-command.

"You think I'm a natural leader, then?" It was a hesitant question, self-mocking.

Charlie looked him straight in the eye and said, "No, darling, I don't. But I think you'd soon turn into one when you had the responsibility. That's all you need. To be given the job, and you'll do it. Grant will be a mess. Besides, he's an old queer deep down, and that's not proved very reliable, has it?"

"You've no reason to say that," Kidson murmured. "And no proof."

She shrugged. "I don't need proof," she said. "He hates being touched by a woman, haven't you noticed? When I shake hands, he pulls back as if he'd got hold of a scorpion. I know when a man's queer, and he certainly is. Not actively, darling, not even consciously, but underneath." She hesitated for a moment. "Has it ever been suggested? At the office, I mean?"

"Good God, no," Kidson said. "He's just looked on as a sort of neuter, that's all."

"Well, why don't you drop a hint to Sir James—that ought to put Humphrey out of the running."

"Charlie," he said, "you amaze me." He sounded stern and disapproving. "That would be the most bloody awful thing to do, just to get ahead myself."

"Only if it wasn't true," she pointed out. "I think you're being silly, John. And I'm sure he'd do it to you if he had anything against you. You want this so badly, why won't you fight for it?"

He didn't answer at once. He was shocked at her. And at himself, because part of him was listening and agreeing. "Because I don't live by the law of the jungle," he said at last.

"You live in it," Charlie said quietly. "You can't have two standards, my love, without being a plain hypocrite. I wouldn't hesitate if I were you. And I know you're going to say I haven't any morals, and I don't care. I don't pretend to have any. You do, and it's time you stopped. Now I'm going up to bed because you're cross. Good night, darling."

He kicked the fire, but it wouldn't break into flame. He had ash over his shoe. He was angry with Charlie. Very angry. He didn't want her to show the ruthless side of her he knew existed. He didn't like to be told he was a hypocrite, and had no morals, as if she were humoring a boy who wouldn't face the facts. He wanted her soft and loving and gorgeous to look at—she had no right to remind him that she was still Davina Graham's sister. They weren't alike; he wouldn't have it. And yet she drew aside the veil from time to time and showed a face that wasn't hers. "You live in the jungle." The remark hurt because it was so true. He lived with lies and betrayal, and no moral values except the belief that what was done was necessary. And no KGB assassin would disagree with that. He wanted to succeed Sir James White. His wife had taunted him because he wouldn't fight to get what he wanted. If he didn't fight, she would despise him. He should never have mentioned it in the first place. Women didn't understand. They didn't accept that there was such a thing as loyalty between colleagues, lines that no decent man would cross, no matter what he stood to gain.

And then he raised his head and said out loud in the quiet room, "You bloody liar. Grant isn't a colleague—you don't even like the miserable bastard. He's a rival, and Charlie's right. Go out to get what you want. You need it, Kidson, you need it very badly. And instead of sitting here in judgment on her, be bloody glad you've got a wife like Charlie on your side. . . ."

He went into their bedroom very quietly in case she was asleep. He knew by her breathing that she wasn't. He sat on the edge of their bed and reached his hand over and touched her. Their fingers gripped and intertwined. "I'm sorry," he whispered. She sat up and took him in her arms.

Later, just before they drifted into sleep, she said, "If he was being serious about Davina, you mustn't hold back because she's my sister. You come first with me."

The night staff came on at six-thirty at Queen Anne's Gate. Davina waited until eight o'clock, when she was sure the offices would be empty, and then she walked to the side entrance and rang the bell. It was opened by a security guard. She handed him the pass. Humphrey had made it out in the name of Burgess, under her photograph in the plastic window. The guard was polite but cautious. He let her inside after he had studied the likeness and checked Grant's signature.

She walked into the hallway; nothing had changed. The same faded green paint, reproductions of Bartolozzi engravings on the walls, a handsome antique mirror over the fireplace. "Thank you," she said briskly. "I'm going upstairs. I'll see the duty officer."

She ignored the creaking elevator and hurried to the second floor. The duty officer had a small room next to the switchboard. She had no intention of going near him. The filing room was in the basement, and that was her objective. By the broom closet on the second floor was a little door that led to the back stairs. It was unlocked, and she went through and down, bypassing the hallway and the man on duty there. The key to the filing room was one of three. James White, Grant, and the chief filing clerk were the only people able to open that room at will. She didn't waste a moment; she got out three files. The basement was invisible from the street; nobody would see the flaring fluorescent lights, but they were bright enough that she didn't need to use a flash as she photographed. It took just under half an hour, and she had hurried, aware that her hands were trembling slightly. The nerves got out of practice, she thought. She'd spent too long in the peace of her parents' home in Wiltshire looking after Colin and believing that this side of her life was ended forever.

She finished. In her haste, one of the dossiers fell on the ground. It was James White's personal file, and if she hadn't been clumsy, she wouldn't have noticed from the subsequent photographs that a section in the last part had been removed. There were numbers in series at the top-left-hand corner of every page. These corresponded to computer keys which stored the information.

The margin above and below the script was three inches wide, and the number was high up near the edge of the page. She knew she had aimed the lens below it to take in the script. Therefore no discrepancy would show up in the photographs. It had caught her attention only because the folder had fallen open, and she saw that there was a four-digit difference between the facing pages. Davina looked at her watch. Half an hour, nearly forty minutes.

One file had been tampered with. What about the other two—Grant's and John Kidson's? All three had sections missing, and in more than one place. Over a period of years, there were sequences that didn't match, sometimes only a page. She gathered them together and replaced them. Only the silent computer in the far end of the room possessed the information that someone had been so anxious to hide. And without the key, it couldn't be operated. She switched out the lights and went out, locking the door behind her. Someone had got there first and made certain she would find nothing.

Unless it had been done over a long time, careful editing of material that might provide a questioner with ugly answers. She couldn't know which. If it hadn't been for a less-than-steady hand, she wouldn't have realized the deception at all.

It would be interesting, but sterile, to see how the photographs read. She went up the back staircase and let herself out onto the second floor. The lights showed through the glass door of the duty officer's room. She could hear voices. She walked very quickly past the door and slipped down the main stairs to the hall. She showed her pass to the security man, who unlocked the side entrance and let her out. It led into a little passageway that came out on Birdcage Walk. Only the initiated used it; any tourist happening to turn in by mistake would be delighted by the cobbled path, the narrow walls, and the leaning houses of a genuine eighteenth-century street that ended in a cul-de-sac.

"Look, darling—isn't that Davina?"

Kidson was driving, and it was Charlie who saw her sister emerge from the passage and walk hurriedly away toward the barracks.

"My God," he said, and he slowed down, "so it is—what the hell was she doing coming out of Anne's Yard?"

He was watching her through the rearview mirror, seeing her back view stop by a parked car, open it, and get inside.

"What was she doing at the office?" He almost asked himself the question.

"Darling, you're going to shoot the lights if you're not careful," Charlie pointed out. "Why shouldn't she go to the office? Except that it's closed."

"No reason." He pulled himself together. He smiled at his wife; they were on their way to dinner with friends. Davina should have waited till it was dark. She was losing her touch. . . .

"No reason at all," he said. "Bloody Parliament Square—it's always blocked!"

"It won't matter if we're late," Charlie said. "They never sit down before nine-thirty. I do hate having dinner at Spanish hours."

She took out a mirror and examined her beautifully made-up face, flicked a wayward strand of hair into place. Kidson negotiated the traffic without saying any more. But she noticed that he was unusually silent during the evening.

"Nothing," Davina said. "Everything we wanted has been taken out."

"Which proves beyond doubt that we're on the right track," Lomax reminded her. "The sections deleted dealt with Harrington, Sasanov, and Mexico. The bastard was connected with both operations; what he's done is remove the evidence of how he sabotaged them. Or tried to."

"The computer," Davina countered. "It'll be in there."

"Don't bet on it," Colin said. "Whoever doctored those files would have access to the computer key. It's not difficult to erase the memory bank. My guess is, they'll have interfered with the whole process of filing over the last six years, to make it look like a computer error."

"Then what the hell am I to do?" she demanded. "Humphrey knew I was going to look at the files. He's the obvious suspect. So obvious that I don't believe it for a minute. John doesn't have a key, but he could easily get in on a pretext. There's always a file clerk on duty during the day. He couldn't have touched the computer, if you're right about that. But he could have fiddled with the ordinary files over a period of time. And then we have James White."

"Who has access and could use the computer," Lomax said. "But we've no proof of anything. Unless I'm wrong and the computer hasn't been told to erase. Maybe only the files were tampered with . . ."

"Because they were going to be inspected," Davina finished for him. "Which means Humphrey, doesn't it? He edited them before I got there. . . . My God, I can't think straight anymore!"

"Let's see what's missing," Colin said.

"You look at it." She got up. "I'll make coffee, my head's spinning . . ."

He looked up when she came back. "I've been going back," he said slowly. "There have been alterations made long before you joined. I've found half a dozen dates and serial numbers that aren't in sequence. Right back to the time of the brigadier's predecessor—Osborn."

"He was suspected," Davina said slowly. "That's why he retired. Nothing was proved against him or even investigated, but there was talk that he'd let Philby get away."

"So whoever the mole is, he was there before you or Harrington joined. He's covered himself right back to Osborn's time."

"That cuts out Humphrey," Davina said. "Sir James recruited him."

"But it leaves Kidson." Lomax reached for a cup of coffee. "How do you feel about that?"

She got up and moved restlessly around the small room. "It couldn't be him."

"Why not? Because he's married to your sister?"

"Don't be silly, Colin, it's nothing to do with that! I *know* John; all right, I accepted that he had to be considered, but I didn't take it seriously."

"Well, I think you should," Lomax answered. "Because he had every opportunity to act as a double. And he was there early on. He was a Cambridge man, wasn't he? Yes, it's here. Educated Rugby and King's College, Cambridge. Went up in 1946, just after the war. The Communists were still busily recruiting at that time."

"You make it sound as if everyone who went to Cambridge was a Soviet agent," Davina said impatiently. "John wasn't there with Philby or Burgess or Blunt. He's much younger."

"It was supposed to be a don who did the recruiting," Lomax said. "I'll bet he was still there in Kidson's time. . . . Listen, darling, I know you don't want to hear all this, but you've got to. Let me ask you one question, and then I'll shut up. If you thought Kidson was guilty, what would you do?"

Davina lit a cigarette. She didn't want to remember her husband, Ivan Sasanov, or the night he was assassinated. She wanted to answer Lomax honestly and objectively. If she thought of Sasanov and of others who had suffered, then she had to balance it with Charlie's happiness and the baby, Fergus. None of which was right. If she had to make a decision, it had to be influenced by nothing but her professional allegiance and her patriotism. "If it is John," she said at last, "I'd do exactly the same as for Humphrey or James White. I'd turn him in."

"That's what I thought," Colin said gently. "And you'd be right. Whoever this joker is, he hasn't shown any qualms about you. Now, sweetheart, seeing as you're tired and worried, I'm going to make a few suggestions. Say nothing to Grant about the files. I'll give him his key back and say we're working on them. I won't sound hopeful. And let me talk to Harrington next time you go. Put your feet up and listen. I've got an idea."

"Why on earth do you want to meet Tony Walden, James?"

The brigadier saw the frown on his wife's face and said pleasantly, "Because he's a very interesting man, my dear. Born in Poland, did you know that?"

"No," Mary White said. "All I know about him is what I read in that nasty gossip column in the *Mail*. He sounds the last sort of person you'd have anything in common with!"

"You mustn't take any notice of all that business about yachts and whiz kids buzzing around in a private plane. That just sells newspapers. I know it's a bore for you to spend an extra day in London, darling, but I promise you it'll be quite amusing."

She looked at him and said sharply, "James, you're up to your tricks again. I've been married to you for thirty years, and I know perfectly well that it won't be amusing and I shan't enjoy it, but you want to meet this man, and that's why we're going. And if I have to cope with Mrs. Walden, you'll have to pay for a new dinner dress!"

"I'll be only too delighted," he said, and laughed. "You're quite right, of course, Mary. It is business, in a way. I can put the dress down to expenses!"

She laughed too. They had a very close relationship, and in spite of her unpretentious domesticated life in their Kent house, she was sharply intelligent and very well-informed. She had been exceptionally pretty as a girl, but James White would never have married a fool. His associates would have been amazed at how much he confided in her about his work.

"What is your interest in Walden, then?" she asked him.

James White locked his hands behind his head and stretched his legs out toward the fire. The late-April evenings were still cold. "You know Davina Graham is working for him?"

"How should I know? You didn't mention it. What a funny job for her. I can't see her selling things."

"Nor can I," her husband remarked. "I can't see her in that kind of world at all. Publishing, perhaps; or one of the quieter professions. She's the last type of woman to enjoy a life of hustle and bustle and high living. I don't see her on the famous yacht, do you?"

"No, I don't," his wife said. "Not that I ever knew her well. A very reserved girl, even as a child, wasn't she? Now, if it were Charlie!" They both smiled at the idea. They had known Captain Graham and his family for many years; it was an intermittent friendship, interrupted by Service postings, but easy to resume however long the intervals. And it was James White who had seen the potential in the clever, introverted Davina Graham and asked her to work for him.

"Yes, Charlie would have fitted in beautifully," he agreed. "Amazing how she's settled down to married life with John. Personally I gave it about six months before she bolted with someone else. I will never, ever understand your sex, my dear."

"I should hope not," his wife said. "If you're dragging me up to London to meet Walden, I suppose you won't tell me the real reason?"

"I'm not sure what it is yet," he answered. "There are several things I'm curious about at the moment, and the connection between Davina and a man like Tony Walden is one of them."

"And what about the others? Anything I may know?"

"I have never kept secrets from you, my dear. Only state secrets. And there's nothing secret about my retirement."

"You haven't the slightest intention of retiring," his wife said firmly, "so don't talk nonsense."

"Perhaps, perhaps not." He smiled at the fire and stretched again. "But I hadn't realized until the other day how much John Kidson wants my job! Good Lord, it's past eleven—time for bed."

"He'd need it," Mary White said, getting up and tidying the paper and collecting their coffee cups. "Charlie must be a pretty expensive wife to keep."

"I don't think that's the reason," her husband said. "I think it's just naked ambition. And he's kept it hidden all these years. I'll put the lights out and lock up." Methodically he locked the doors and checked that the locks were down on the windows.

It had taken some maneuvering to arrange a meeting with Tony Walden. They had a mutual friend, a senior partner in one of the City's prestigious broking firms. James hinted and his friend set up a dinner party in London, arranged around the Waldens. Mary was very good about that sort of thing, he thought affectionately. She loathed going to London, and the kind of superficial, overmoneyed company around their host's table would be a genuine bore to her. He hoped she chose a really nice dinner dress. The remark about expense had been a joke, but it was time she had something new.

They switched out their bedroom lights, but James White didn't sleep for a long time. He was not a person who indulged in memories unless they had a bearing on the present. He was the most unsentimental man alive, and he said it as a boast. His enemies, and some of his friends, insisted that he was also the most heartless and unscrupulous head of British intelligence since its Elizabethan founder, Walsingham.

That night, lying awake in the darkness, Mary curled up peacefully beside him, James White deliberately looked back. A distinguished Army career had ended prematurely when he was at the Ministry of Defense and the approach was made to him to head SIS. He had taken over a demoralized mess, with a man suspected of Soviet sympathies slinking into retirement. White smiled a little, thinking of the morning he took over the office in the house in Queen Anne's Gate.

He could have risen to the rank of a full general if he had stayed in the Army. The salary at SIS did not compare, nor did the pension. And he wasn't a rich man by any means. The speed of his acceptance surprised the people who had offered him the job. The Mandarins, as they were known, moved at a stately pace themselves; the Army relinquished him with regret, and a new life of secrecy and intrigue began for him at the age of forty-seven. He was well fitted for it, he said to himself; he had a natural bent for political trends and a knowledge far beyond that of the average Army officer of his rank. He spoke three languages fluently, and had passed out of staff college with the highest marks seen in twenty years. He was a very clever man with a peculiar twist to his personality; nobody, not even his wife, who was very dear to him, understood what the twist was. He had always found it difficult to understand it in himself, and he had tried to over the years. It had shaped his life.

He loved to deceive. He loved to baffle and bemuse and mislead his fellow human beings. He loved the world of lies as the alcoholic loves drink and the gambler needs to lose to be satisfied. He couldn't help himself. He had sometimes said that inside every man or woman there was a mainspring that kept them alive and directed their lives. Once that was broken, a man soon died. His own mainspring was a passion for deception. And when he retired, his mainspring would be broken. Or need it be? Until the moment of decision came, he could manipulate and mold the future through the weakness and ambition of the two men who hoped to succeed him. And then there was Davina Graham. Thinking of her, he gave a little sigh. Capture by the KGB, the death of Sasanov, and a miscarriage—in spite of all these blows, her mainspring was unbroken. She had retired once before, and he had maneuvered her into going back to work. Now she had retired again. Or so she said. She had given up her work to nurse her lover, who was dying. Only he hadn't died; he'd recovered from a remarkable operation and was very well indeed. And she was acting as personal assistant to a former Polish refugee who had turned himself into a ready-made Englishman at the head of a huge advertising empire.

Retired. James White didn't believe it. Somebody was using Davina as he had used her. And he intended to find out who it was. Instinctively he knew it would be connected to Tony Walden. On that final reflection, he fell asleep.

The night staff went off duty as the day staff came in. The security guard was hanging up his coat and preparing to go home when John Kidson approached him in his cubicle off the hall. He didn't know Kidson, and he hadn't been at what was known as the Office more than three months, but he recognized what he privately called "management" when he saw one.

"Good morning—you're just going off, I see."

" 'Morning, sir. I'm signing out now."

"Yes, of course. I'm early this morning. You saw Miss Graham last night?" The inquiry was made in Kidson's most beguiling way; he was smiling and casual, asking rather an obvious question. The security guard hesitated. "No, sir. There isn't a Miss Graham in the building. I know everybody's name. Which reminds me—can I see your ID card, sir, please?"

Kidson laughed. "Well done, you. 'Course you can." He produced the little gray card with its photograph and signature. "You don't have to worry. I signed the book when I came in." His eyes said kindly: I'm not checking up on you, old chap. I know you're doing your job.

"Thank you, sir. Regarding your inquiry . . ."

Oh, Christ, Kidson said to himself. He'll ask about my vehicle next. Aloud he said, "Yes, Miss Graham. Didn't she come in last night? About nine o'clock."

"A Miss Burgess came to see the duty officer." The reply was stiff and much on the defensive. "She had a pass and she signed the book, sir. In and out."

"That's my mistake, then," Kidson said, and shrugged. "I thought Miss Graham was coming. Very blond young lady." He gave almost a wink. "Very nice-looking indeed. You certainly wouldn't mistake her."

"I wouldn't mistake anyone who came in while I was on duty, sir."

Oh, Jesus H. Christ, Kidson murmured inwardly, using one of the odd American blasphemies he'd picked up in Washington. And then his faith in the stupidity of human nature was restored.

"Miss Burgess was certainly not blond, sir. Sort of browny-ginger."

"Definitely a different girl," Kidson said lightly. "I'll bet the duty officer was disappointed." The reply was stony and disapproving. Jokes like that were not made by senior officers or bloody "management" or whatever they were called in this new outfit. He wasn't familiar and he didn't like people who were.

"I wouldn't know, sir. I'll be getting off home now. I'm ten minutes late, and I'll miss my bus."

Kidson said pleasantly, "Thank you. Good morning."

It was easy to flip through the night book. There were the usual signatures. Security. Telephone and telex operator. Duty officer. And one almost illegible scrawl. She'd done a good job disguising her own rather sharp handwriting. This was little more than a flat pen stroke with a line underneath it.

You bitch, he said to himself. You lying, devious bitch—what the hell are you up to? And the answer was too simple. Angling for the brigadier's job. Going out on her own on some head hunt which would put her ahead of him and Humphrey. He had always liked Davina. Admired her professionalism and respected that steely integrity which was her trademark as an operative and as a person. But he had never thought of her as a woman, never connected her as bone and blood with his beautiful wife, and didn't want to see any resemblance. Two men had loved her, and Kidson couldn't for the life of him see why. But he realized how a man could hate her so that the bile of it burned his throat.

In his office he sorted his letters and memos, glanced briefly at the appointment book, which his secretary had left ready, and found he couldn't concentrate. Should he go and see Humphrey, alert him? He pushed his chair back and took a deep breath. Was he taking too much for granted because Charlie had seen her sister coming out of the little yard that led to nowhere? He had dismissed the signature as a forgery because he had made up his mind that no such person as Miss Burgess existed . . . and yet the name suddenly rang a bell. Of course, there had been a Miss Burgess who worked as a secretary and had left three or four years ago; he couldn't quite remember—he couldn't picture her in his mind, either. Browny-ginger was a nondescription, a negative response to his suggestion that the woman was a blond. The whole thing could just be the product of his own irritable suspicions. Just. He looked at his watch. He might catch the duty officer before he left. The security staff always arrived and went off earlier than the clerical.

"Jim?"

"Oh, 'morning, sir."

"Any dramas in the night?"

"No, nice and peaceful. There'll never be a nuclear attack while I'm on duty."

"That's good to know. By the way, did you see Miss Burgess? She said she might come over last night."

He saw the other man's head begin to shake, and his stomach lurched once. It was his particular alarm signal.

"No, nobody came last night. It was dead boring, actually." He was a very pleasant young man with an engaging manner and a cheerful grin.

Kidson didn't feel like grinning back, but he managed it. "Don't worry, you'll get your fill of excitement one day. And the best part will be waking up the Chief at three in the morning!"

He went back to his room. His instincts had been right; they nearly always were when things weren't what they seemed. Davina had gone into the office on a forged pass. She couldn't have got that for herself. He sat very quietly until his secretary came in. He had decided to say nothing to Humphrey. Let Humphrey look out for himself. He partly listened to what his girl was saying, while asking the same question over to himself. What was she looking for? And at the back of his mind he knew the answer. The filing room. Only Grant and the brigadier had keys.

"Mr. Kidson? Sorry, but did you want to send an answer to that?"

He said, "I'm sorry, Jane. I wasn't paying attention. Say that all again, will you?" It was the brigadier; he was certain of that. Playing one of his devious games, moving his own people about like pawns on a board. He was using Davina, but against whom? He made a great effort and put the whole issue aside. He worked hard and single-mindedly for the rest of the day. But when he got home, he knew he had to tell Charlie. Because if he was going to engage Davina in a power struggle, his strongest ally would be her own sister.

"I can't do any more," Peter Harrington insisted. "I've reread your bloody report till I'm quoting it in my sleep, and I'm stuck. So were you!"

"Maybe," Lomax said. "But I picked up enough in six months to see what none of your lot even guessed at—I needed facts, and don't tell me you haven't got some." He leaned toward Harrington. "You can try that I-don't-know bit on Davina, but you won't get away with it with me. I haven't got a lot of patience, Harrington, and I don't like your type anyway."

Davina had her back to them and was looking out of the window in the governor's office.

"And who the hell are you, anyway? You're just a glorified bloody hit man!"

"If you say so," Lomax remarked.

Harrington recognized the type. Tough and merciless. He'd seen men like Lomax on both sides. He was frightened, but he wasn't going to show it. "You don't have anything to say but 'Yes, sir' when you get your bloody orders, so don't try to bluff me!"

"You haven't told him, Davina?"

She turned around and walked back to them. "No," she said to Lomax. "I thought I'd wait."

"Told me what?" Harrington demanded. His heart had begun to flutter and bump. He looked from one to the other and cursed them both inwardly. Bastards. Cold-blooded, tormenting bastards. . . .

"The official investigation has been closed down," Davina said. "They've given up on you, Peter."

He sagged in his chair and gave a loud moan. "Oh, Christ, no."

"I warned you it would happen," she went on. "We needed results, and quickly, if the whole thing wasn't going to be shelved."

He looked up at her and said slowly, "Then why are you here? What's *he* doing here?"

"Because we've decided to go it alone," she answered. "Your Mandarins, as you call them, want this swept under the carpet. I don't, Peter. I want to get the man who helped them kill Ivan. You want to get out of here, don't you?"

"No," he mocked bitterly. "No, I love it here—wild fucking horses wouldn't drag me away."

"Mind the language," Lomax said quietly.

"You've got to stop playing games," Davina said. "You've got to cooperate."

"What do you want?" he asked her. "What does 'cooperate' mean?"

"It means you've got to tell us everything you know," Lomax answered. "And we take it from there. The only promise is, you'll end up with your own dirty lot on the other side. If you don't like the option, we won't be coming back."

"Give me a cigarette," Harrington muttered.

"No."

Harrington glared at Lomax and then looked at Davina. "You can't help me—not without the office behind you. If they've pulled out, that's the end of it."

"Think about it," she said quietly. "I'll be back."

"Suit yourself," Harrington said. He didn't look up when they were let out of the office and the guard came to escort him back to his cell.

Harrington needed an answer to one question. That question could determine whether he was free and broke or living a comfortable life in some pleasant Swiss canton. How much was he to tell Davina Graham about Albatross? Was Albatross expendable? He condensed the message into a few lines and scribbled them on the margin of the eighty-third page in the book on Grinling Gibbons' carving which Wood had brought him.

As Wood was leaving that evening, Harrington said, "You couldn't come back next Friday, I suppose? I've been feeling a bit down lately. I'd like an extra visit."

"I'm sorry about that, old chap," Wood said kindly. "I'm sure that'll be all right. I'll have a word about it. Want me to bring you anything? Got enough to read?"

"I've got plenty. But if you think of something funny, I'd like that—cartoons, anything with a bit of a laugh in it."

"David Niven's new one," Wood said eagerly. "I've got it for myself. You won't feel under the weather if you're reading that. I really laughed over the other one—*Bring on the Empty Horses*. Anyway, I'll see you on Friday. I'm sure that'll be all right."

Outside he said thoughtfully to the prison officer, "I think he's suffering from a bit of depression, you know. Looked very sorry for himself tonight. I'll ask for an extra visit. How's my other fellow?"

"Fair to middling," was the answer. "Always easier after he's seen you." As he unlocked the cell door for Wood's second prisoner, the officer thought what a decent man he was. Never missed a visit; very friendly to the prison staff, unlike some, who kept their distance. People like Stephen Wood did a lot of good. He wouldn't hear a word against that type of prison visitor.

"What you're saying," Humphrey insisted, "is that you're giving up."

"If that's how you want to put it, yes." Davina turned away and stared angrily out of the car window. She felt if she had to look at that particular piece of grass and flowerbed in Regent's Park once more, she would start screaming.

Humphrey looked and sounded genuinely shocked. "But there *is* somebody; we know that, from Lomax's report! How can you sit there and tell me you're not going on with the investigation!"

"Because I'm not sure myself anymore," Davina said. "I know Colin's deductions made it look as if we had a mole working inside. I know exactly how it all fitted together, but there's nothing else, Humphrey! There's not a shred of outside proof that I can find. The files showed nothing."

"Harrington," he reminded her. "Harrington confirmed that there was a Soviet plant."

"Harrington," she said acidly, "would say anything to get himself out. He couldn't back it up when I pinned him down. All he kept on about was being moved. It's no good, Humphrey. I'm wasting my time. If there is someone, they're so well covered that I can't find them, and that's that! And you needn't think I like giving up on it, because I don't!"

"Very well." He snapped out the two words and then repeated them. It was a maddening habit. "Very well. We'll drop the whole thing." He leaned across and opened the car door for her. His face was set and furious.

She got out and leaned down toward him. "Thanks, Humphrey. Luckily I haven't got far to walk."

He pulled the door shut and drove off, banging through the gears. Davina stood for a moment looking after the car. Genuinely angry or secretly relieved that he had blocked his own exposure? It was a sickening situation. Colin was right. She either carried on alone or she gave up. Thank God she had him to support her.

"Davina?" She hadn't heard the car draw up beside her; she had been walking slowly, miles away from her surroundings in her thoughts.

Tony Walden leaned across and called her name again. She stopped, startled to see him. The car was a big blue Mercedes.

"Oh . . . hello, Mr. Walden."

"Get in and I'll give you a lift," he said.

She hesitated. She felt suddenly low and tired of walking by herself. "Thanks very much." He was a smooth driver; the big car sped along and turned out of the park. He hadn't spoken since he picked her up. She said, "I thought you'd have a driver."

"Why? Do you think I'm too grand to drive myself? I like driving Other people make me nervous. Why were you looking so depressed, walking along with your head down and your back bowed? I've never seen you like that."

"I was thinking," Davina replied.

"Not very happy thoughts, then," he said.

She didn't answer; glancing out of the window, she saw they were heading toward Marble Arch and had missed the turning to Arlington Place.

"Aren't you going to the office?" she said quickly.

"No. I'm meeting a very important client in Kensington Palace Gardens. It will be nice to have you with me."

"I haven't got much choice," she retorted.

"You can jump out at the next traffic lights," he suggested. "But this meeting might amuse you. What do you know about Arabs?"

"Nothing at all. Except that they're rich."

"That's the first thing I knew about them too," he said. "And the second is equally simple. Don't expect them to be like anyone else you've dealt with. Put every accepted business and social practice to one side and start from the very beginning."

"You sound as if you know rather a lot about them," Davina said. She had begun to feel less low-spirited. He had been right when he said she was depressed. He had a natural optimism which lifted other people up. She recognized it, and in spite of herself, she was grateful. The more he talked about his Arab client, the less she remembered that awful empty sense of isolation after leaving Humphrey Grant.

"I know quite a lot about the man I'm going to see," he agreed. "He is one of the most powerful men in the Middle East. A younger prince, but much favored by his father. Full of enthusiasm for Western ideas and anxious to modernize his country on Western lines. But without antagonizing his elder brothers. They are strict Muslims. At home, anyway."

"And where does the agency fit in?" she asked him.

"In a discreet campaign to promote the country in the public eye," he answered. "Television programs, articles, features in important magazines. All showing how the kingdom has come into the modern world. Hospitals, technology, schools, transport—you know the sort of thing. Fine hotels. One of the biggest aluminium smelters in the world. Skyscrapers and palm trees. Doesn't it fascinate you?"

"Not really." She smiled slightly. "It's too much of a man's world to attract me. I've never suffered from the sheik-in-the-desert fantasy, I'm afraid."

"No," he agreed. "I wouldn't expect you had. Tell me, what kind of man would he have to be to carry you off into the night?"

"I've no idea," Davina retorted. "I prefer to walk where I want to go."

"You're not a romantic. What a pity." He looked around, and he was laughing at her.

Immediately she felt defensive. "Mr. Walden—" she started, and he interrupted her immediately.

"Not that tone of voice, please. Let me have my little joke—it helps me concentrate on the important things. Like my Arab prince."

"I'm glad to act as light relief," Davina said. "But I don't enjoy being talked to like a fool."

"You mean you don't enjoy being flirted with," he said lightly. "That's quite different. I'm sorry. Most of the women I know expect it."

"Now you can see that I don't," Davina pointed out. "There's the turning into Kensington Palace Gardens."

"So it is," he murmured. "And of course I saw it. What a bossy lady you are, my dear. And how attractive. There's the Soviet embassy."

"I know it is. I always thought how inappropriate it was to have it in a place known as Millionaires' Row!"

"That shows you believe in all their nonsense about equality," he remarked. "Here we are. Now, remember. You are my secretary; the prince is an enlightened and charming man, but he won't expect you to say anything except 'Good morning, your Highness' and 'Goodbye, your Highness.' In his country, women are still kept in their proper place."

She got out of the car and followed Walden inside the magnificent house. She didn't know whether she was glad or sorry that she had come with him. They were shown into a vast salon with a gilded ceiling and a giant-sized crystal chandelier which was blazing with lights in spite of the bright sunshine outside. Everything in the room was on a massive scale: the velvet sofas seated ten in comfort; there was a modern red-and-gold throne-type chair at the head of the room, and some of the finest Persian carpets Davina had ever seen. An Arab servant asked in good English if they would like tea or fruit juices while they waited for His Highness. Walden asked for tea without consulting Davina. It was watery and aromatic, with a slightly bitter taste. The time went by and Walden looked at his watch.

"How much longer?" Davina started to demand, but he put a finger to his lips.

"Remember lesson one," he said gently. "They all have all the time in the world. We are the ones in a hurry."

They had been sitting there for over an hour when the prince came into the room. He was a small man, handsome in a swarthy way, with brilliant dark eyes and a very hooked nose that gave him a predatory look. He wore Western clothes, immaculately cut, but with the white headdress and black-and-gold binding of the ruling family. He shook hands with Walden, gave Davina one brief, disinterested glance and a nod when she was introduced, and for the next hour she sat and listened.

Twice Walden asked her to take a note of something, and she managed to scribble on the back of her diary. She wondered whether the Arab noticed that she was hardly equipped for secretarial duty that morning. It was a new and alien world to her, and she saw for the first time what had made Tony Walden the boss of the biggest advertising agency in Europe. He was deferential without being servile; he put forward his opinions tactfully and clearly, and withdrew them gracefully if they weren't well received. Above all, he listened. No fast-talking sales promotion; the prince talked about his country and its needs and told Walden what he wanted.

And then, without preamble, the conversation veered into a discussion of the prince's racing interests. Walden knew the names of his horses and the races they had won. She was sure he knew when they had failed to win too, but this was never mentioned.

He himself changed the subject to ask about the progress of the prince's new palace outside the capital. A wonderful building, he enthused, with every conceivable modern amenity, and the beauty of a desert setting—how much he had enjoyed seeing the royal falcons being trained! Casually he asked by name after the prince's two favorite birds. Not once did he include Davina, or acknowledge her existence, apart from the two brief instructions to take notes.

At last the prince stood up; he shook hands and Walden gave a slight bow. Davina was granted another impersonal nod. They left the house and walked down the steps into the sunny forecourt.

Walden didn't open the car door for her. He got into the driver's seat and said, "I'm sorry about the bad manners. I'd lose face if I let you in first."

"I don't mind." Davina was looking at the house. She saw a curtain on the ground floor move as if someone had let it drop back. "I think there was someone watching."

"Oh, there would be," he replied, starting the engine. "There are bodyguards all over the place. The ones who let us in and brought us tea were armed to the teeth under those robes. The prince wasn't alone with us, either; there's always a guard close by wherever he is."

"I didn't see anybody."

"You didn't look behind that handsome Chinese screen, did you? You'd have found two men with loaded pistols. He doesn't like to go round with an escort like some of the other rulers' sons. He likes to seem Western, but he's about as Western as you're an Arab lady of the harem."

"You couldn't have made a better comparison," she said shortly. "Anyway, you've made the deal."

"My dear." She saw his annoying grin appear again. "I said to throw your Western European notions out of the window. We haven't agreed to anything except to go on talking. He knows it is a massive account. He isn't going to hurry, because he doesn't like doing anything until the moment Allah wills. And Allah usually wills when he is in the mood. That mood may last for a few minutes, rarely longer than an hour or so. Arabs get quickly bored; if you let that happen, they are beautifully polite, and you never hear from them again. I want this account, and I can give the prince what he wants. But I have to judge the right moment to ask for a signature on a contract, and above all, I can't have anything else to do at the time. Except be there and be prepared to wait."

"How much will it mean to the agency?" Davina asked.

"About two and a half million, spread over a period of a year and three months. Do you realize it's nearly half-past twelve? I could do with a drink."

"You can drop me," Davina said. "I can take a taxi back to Arlington Place."

"Why?" He pulled up at a red light with unnecessary abruptness and she jerked in her seat. "What pressing work is waiting for you that you can't even join me for half an hour? I spend the whole morning treading on a lot of bloody eggshells, and you expect me to go and drink by myself?"

Davina protested. "Wait a minute, I'm not expecting you to do anything. You're expecting *me* to keep you company."

"And you don't want to. You've had enough, you're bored. You want to go and gossip with Frieda Armstrong?"

"I'm meeting someone for lunch," she said at last, unwilling to explain herself to him.

"I see. Your hard-faced major friend?"

"My hard-faced major friend. He doesn't like me being late."

"Doesn't he trust you?"

She didn't answer; she had arranged to meet Colin at one o'clock at a pub close to Arlington Place.

"I'm going to the Connaught and buy you a glass of champagne. He can wait five minutes for you."

"I don't like champagne," Davina said gently. "Thanks all the same."

"Then you can watch me drink mine," Tony Walden answered, and put the car into top gear. Ten minutes later he steered her by the arm into the Connaught Bar to a table by the window.

"You're the only man I've ever met who manages to get me into a corner, one way or another," Davina said suddenly. "I didn't want to come; I'm going to be late, but goddammit, here I am!"

"It's my charm," he said, and beckoned the waiter.

"It's your persistence," she countered.

"Two glasses of champagne," he ordered, and added, "The first time I met you, you said it was your favorite drink. In your flat with Humphrey and your major. So I didn't take any notice of that nonsense in the car. Have an olive, they're very good."

"I can't pretend I don't like those," Davina admitted. "You know, Mr. Walden, you look tired. I'm beginning to think you're human after all."

"I'm glad to hear it," he said. "That's why I needed this, and you to share it with me. You do make me struggle for very little, don't you?"

He did look tired: there were rings under his eyes that hadn't been there when she got into the car.

"There's often a feeling of deflation when something's gone well," he said. "The day I come away with that contract in my pocket, I shall fall into the depths of depression. I always do when the battle is won. Have you ever felt that?"

"No," Davina answered. "When I've succeeded, I'm quite the opposite. I get euphoric, excited. Failure is what depresses me."

"And had you failed when I saw you this morning?" He asked the question quietly.

She looked at him and said, "I don't know. But I think you'll be getting a call from Humphrey Grant."

The look was quick and shrewd, and he put his glass down without drinking. "What to say?"

"That you don't have to go on fronting for me," Davina answered. "I wasn't going to mention it, but I think I should. You've been very good and it's been a tremendous help. I'd like to thank you, for myself."

"I see. So whatever Humphrey Grant wanted hasn't come off, is that it? So I am not needed anymore. I can give you the sack tomorrow morning."

"This afternoon, if you like," she said.

"You wouldn't like to go on working for me, I suppose?"

"I'm not working for you," she said. "There was never any job."

"There could be," he countered. "Unless you hate the agency. Or me. I have annoyed you quite a lot, haven't I?"

She faced him and said suddenly, "Yes, you have. You've muddled me, and I don't like that. But the truth is, I've rather enjoyed it too."

"Then I shall tell my friend Humphrey to take a running jump,"

Walden said. He didn't actually give her time to reply because he looked at his watch and said theatrically, "My God! It's long after one! You'd better go or your major will be coming after me with a gun. The doorman will get you a taxi. I've seen someone come in I want to talk to . . . Ah, Jack! How are you, my dear boy? Looking great . . ."

She heard his voice, full of warmth and good humor, and thought: Christ, he has to act the whole time—it must be the most awful strain. Colin will be furious if he knows I was here with him. And in the taxi she shrugged as if she were arguing with Lomax. Why should he mind? There was no harm. Walden was lonely and drained and needed somebody to talk to. Of course she'd leave the agency. There was no reason they should ever meet again once she had gone.

It was Thursday morning. The sky above Moscow was gray, and a thin rain fell, making the streets greasy. The eight golden cupolas of St. Basil's Cathedral gleamed under the coating of rain. The bells chimed as always on the hour. In the big room on the second floor of the modern building inside the Kremlin walls, the Politburo was in session. There were nine men seated around the heavy table; between them they were responsible for every aspect of life in the Soviet Union. Transport; Communications; Finance; External Affairs; the Army, Navy, and Air Force combined; the Foreign Ministry; Internal Security; and the huge network of Russian intelligence throughout the world. The Chairman and General Secretary of the Party sat at the center of the oval table. Zerkhov was built like a peasant: heavy-shouldered, clumsy in movement, with a large head and deep-set eyes that had no expression in them. On his right sat his protégé, the all-powerful Igor Borisov, young by Politburo standards, disliked and resented by many of the old men sitting around the table. On the left of Zerkhov, two places down, the Foreign Minister, Yuri Rudzenko, sketched a face on the pad in front of him. He was a thin, tall man with a drooping mustache and dark hair that was only flecked with gray in spite of his sixty-eight years. Albanian blood was evident in the dark skin and the thin features; his eyes were hooded under heavy lids, but they were black and fierce. He was an admirer of Stalin and dedicated to the ideology of prewar Communism. He regarded detente with the West as a betrayal; his views on dissidents and Jews and the human-rights activists reminded Zerkhov of the worst days of Stalinist terror, when as a young, ambitious man he had entered the dangerous arena of Soviet political life.

Business had been concluded for the morning. Zerkhov sat on for a time, listening and saying little, while his colleagues relaxed. There was a burst of laughter at one moment, from the iron old Soviet General Gagarin, who loved a dirty story. Rudzenko looked at him and scowled. Nobody would have laughed had he been General Secretary. Zerkhov nudged Igor Borisov with his elbow. "Gagarin has heard the one about the engine driver from Kharkov," he remarked, and his heavy face split in a brief smile. "Have dinner with me tonight, Igor. Come at nine o'clock." He pushed his chair back to end the meeting, and the company broke up.

Rudzenko swept up his memoranda and stalked out, followed by two of his supporters. Both were men of rigid ideas, dedicated to oppression in the cause of a pure ideology. Rudzenko was their leader now that the guardian of Marxist principles, Anatoly Braminsky, had died. There was no secret about their alliance or their opinions. But one thing even Rudzenko dared not do was arouse the suspicions of his General Secretary. He did not plot; he fought openly for his policies and his beliefs.

Zerkhov had accepted an invitation to visit West Germany. Rudzenko and his allies had opposed it. It would appear, they argued, that Russia was courting favor with the Germans because of the reaction to military rule in Poland. Borisov had made a clear and devastating rebuttal of all Rudzenko's points, taking them one by one. He reminded the Minister that his insistence on direct Russian intervention had been proved wrong. Poland was solving her difficulties in the way that Russia wanted, but without a single Red Army soldier being involved. The rest of the world could accuse and condemn, but they had no proof and their cries were hollow. Poland would be left to her fate. Order would be maintained and Soviet interests protected without the extreme measures the Minister favored. The wisdom of Comrade Zerkhov's policy had been proved again, and an essential part of that policy was to divide West Germany from the Western alliance as deeply as possible. The visit to the West German Chancellor was part of that plan, and nobody would mistake anything the President did for weakness. Rudzenko and his colleagues were overruled, and the members of the Politburo endorsed Zerkhov's decision. The invitation to a private dinner was Borisov's reward. In the privacy of his apartments in the Kremlin, the President would express his thanks, and things could be said that nobody else must hear.

Borisov went home to his family early that evening. He told his wife he had an important meeting; she showed on her face what she thought that meeting to be, and he said in a burst of irritation and guilt that he was going to dinner with Zerkhov.

She was excited, and tried to talk to him about it, but he brushed her aside, saying he must bathe and change and had no time. Did she want him to be late? She was a fool; he couldn't discuss anything with her. He had Natalia to confide in; she understood his world. He got into his Zim, and the driver took him back to the Kremlin.

Unlike his predecessor, Zerkhov did not use the old palace building for his private apartment; he had the top floor of the modern offices. He had been born on a farm in the Ukraine and had grown up in conditions of sparse food and grinding labor. Now, seventy-two years later, he lived with a private collection of Impressionists among magnificent modern furniture, and his wife swathed her plump old body in very expensive Paris dresses. They had no children; they lived the private part of their lives in the superb penthouse overlooking the great city, and indulged in the perquisites of his enormous power. Borisov knew that he was not only privileged but also wholly trusted, to be allowed into that sanctum.

The food was simple; Madame Zerkhova presided over the table, helped by an impassive member of the Presidential Guard in mess orderly's uniform. Watching him serve them, Borisov was reminded of the old Preobrazhensky Guard, the troops who had guarded the tsar since the days of Peter the Great. Times changed, he thought, but Russia remained the same. He was a scholar of Russian history; unlike the arch-puritan Rudzenko, Borisov saw much that was glorious in his country's pre-Lenin past. They drank vodka with the cold hors d'œuvres and the borscht. Zerkhov drank heartily, pushing the bottle toward his guest, anticipating the servant as he moved to help them. Unlike Stalin, who toasted his rivals in plain water while they succumbed to ninety percent pure alcohol, the present ruler of Russia enjoyed drinking and eating. He liked the fresh Crimean wines which went with a homely mutton stew, heavily spiced. The talk was general; his genial wife had little to say but trivialities; she had a motherly smile and showed her fondness for her husband, quoting little anecdotes of their early life. There was a close bond between them, Borisov decided. They had shared the hard years and the dangers that followed when Zerkhov was ambitious and climbing toward power. She might indulge herself in Paris-made dresses in private, but not the cleverest dressmaker could disguise the strong mother image of the Russian peasant woman. He thought of his own wife, and envied Zerkhov his marriage.

When the dinner was finished, Madame Zerkhova got up and said good night.

"We will sit here," the old man said to the orderly. "Bring Turkish coffee and brandy." He said to Borisov, "I miss the old table in the kitchen with the samovar always alight. But this does as well." And he laughed.

"I admire your taste in pictures," Borisov said.

"I like the Renoir best," Zerkhov admitted. "He gives peace; looking at his pictures is like having a gentle dream. Manet is more powerful, not so soothing. I hate Van Gogh; his madness screams at you from the canvas."

"Still, you have two," Borisov countered.

The old man shrugged slightly. "Only to please Anna, she likes them. She does not like Picasso except in the Blue Period, so I keep those in my office up here. I like contemporary art, but it's more difficult to collect without arousing criticism. I have been waiting to get a very good Francis Bacon for nearly two years, but the owner still won't sell. It's an American." He chuckled. "They wouldn't like to know it would end up here," he said. "Put another bottle of brandy on the table, Ivan, and you can go. Good night."

The orderly saluted, ramrod stiff, never looking directly at the President. The Guard were the crack troops in the regular army.

There was no love between them and Borisov's militia. There was silence for a while; both men drank the sweet thick Turkish coffee and emptied the first bumper of brandy.

"That's the difference between us," Zerkhov said suddenly. "I believe in the modern world. Rudzenko hates it. I believe that we are progressing, that while we overtake our enemies we have a lot to learn from them and put to use. He sees nothing good after 1953."

"And nothing good before 1917," Borisov remarked. "He would like to petrify Russia like a fly in amber, from Lenin to Stalin's death."

"Yes," the old man sighed. "When Braminsky died, he gave his hat to Rudzenko. Unfortunately, it fits him even better. You spoke very skillfully today, Igor; he won't forgive you for making him look a doctrinaire fool. Every time he tries to attack me, you rip a piece off his reputation as a responsible politician. Your exposition of the Polish situation was a masterpiece. You've become cruel as well as subtle."

"Would you rather I changed?" Borisov asked him. The alliance between them had grown up through Borisov's first failure when he took over the KGB. He had never forgotten the advice of Natalia then, when he faced ruin. "Tell him the truth. Go to him as a father." He had done exactly that, and he asked now, as a son would to his father, "I want your criticism, Peter Petrovich. Tell me."

The heavy-lidded eyes opened a little; the first bottle of brandy was nearly empty, but the eyes were bright, their look intense. "I have no criticism, only a suggestion. More subtlety, more cruelty. Attack as often as he gives an opening. Matters must come to a head before the meeting of the Supreme Soviet in the autumn."

Borisov put the glass down, wishing he hadn't kept pace with Zerkhov. He couldn't believe what he had just heard. "If that's what you mean, I'll make sure it's done," he said. "But why? Surely we don't want an internal crisis at the moment? Poland—"

"Will explode before the end of the year!" The interruption cut across him. "That is what Rudzenko is hoping for, and that's what he is trying to initiate. He has allies in the Stalinist clique in Poland. They will force an uprising and overthrow Jaruzelski. And that, Igor, my friend, is when Rudzenko will make his bid for power. At my expense." The heavy head tilted forward on its short neck like a turtle leaving the shell. "And yours. You won't keep your place a month after Rudzenko wins. In fact, I wouldn't give much for your life, either, or mine. He would bring back the old ways, don't you think? The state trial, the confession in public—and click!" He snapped his fingers like a pistol shot.

"He won't win," Borisov said. "If I thought there was any danger of that . . ." He stopped himself in time, and the old, cunning face opposite him twitched once.

And Zerkhov said softly, "What would you do, Igor Igorovich?"

"I would stop him," Borisov answered quietly. "I will stop him. He'll never harm a hair of your head." He wasn't aware of the fierce emotion in his voice. A gleam of genuine affection passed from the old man to the young one, and Borisov said in a very low voice, "I am your man. Leave him to me."

"That is what I'm going to do," came the answer. "But not yet, my son." The last two words hung on the air. Borisov felt a prick of tears in his eyes and a wild exultation in his heart. My son. He knew what that meant in terms of his future. "I will tell you when," the voice went on, flat and droning. "I am no Stalinist. I don't believe in paddling in my comrades' blood." For a moment he paused. "I won't give you the order unless I must; you can believe that. But I know there is no choice."

"How?" Borisov felt bold enough to ask anything. "How do you know?"

"Because of what I have discovered," Zerkhov said. He got up from the table; he was slow but perfectly steady. "We'll relieve ourselves first. Then I will explain everything to you."

"I suppose," James White said reflectively, "that I should have expected to lose Davina in the end—but you know how it is. One takes people like that for granted."

Tony Walden eyed him across the table and said, "Does one? I don't, Sir James."

"But then, she hasn't been with you for more than a few months, has she?" he countered. "Davina worked as my secretary for twelve years. It was a great shock to lose her. Tell me, Anthony, does she really like advertising?"

"Tony," Walden corrected him. "Yes, I think she quite enjoys it. I hope so, anyway."

White smiled pleasantly at him. "You obviously intend to keep her," he murmured. "What a pity. I may still try to tempt her back."

"Try, by all means." Walden's answering smile was bleak.

The hostility between him and James White had begun immediately when they met. Their host, who had obliged Sir James by arranging the party, cursed them inwardly for spoiling it. He had never seen Tony Walden in such an aggressive mood. Normally he radiated charm on social occasions, especially if there were important fellow guests. This time he was far from charming. He contradicted everything James White said during dinner, and bristled openly when the subject of his assistant Davina Graham was mentioned when the men were sitting alone with their port. It was as if Sir James were deliberately baiting him. His remarks grew milder and yet more provocative, accompanied by that eternal empty smile that was a sort of insult in itself, as if he were talking to someone very stupid who had to be humored. Their host decided to break in and ease the atmosphere. "She must be a real treasure, this lady," he said in a jolly voice. "I've got a lovely girl working for me as a temp at the moment. Not a brain in her head, and has to be told everything twice. Thank God my regular girl comes back from holiday next week! Now, Tony, how are your negotiations with the prince getting along?"

"What prince?" Sir James inquired. "Ah," he said, hearing the name. "And what do you intend promoting for him, Anthony?"

"His country," Walden answered. "And for the second time, Sir James, please call me Tony."

"I'm sorry," he apologized. "I hate to shorten a good Christian name."

"In my case you needn't worry," Walden answered. "I happen to be Jewish."

Oh, Christ, the host murmured to himself. I'm going to cut this short. "I think," he announced, rising from his chair, "that we'll join Julia; she doesn't like being left with the girls too long."

The Whites excused themselves before midnight; they had to drive down to Kent, Mary White explained. Both were profuse in their thanks for a lovely evening, and Sir James made a point of going up to Walden and shaking hands.

"So nice to have met you at last," he said. "And good luck with putting the kingdom on the map! Give my love to Davina—perhaps my regards might be more appropriate." He turned away before Walden could think of a retort.

"Well"—Mary White turned to her husband in the car—"was it worth it?"

"Yes, I think so. Didn't you enjoy it, dear? I thought you looked rather bored once or twice."

"Bored to tears," she retorted. "Except when you were scoring points off that man Walden—he's an odd sort, don't you think?"

"I know what *I* think," Sir James said, "but I'd like to know why you say he's odd. He's very successful, a bit flashy, Cartier watch and all that kind of thing. Rather aggressive, on the defensive." He was almost musing now, as if he'd forgotten about his wife's opinion. "Not at all smooth, as I'd expected. But why odd?"

"Because he *isn't* smooth," Mary pointed out. "People like that make an effort; after all, charm is part of their business. He looks the part, just as you say, but somehow he doesn't fit into it. You said he was born in Poland. You wouldn't know *where* exactly."

"He said he was Jewish," White remarked. "I wonder whether Prince Ahmed knows that he's employing a Jew?"

"Now, James"—she switched the car into top gear as they left London—"you're not going to ruin the poor man's business just because you're annoyed about Davina!"

"Not unless I have to," he said gently. "He was very touchy about her, wasn't he?"

"You both were," his wife said.

"I have reason to be," Sir James said. "She was one of my most valuable operatives. I had great things in mind for her. She behaved very badly, for the second time."

"I imagine she'd say the same about you," his wife said. "I thought Walden was a bit too on edge about her, if she is just his assistant. He seemed to take it all personally."

"He did indeed." The brigadier smiled in the darkness. "Wife's very beautiful, too. . . ."

"Beautiful, and thick as two planks," Mary White retorted. "She's an accessory, like the watch, that's all."

"Hmm. They hardly said a word to each other the whole evening. An accessory, that's very clever of you, dear." Privately he thought his wife had been a little sharp in her judgment of Mrs. Walden. Now that he had met Tony Walden, he was convinced that his instincts about Davina Graham's job were right. Something was going on. He knew her too well to accept the obvious explanation that she and Walden were having an affair. She wasn't the type to involve herself with two men at once. He knew how devoted she was to Colin Lomax. She had taken a highly paid job, which was quite out of character. So was the man she worked for. Self-made, alien, an aggressive type that instantly made James White's conservative hackles rise. Davina had been schooled in secrecy. She would never fit happily into a world of publicity and promotion like the Arlington Agency. She belonged in the brigadier's world, at the end of a string attached to his finger. He would teach Mr. Anthony Walden a lesson in manners and not taking what didn't belong to him. He settled into his seat and dozed till the car pulled up in front of the house.

"I think you'll find this welcome news," the governor said. "You're leaving us, Harrington."

Harrington stared at him for a second and then said, "I am? Where am I going, sir?" His knees felt suddenly weak, as if they might buckle under him. *Leaving*. Davina had said they'd shelved the whole thing. . . .

He heard the governor say, "Shropwith. It's an open prison; very nice country up there. It's a good sign for your parole prospects, by the way. The Home Office doesn't send a man there unless they're well disposed towards a parole at some later date. I may say, Harrington, I put in a good report about you."

"Thank you, sir." Harrington had control of himself. He managed a big friendly smile and said, "I won't say I'm sorry to leave, but I've made friends. I'll miss them. I'd like to thank you for all you've done to help me rehabilitate myself, sir. I shan't forget it."

"That's what my job is all about," the governor said briskly. "Helping a man to get back on the right road. One word of advice. I know the governor of Shropwith. He's a very fine chap, but he runs the place on trust. He never gives a man a second chance if he lets him down. So stick close to the rules, Harrington. Anyway, I'll see you before you go."

"When will that be?" Harrington couldn't hide the shrill eagerness in his voice. Out. He was getting out of the Scrubs, where he couldn't possibly be sprung. . . . Shropwith Open Prison. He felt like laughing out loud.

"You'll go up at the end of the week," the governor said. "By the way, you'll have your visitor, Mr. Wood, this evening. We let him know you'd be leaving and he asked if he could make a special trip in to see you."

"Yes . . ." Harrington beamed at him. "Yes, I'll miss him too. Thank you again, sir."

He was taken out and the governor paused for a moment before starting on his daily report books from the four cellblocks. Strange that a man of Harrington's type should have turned traitor. Not at all the fanatic. Rather a simple man, peaceable, clever with his hands. Perhaps he really had gone through a change of heart during the last six years. He hoped so; he hoped that in some small way he had been responsible for setting him straight.

"I shall be sorry to lose you," Stephen Wood said. "I've enjoyed our visits."

"So have I," Harrington said loudly, for the benefit of anyone who might be passing the cell door. "Still, Shropwith isn't that far. Maybe you could come up one day."

"I don't know." Wood shook his head. "It's a fair old journey. I'd have to see. I brought you the new David Niven—made me laugh like a drain when I read it."

"Thanks." Harrington took it from him, flipped open the title page, and his jaw went slack for a moment. "Our friends have arranged the move. You will be collected."

"You haven't read it, have you?" Wood asked anxiously.

"No, no, I haven't. But there's not much point in your lending it to me, because I'll be leaving in a couple of days' time. I expect they have woodwork at this new place. I'll make you something, just to remind you of the last few years."

"It's supposed to be very good," Stephen Wood said seriously. "If you settle in as well there as you've done here, you'll be considered for parole. That's what I hear about it. So you may not have to stick out the whole sentence. That's something to hope for, anyway."

"It certainly is," Harrington said. There were times when he listened to that rather unctuous voice saying the right things and wondered whether he was imaging the books and their messages. At that last moment he stared directly into Wood's brown eyes, beaming a communication at him. Come on, for Christ's sake. Look at me, we both know what you are. Nobody can see, if you just *look*. There was no response. Nothing changed; the dull face didn't alter in expression, the eyes didn't blink, and the annoying voice went on talking.

"I don't know who I'll be seeing instead of you. I hope it's a pleasant chap. Personally, I've enjoyed our weekly chats. Well, I suppose I'd better be on my way. I'll say *bon voyage*, then, and good luck." He held out his hand and Peter shook it. Every cliché in the English language except "God is love" and "Gentlemen, please adjust your dress before leaving." Churchill had said that about one of Attlee's speeches. He ought to have listened to Stephen Wood for the last four years. . . . *Bon voyage*. Oh, Jesus Christ . . . he was actually laughing as Wood was let out of the cell. Over his shoulder, Wood looked back at him with disapproval. Then the door closed and locked, and Harrington was alone. He laughed till the tears stung in his eyes.

"Colin—he's gone! He's been moved!" Davina shouted through from the bedroom. She still had the phone in her hand, although the connection had rung off. He came quickly to the door.

"What? Moved where?"

"To Shropwith Open Prison," Davina said. "I've just spoken to the governor!"

"Wait a minute," Lomax said slowly. "Wait a minute, this doesn't make sense—you told Grant you couldn't find out anything. The whole thing was washed out so far as he knew. Harrington the same. For Christ's sake, why would he be moved now?"

"Humphrey must have set it in motion," she said at last. "The Home Office just went ahead. That must be it. But it isn't, is it? He never said a word about moving Harrington from the Scrubs! But somebody arranged it. Somebody's got Harrington out of the top-security prison and into an open one. And that means one thing. He's going to be got out."

Lomax came and sat on the bed beside her. "Before he can talk," he said quietly. "Humphrey was the only one who knew you were seeing him."

"How do we know that?" she countered. "We can't be sure of anything. The files were doctored. Now Harrington's moved, so he can be lifted out. That's what is going to happen, isn't it, Colin? He'll disappear, and we've lost our best chance of finding who this rotten bastard really is. We've got to do something!"

"Yes," he said quietly, "we have. And pretty quickly."

"Colin," she said, "I know that look on your face—I know what you're thinking. It wouldn't work!"

"I think it would," he said. "If Harrington's going to be lifted, then we're going to do the lifting. Or rather I am. Before the opposition gets there first. There's no other way. And you know it."

"It's the risk." Davina looked at him. "The risk to you. And the idea of doing something like this without official backup." She hesitated and then said simply, "We're breaking the law, and I don't like it."

"Listen, darling." He reached out and held her hand. "We talked this over before we saw Harrington, didn't we? And we agreed then that if you were going to find this traitor, you couldn't work with anyone. You can't trust anyone. You realized that yourself after you found those files had been doctored. The very man who sent you in to look at them could be responsible. Or your own brother-in-law. Or the head of the whole damn organization. It's an impossible position. The only way to do it is this way."

"To break Harrington out ourselves? Colin, if it goes wrong, we'll go to prison for the maximum sentence!"

"You won't," he said quietly. "You're having no part in any

jailbreak. Your job is to use your brains, my love. I'll be the brawn. There won't be any problem." He squeezed her hand. "You want to find him, don't you? You don't want to give up?"

"You know I don't!"

"Then stop worrying about my end of it."

Davina said, "You're going to enjoy this, aren't you?"

"I suppose so," he admitted. "I've been out to pasture long enough. I could do with a bit of excitement."

"God help us." She shook her head. "Are you going to tell me how you're going to do it?"

"No, I'm not," he said firmly. "The less you know, the better." He saw the expression on her face and smiled. "You'll have to sit back and be the little woman waiting at home till it's done!"

"You really are the worst kind of macho idiot," she said. "Thank God."

It was a noisy pub. Colin pushed his way through the crowd at the bar and ordered two whiskeys. The atmosphere was thick with smoke and body heat; a jukebox was playing in the corner, and he had to squeeze between the little tables to reach the one nearest the door and farthest from the crowd of people standing at the bar.

"Thanks," the man said, taking the drink from him. He was older than Lomax; thick-necked and heavyset, with cropped dark hair and a nose that had been broken at some time. It had taken Colin several telephone calls to old comrades retired from the regiment to find him. His name was Fraser, and he had reached the rank of captain before he left the Army and set up his own business.

"Long time," he remarked to Lomax. "Nearly three years, isn't it?"

"Four," Lomax corrected him. "You left just after we went to Ireland."

"Bloody right, too." Fraser grinned. "It wasn't too healthy for you, old friend. You got through all right, though."

"Up to a point," Lomax said. "Off I went into civilian life and got into more trouble than I ever did in the regiment."

"What sort of trouble?" Fraser asked the question quietly.

"Legitimate trouble," Colin answered. "I'm still in it. That's what I wanted to talk to you about. First, drink up, and tell me how it's going."

"I've got a good business," Fraser said. "And a very good staff. All top-class men, absolutely straight; they have to be, as you'll appreciate."

"The bloody world's gone mad," Lomax remarked. "Mugging, kidnapping; in the old days the burglar ran away if anyone disturbed him. Now he bashes you on the head with an iron bar. Do you do any banks, or just private businesses?"

"Jewelers mostly," Fraser answered. "Hatton Garden. My chaps escort the buyers to and from the office and on the monthly buying expeditions to the Diamond Corporation. We drive the cars, and if anyone's got a valuable consignment coming in, we stick with them till they leave the office and see them home. One poor devil last year found a couple of heavy types waiting for him in his flat. They'd tied up his wife and daughter and they grabbed him and got the keys of his office and the safe. And *then* they beat the hell out of him just for fun!"

Lomax scowled. "It makes me boil when I read some of the things that happen. Old women, kids, anyone who can't stand up for themselves is fair game. By Christ, if I were a magistrate . . ."

Fraser grinned. "You'd go easy on probation," he said. "That was my biggest headache when I started the business. I had to be sure of every man. A few no-goods slipped into the security services when they first started. There were big pickings for inside information. They got weeded out pretty quickly, but not before there'd been a few big robberies and a Securicor man put in hospital with bloody awful head injuries. This kind of job is all personal. One man looking out for a man and his family. They've got to feel involved, because it's people, not just money they're protecting." He leaned forward. "Most of them are from the regiment."

"That's what I hoped," Lomax said quietly. "I need help."

"What kind of help?"

"I need three top-class men, in combat condition."

Fraser finished the last of his whiskey. "What does 'legitimate' trouble mean? I've got to know that before I listen to any more."

"Government service," Colin answered. "The civilian branch of what we used to do."

"Then why come to me for recruits?" Fraser was watching him warily. Major Colin Lomax, George Cross. Invalided out of the

Army after a booby-trap bomb in Northern Ireland. Even men with that kind of record could go wrong.

"Because I have to get a man out of jail," Colin answered. "And it can't be official. Or traced back to the department."

Fraser half-pushed his chair back. "Doesn't sound like my sort of job. You'll have to try someone else."

"You don't trust me?"

"I didn't say that. I don't like the idea, that's all."

"There isn't any money in it," Lomax said quietly.

"Wouldn't make any difference if there were," Fraser said bluntly. "I run a respectable, registered security service. We're not bloody mercenaries for hire. Sorry, Colin. Not interested." He prepared to get up, when Lomax reached over and put a small brown plastic card facedown on the table. Fraser hesitated, then picked it up and turned it over.

"You'll remember those," Lomax said. "I told you, it was legitimate."

Fraser passed it back to him. The bearer of those special ID cards was entitled to help from any member of the armed services or the Diplomatic Corps. They were rarely used.

Fraser said slowly, "I'm sorry, Colin. But I had to be sure."

Lomax grinned, putting the card away. "Too right. You can get the next round."

"It'll be a pleasure," Fraser said. He came back with their drinks and said, "I've got just the men in mind. You know two of them. Both sergeants. Hicks and Sutton—remember them?"

"I do," Lomax answered. "Why did they leave? They were good types."

"Got married," Fraser said. "It's not an outfit for married men. They've worked for me since I started. There's another lad, ex-marine commando. Simpson. He'd do for you. How much can you tell me, or is it an in-and-out job, no explanations?"

"I can tell you where the prison is, but that's all. Shropwith Open Prison. In Lancashire, five miles outside Shropwith."

"That'll do. How long will you want my blokes?"

"From the eighteenth to the twentieth. I'll come in on Wednesday and see them, if that's all right with you. You brief them first, and say as little as you can get away with. I'll tell them the details of the job when we go up there."

"That's fine," Fraser said. "They won't let you down. And don't you bloody well drop them in it, either!"

" 'Who dares, wins.' " Lomax raised his glass and they drank together to the motto of their regiment.

CHAPTER 4

"DAVINA? LISTEN, I'm just around the corner from you—why don't we have lunch?"

She was caught unprepared by Charlie's telephone call. To her surprise, Walden had deluged her with work as soon as she started what should have been her last week at the agency. He had breezed in and out of his office, refusing to discuss her resignation, and because there was nothing for Davina to do while Lomax was in the north, she let him win the preliminary round, and concentrated on her work. She hesitated, and then said, "Yes, why not—where shall we meet?"

"I'll collect you," Charlie said promptly. "I'll be round at one."

Davina didn't want to go out to lunch with her sister. She was not, as she described it, a "lunch person"; it seemed a waste of time when there was work to do, and she begrudged the expense of the average restaurant with its indifferent food, noise, and high prices. But she didn't want to seem offhand with Charlie. From being bitter enemies they had become friends at last, and Davina valued this. They had nothing in common, but they were sisters, and a curious affection had grown up between them since Charlie had married and Davina found her own happiness. She hadn't seen Charlie since the evening they had gone to the Kidsons' for dinner.

At ten to one she tidied her work away, slipped into the staff cloakroom to do her hair and put on a little makeup. She was used to walking in Charlie's spectacular wake, and it didn't annoy her anymore. Ivan had given her confidence in her looks, and Lomax was a man who noticed.

When she came back to the office, she saw that her sister was on the other side of the door, talking to Tony Walden.

"Davina? You didn't tell me you had such a beautiful sister. Does she always keep you hidden, Mrs. Kidson?"

Charlie giggled; she loved being flattered.

One thing, Davina thought with unusual acidity, she doesn't pretend to be modest. "We're having lunch together," she said, and Walden took his eyes off Charlie just long enough to say, "Oh, how nice. Why don't I take you both out?" Before Davina could protest, Charlie did something so uncharacteristic that she stared in amazement.

"That's sweet of you, Mr. Walden. Another time, I'd love to—but I've got a lot of family things to talk to Davy about. Do ask me again, won't you?" And she smiled her seductive smile and gave the little sexy laugh that men found irresistible.

"I'll hold you to that," Walden said, and then added as an afterthought, "We'll ask Davina along too."

Outside in the street, Charlie waved and immediately a taxi cruised up and stopped for them. She had that magic-wand capacity for getting taxis, tables in restaurants, seats on planes, and hotel reservations when the rest of humanity waited, queued, and argued in vain. It was as if life recognized a winner.

"Where are we going?" Davina asked.

"Claridge's," Charlie answered.

"Charlie, for heaven's sake—don't be ridiculous! I can't afford—"

She interrupted Davina with a brightly determined "I *can*, darling. I got a delicious dividend from poor Edward's settlement this morning, and I'm going to treat us both. Besides, it's the Causerie, not the restaurant. That's always full of ghastly people these days, nobody nice can afford it. Here we are. All right, Davy, you can pay the taxi." And she gave her sister an affectionate pat on the arm.

Inside the famous Causerie, with its magnificent table where the customers helped themselves, they chose a center table, and Charlie ordered wine. She looked at Davina and said, "Do relax and enjoy it, Davy. Honestly, I got a fat check this morning. I felt like celebrating, and we don't see each other all that often, do we?"

"No," Davina agreed, feeling ungracious and guilty, "we don't. It's a lovely idea. But you could have let Tony Walden take us out. I couldn't believe it when you refused."

"It's not like me to turn down an invitation from an attractive man, is it?" her sister added. "But I didn't feel like sharing you with anyone today. I made up the bit about family things, I couldn't think of anything else."

"I haven't been home for a while," Davina said. "How are Mother and Father? I must go down and see them soon."

"They're fine," Charlie assured her. "John and I went down to lunch last weekend and took Fergus. Mummy's besotted with him. They asked about you and Colin and I said we'd seen you and you were both well. They're very fond of him, you know."

"I know," Davina said. "They were wonderful to him while he was convalescing. He's just Father's type, of course. I suppose they asked when we were getting married?"

"Not when, if. We said we didn't know. Why don't you marry him, Davy? You're out of the cloak-and-dagger thing now, you've got a marvelous job—that Tony Walden is madly attractive, by the way—don't you want to settle down? I'm sure Colin does."

"We're happy as we are," Davina answered. "There's plenty of time."

Charlie looked at her a moment. "It's not Walden, is it? Not that I'd blame you—"

"It's not anybody," Davina said. "I shan't be working there much longer anyway."

"Why not? Aren't you earning a fortune? Don't tell me you're getting the sack, darling, you're the most efficient woman God ever put breath into!"

"You always did make me feel like a computer, Charlie," Davina said quietly. "I'm not getting the sack. I probably won't leave anyway." She was irritated at letting the admission slip out. Even more irritated at her sister's suggestion that she was holding back because of Tony Walden. Madly attractive. Charlie would think so. He was just her type. She said, "How's John?"

"Rather uptight at the moment. There's a lot of talk about Sir James retiring. You wouldn't have heard about it now that you've left, of course. But he's due to retire at the end of the year."

"He won't," Davina said shortly. "He loves it. He wouldn't last five minutes if he wasn't pushing people around."

"John thinks he will," Charlie said. "And actually, Davy, there's a good chance that John will get the job." She had beautiful eyes, smoky gray and very large. They gazed at her sister with sweet innocence. "Wouldn't that be marvelous? Don't you think he'd make a marvelous chief?"

Davina didn't answer for a moment. John Kidson to succeed as head of SIS. One suspect retiring, another taking his place. "What about Humphrey?"

"Oh, Sir James rather hinted to John that he wouldn't be recommended. Do you know, Davina, I think you could have got the job if you hadn't walked out!"

"Not in a million years," Davina retorted. "There's never been a woman in the top job. There never would be, either."

"Would you have wanted it, though? Just supposing?"

"No. I don't mind being responsible for myself. Whoever takes over from Sir James has to send other people out to do the dirty work. I wouldn't like that side of it; frankly, I don't think John would either."

"He wouldn't mind," Charlie said. "After all, somebody's got to do it. You could say the same about a general in the army."

"That's why I wouldn't want to be a general, either. If John wants it, I hope he gets it. But I wouldn't bank on anything that man says if I were you."

"You hate him, don't you?" Charlie asked her. "Why? Why, when you've worked with him for so many years? Just because of Ivan?"

"He let Ivan die," Davina said slowly. "When he was no more use, he just shrugged him off his conscience and let the killer track us down. I'll never forgive that, and I told him so. But it's not just that. Not just personal to me. It's the way he thinks and feels, or doesn't feel, I mean. He has no heart for anything or anyone. I should be very careful if he's dropping hints to John. He's got some scheme up his sleeve, and believe me, it isn't necessarily in John's best interests!"

"You don't regret leaving, then? I've sometimes wondered," Charlie asked her.

"I didn't have to go. I chose to. I'd had enough. And I didn't know how long Colin had left. I wanted to be with him, Charlie."

"I know you did," her sister said. "Haven't you ever been back? To see any of your old friends?"

"I didn't have any old friends. Except Peter Harrington; he used to take me out to the pub once or twice. Before he handed me over to the KGB. I haven't been back, no. What for? Charlie, I'm sorry, look at the time—I've got a desk full of work, and it's half-past two."

"If you're leaving," her sister said, "why worry about being late?"

"Because that madly attractive man is paying me a madly attractive salary," she said. She left Charlie to pay the bill, and waited unsuccessfully for a taxi. She had not enjoyed the lunch.

Borisov had the confidential dispatch in front of him. Peter Harrington had been moved. It was imperative, the message said, that he was rescued and got out of England before he gave more information to Davina Graham. A rescue could be organized from Britain as soon as Borisov gave his sanction. Borisov considered for some time. He didn't send for Natalia; he weighed the factors with his usual care. Albatross was desperate to protect himself; yet Borisov had already decided that his effectiveness was coming to an end. Suspicion was enough; sooner or later it uncovered clues, and though it might take long and patient investigation to produce an answer, any suspect was excluded from anything too confidential until his innocence was proved. Albatross was nearing the end of his service with the KGB. Peter Harrington was due for the reward promised him for his: release from prison and a haven in Moscow. Both agents were owed Borisov's support; the KGB never abandoned their servants, even if they were captured. Only defection was punished.

Albatross mustn't be exposed; his exit must be unobtrusive, leaving a vacancy for his replacement. Harrington mustn't be bribed or bullied into giving him away. He would sanction a rescue from the open prison. He spoke into his intercom. "Send Major Rakovsky in."

Natalia's voice murmured back. "Yes, Comrade General."

He spent ten minutes with the major. His instructions were brief; he didn't bother with details, that was subordinates' responsibility. When Borisov had issued his orders, the major asked only one question. "How quickly do we arrange this?"

"At once," Borisov answered. "You have the resources; mobilize them."

The major saluted and went out. A few moments later Natalia came into the office. She approached him timidly; her blond hair was like a fluffy golden nimbus around her head as she came to his chair and laid a light hand on his arm. "Do you need anything?" she said in her soft voice.

Borisov looked up at her. "What I need must wait till tonight," he said.

She blinked and smiled. "I've missed you. Don't be angry with me, will you? I know I shouldn't say that to you here."

"I've missed you too," he answered. He put his hand up and stroked the front of her blouse. "We'll be together tonight," he said. "I promise."

"I saw Major Rakovsky going out," she murmured. "He looked full of purpose. You know the way a man walks when he's got something important to do? He walked like that." She giggled slightly. "I said good morning, and he didn't even hear me."

"He has other things to think about," Borisov said gently. "Important things. I'll tell you about them this evening."

"I'd like that," she whispered.

She went out of the office, and Igor Borisov watched her go. The pain of his love for her was very hard to bear.

Restrictions at Shropwith were minimal. Most of the work was agricultural; there were no cellblocks, no high-walled exercise yards. The prisoners lived in barracks, each with his own cubicle, and a red-banded trusty was in charge.

The food was no better than inside the Scrubs, which surprised Harrington. With all the produce being grown and a bloody complex of heated greenhouses, you'd imagine they'd get some of it on the menu, he grumbled to another inmate. It went out to the local markets, was the explanation. Harrington had bitten back a jibe about living off slave labor. He didn't know or trust anybody in his new surroundings, and his contacts with the new governor confirmed the previous one's warning. He believed that treating men fairly and giving them responsibility brought an honorable response. But God help the man who tried to take advantage and abused his privileges. Harrington set out to be a model prisoner. It wouldn't be for long, he comforted himself. But how long, for Christ's sake, and when? There was no contact with the outside now. No successor to the human cliché Stephen Wood handing him books with his maddening cheeriness. No word, just the promise. And his service kept their promises. All he had to do was obey the rules with scrupulous attention and be ready to move when the signal came.

He started passing the sleepless hours by trying to plan his own escape. The prisoners who worked in the greenhouses were lightly guarded by a single officer, who tried to be as unobtrusive as he could. The longer-term offenders with a good record worked in the open fields, unsupervised except by trusties. There were no wires, no barriers to prevent a breakout. And there were weekly expeditions into Shropwith, when the blue battle dress was exchanged for civilian clothes, and money earned in the prison could be spent in the local shops. They drove into the little town in a plain bus, and were allowed to walk about in twos, provided they rendezvoused at the bus at a certain time. The man who was even five minutes late forfeited the privilege for a month. Harrington was given this opportunity to see the outside world after he had been at Shropwith for a fortnight. His companion was a prison officer in plain clothes. He was marked as a special-category prisoner, and he wasn't allowed to roam without a guard by his side. The experience wasn't exhilarating. He found himself nervous and uncertain, not sure how to choose the cigarettes and chocolate bars in the supermarket. The checkout confused him, and he felt like bursting into tears.

The officer was kind; he understood the effect that a sudden reentry into freedom could have on a man who had been locked up in a top-security jail. He had seen men turn and run out of shops and stand shivering in the street, asking to go back to the bus. He sympathized with Harrington's shaking hands and hunted look. He believed very strongly in a reformed penal system where the more savage regimes of confinement and rigid discipline were replaced by centers like Shropwith. "Come on, just hand over the goods and pay for them," he whispered. "Nobody's looking at you. Go on, it's nothing to worry about."

Harrington stood his ground, paid, picked up his meager parcel in a plastic bag, and shuffled quickly outside.

Afterward, when the second and third visits had given him confidence, he decided that this was where he would be picked up and taken to freedom. A month had passed. He was what the governor called "settled in." His guardian on that first outing had become quite attached to him. They sat together on the bus journeys and talked about snooker. *Pot Black* was a great television favorite with the staff and the inmates. Yes, Harrington convinced himself in the lonely night hours, they'd come for him when he was in Shropwith town. They were undoubtedly watching him already, getting a routine worked out to a split second. They wouldn't use violence. No fuss, no commotion. Just a lightning move to separate him, a planned jostle in the supermarket, say, and then the waiting car and the escape. There would be roadblocks. Not a car, then, a van maybe, with a compartment where he could be hidden. Or a helicopter—that would be best. He'd be lifted out of the place and beyond any chance of pursuit. The idea made him sweat. He didn't want a helicopter. He had been shut up too long, and his nerves cried out for something familiar like a car. He couldn't stand heights, and those things were like being suspended on the end of a string with nothing but boards under your feet and a plastic bubble holding you together inside. He hated bloody heights. Davina had been terrified of enclosed spaces . . . he didn't want to remember that. He put it out of his mind. She'd survived all right. Survived well enough to go off to Australia with her Russian and get married. They hadn't connected Albatross with the KGB's murder of Ivan Sasanov. He had heard about it, in his isolated cell, and grinned in satisfaction. That was something he could have told her. That was a clue she would have appreciated. Along with the other clues he hadn't given. Now he wouldn't have to tell her or that hard-nosed Scotsman anything. The investigation was off, they'd said. They'd enjoyed seeing him wilt and suffer. You'll have to go along with us and tell us everything, or you'll be left here for the next twenty-odd years. . . . He gurgled with silent laughter in the night, thinking of that. He felt almost hysterical at times, imagining her frustration, her disappointment. She wanted to revenge Sasanov's death. Hadn't taken her long to pick up with someone else, though. . . . His thoughts were obscene, bitter. Not quite sane sometimes. But it wouldn't be long now. Albatross had put him in place. Moscow would do the rest.

Natalia had never looked more appealing. She had brushed out her hair, letting it flow around her shoulders, and her beguiling body was lightly clothed in a thin silk dress that clung and showed the shape of breast and thigh to Borisov when she moved.

She had prepared him dinner and filled his glass again and again with wine. Her scent was pervasive, her touch constant and suggestive. Watching her, Borisov felt the ache of desire. She came to him, murmuring erotic words of love play, unbuttoning his shirt, touching him with hands that were skillful and sensitive to every tension in his body. He took her to the bedroom and they made love. She drowsed with her head on his shoulder, and he lay awake looking at the shadows on the ceiling overhead. When she woke, she switched on the light and smiled in contentment at him. "You're the best lover in the world," she said. "The strongest . . . the best . . ." She leaned over him again. Later still she brought him wine and placed a lighted cigarette between his lips. Curled up beside him on the bed, she said, "You promised to tell me about Major Rakovsky."

"Ah, yes," Borisov agreed. "So I did. He had a purposeful walk, you said, my darling. You were right, as always. I had just given him some important instructions. If he does well, it will mean promotion."

"What does he have to do?"

"Rescue one of our agents from a British prison," Igor said. "Harrington—you know the man."

"Oh! But weren't the British interrogating him about Albatross?" she questioned. "Isn't it very dangerous to attempt a rescue?"

"Not as dangerous as letting the SIS find out who Albatross is," he answered.

"But you said you were going to replace him," Natalia demurred.

"You said he wasn't useful anymore because he'd be discovered sooner or later."

"Your memory has always amazed me," he said gently. He stroked her cheek with one finger. "You remember every word I say, Natalia. You're right again; I am going to replace Albatross. In due time. In due time I shall put another agent in his place. Would you like to know who it's going to be?"

"If you'll tell me," she whispered. Her eyes were wide, sparkling with interest.

"I'll tell you," Borisov said gently. "If you'll tell me something. How long have you been spying on me for Rudzenko?"

She lost every vestige of color. Her face changed to a deathly white, and the wide eyes opened and closed as if she were going to faint. Borisov got up. She stayed on the bed, half-crouching, looking up at him. At last she said, "Igor . . . what do you mean?" And terror turned her voice into a croak.

"You are Yuri Rudzenko's spy," Borisov said quietly. "One of the little pool of whores he keeps in reserve to inform on his enemies. When did he recruit you, Natalia? After you began working for me, or before? Tell me. Hold nothing back. He forced you, didn't he? Blackmailed you? Tell me how it happened."

He had dressed while he was speaking. She opened her mouth and wet her dry lips. He saw the nervous swallowing in her full throat. There was a red mark on it where he had bitten lightly into the white skin.

The tears began to fall. "He made me do it," she said. "He threatened me. He said he'd punish my family if I refused. . . ." She was crying like a waterfall; Borisov had never seen such a volume of tears. Niobe, he thought dispassionately, whose tears became a river. . . . She slid off the bed and came toward him; she knelt and clutched at his legs, naked and begging at his feet. "Forgive me . . . oh, forgive me, Igor, my love, my darling. . . . I didn't mean it, I was so frightened, I didn't know how to tell you. . . . Oh, forgive me. . . . Kill me if you like, but say you forgive me for what I've done. . . ."

Borisov leaned down and helped her up. "Get dressed," he said quietly.

She did as she was told. She was shaking so badly that she couldn't fasten the buttons on the silk dress. Borisov poured a glass of wine and sipped it thoughtfully.

"Rudzenko didn't threaten you," he remarked. "Your family weren't in danger. You didn't betray me out of fear. You were recruited five years ago, by one of my colleagues who was a Rudzenko man. You went to Tashkent to train when you were only nineteen. It's not a place where anyone would expect to find a school for spies and *agents provocateurs*. That's why it was established. They taught you how to look after a man there, didn't they? How to memorize and collect information, how to be an efficient secretary . . . how to lie and flatter and insinuate yourself into your quarry's confidence. You learned very well, my little Natalia. You were set to catch me, and you succeeded. Was it money? Did they put money aside for you? What was the reason? I'm curious. Tell me why you did this."

She was standing in front of him, her hands clasped, her face distorted with tears, and for a moment he thought she was going to throw herself down and beg again.

Suddenly she straightened up. With a hand visibly trembling, she wiped her eyes, pushed the wild hair out of the way, and took a breath to steady herself. "Can I have a drink?" she said.

He nodded. "Help yourself."

She turned back to him and said, "I've been a coward. It was the shock, you caught me unawares. And I was told to go to pieces if I was discovered . . . just in case you'd believe me. Why did I agree to work for Rudzenko? Because I believe in his Russia, Igor, not in yours. That's why."

"You are a Stalinist?" he inquired.

"I am a Stalinist." She drank the vodka down. "I loved you as a man," she said softly. "As a Communist who was betraying the Revolution, I worked against you. That's all I have to say. Now, I suppose, I'm to go to the Lubyanka."

"No," Borisov said. "You are not going to be arrested, Natalia. Rudzenko is not going to know that his agent has been discovered."

Fear showed on her face again. He thought suddenly, furiously, that she looked sallow and ugly; his rage shocked him. He was glad that he would soon be out of the flat, or he might have lost control of himself.

"What are you going to do?" she said.

"I'm going to tell you what you wanted to know," he answered, and he got up. "The name of the person who will replace Albatross." He said it, and went to the door. "But you won't be able to tell Rudzenko this time." He opened the door and she saw two men standing outside. He heard her little gasp of fear as they went inside and he closed the door and left her with them.

Natalia died at three A.M. Twenty sleeping tablets and three-quarters of a bottle of vodka were siphoned into her stomach by one of the men while the other restrained her. They held her down on the bed till she lost consciousness. After an hour, one took her pulse, nodded to his companion, and they settled down in the small sitting room to wait.

A final inspection showed that she had vomited and choked to death while she was unconscious. Silently they left the flat and slipped out of the entrance, watched by the old *dezhurnaya* in her cubicle. She had seen them come in and go out, but there would be no entry in her book for the police detailing the movement of all occupants of the building. She had been shown the shield with the crossed swords.

When the girl was found dead of an overdose the next day, it was reported as a suicide. Borisov went home to his wife in the evening for the first time in almost a year. He sent a private word of thanks to Zerkhov for his warning about Rudzenko's agent and stated that the matter had been dealt with. He was silent and unapproachable for a long time, and several times he wept when he was alone. She was dead. But he had loved her.

"She said she was leaving," Charlie Kidson said. "And then she sort of took it back. I had the feeling she didn't want to talk about the job or Tony Walden. She went rather red when I asked if he was the reason she didn't marry Colin."

John looked up sharply. "Is there something going on there?"

"Not that Davy would admit." Charlie shrugged. "You know what she's like. She'd hate a messy situation. Living with Colin and fancying somebody else. But I think she rather likes him. If she *is* leaving, John, what does that mean?"

"Not much. Except where does she go next? Back to the office, I suspect, having done the Chief's dirty work for him. She denied ever having been back to Anne's Yard—that proves she's onto something."

"She made an odd remark about having no friends," Charlie said. "Only Peter Harrington used to take her round to the pub, till he handed her over to the KGB. She's very bitter, darling, and she can't hide it. She wouldn't listen to the idea of taking on the top job. She spoke about that very sourly too. She didn't think you'd fancy sending other people out to take the risks—that's what she said."

"She's always had a chip on her shoulder," John Kidson remarked. "About you, about her parents, about herself—then Sasanov. She hates the Chief; she says she hasn't a friend in the office after working there for fifteen years. What the bloody hell's the matter with her? Doesn't she ever think it might be some of her fault?"

"I don't think Colin helps," she said suddenly. "He's very chippy too, you know. All these Army specialist people have the same attitude, a sort of contempt for everyone outside their little world. I think they sit together criticizing and carping about Sir James and the office—undoubtedly you and I come in for a fair bit. I can just imagine Davy going back and saying how extravagant I am. I don't think she's after that job, darling. I don't disagree that she's probably working on something; she's very devious, always has been, but I don't think she's a serious rival to you. She's too full of grievance to be credible."

Kidson didn't answer for a moment. "She is, isn't she?" he said. "Grievance with a capital G. She goes to the office on a forged pass; to you she denies having been near the place. She's gunning for somebody, and somebody has put her up to it. I've made up my mind, Charlie. I'm going to take the damned bull by the horns. I'm going to see the Chief and tell him what I've found out. If he's using her to undercut me, I'm going to let him know I know it. If he isn't, and it's Humphrey . . . well, that puts me in a strong position. Either way, I'm going to call his bluff. And Davina's!"

Charlie didn't say anything for a while; she watched her husband. He was agitated, moving restlessly in the chair as if he couldn't sit still for long. It was unlike him to lose his equanimity; he was naturally calm, even placid when he was at home. She had seen him through several crises, including the desperate days in Mexico. He was far more on edge since they saw her sister coming out of the cul-de-sac leading to the office.

"She's gunning for somebody." Charlie got up and poured a glass of white wine for herself. Almost casually she said over her shoulder, "Do you think she's after you, John?"

He jerked as if she had slapped him. He said, "What the hell do you mean by that?"

"I mean, is she investigating you?" Charlie said quietly. "I know you, you're not just worried about the job. I told you, she isn't interested. She wouldn't take it if it was offered. So what are you afraid of?"

He stood up. "Charlie," he said, "just stop this, will you? You don't know what you're talking about, so just stop it!"

"All right." She shrugged. "But I know a lot more than you think, John. If you are in trouble, I want to help if I can, that's all."

"Well, it's very sweet of you, darling," he said angrily. "If I'm working for the Russians, you don't mind—is that what you're saying?"

"If you are," his wife said, "I'd mind very much, but it'd be better to tell me."

"For Christ's sake," he shouted at her, and then stopped. She faced him calmly. He had never in his life laid a hand in anger on a woman. He came close to doing it then. "I think we'll drop the subject," he said. "I'm going out for a bit. Just don't bring it up again when I come back, will you?"

"Not if it upsets you like this," Charlie remarked. "Don't be late for dinner; I've got something rather nice." She went back to the sofa and sat down.

He slammed the door as he went out. Charlie sipped her wine. They had never had a serious quarrel before. She had never seen him so angry, and under the anger she sensed something else. Was it fear? Was it disappointment that she should doubt him and say so? Was he shocked at her lack of moral principle? She didn't know the answer, but she was convinced of one thing as she sat alone waiting for him to come back. She was happy and in love, with a child and a good marriage. Davina was posing a threat to it. That had to be stopped. By the time John Kidson came back from a long walk and a stop at a pub, she was so sweet and conciliatory that he found himself apologizing.

Colin Lomax checked into a motel twelve miles outside Shropwith. He spent the first two days studying the layout of the town itself and the main roads leading to the highway. He frequented the pubs and got into conversation with the barmaid in one and a convivial married couple in another. He was thinking of setting up in a small business in the area, he said. He'd been looking at empty shop properties. Antiques, bric-a-brac, not too expensive, a quick, cheap turnover. His listeners were fascinated. He praised the town and the district; he invented a wife and two small children and then said that his only concern was the open prison being so near. The married couple, Jim and Wendy, as they insisted he call them, went out of their way to allay his fears for his family's safety. It was a very good place; there hadn't been one instance of an escapee breaking into a house or doing anything to frighten anyone. The last prisoner to walk out had wandered around for two days and then gone back and given himself up. It wasn't a center where sex offenders or violent criminals were ever sent. How tight was the security? Lomax wondered, not convinced. They had to admit that it was almost nonexistent. The barmaid was more explicit. "No, luv," she said. "They come in here once a week on the bus, do their bit of shopping, and go back again. You wouldn't know they weren't the same as us if you saw one of them wandering about. They've got their warders with them, but it's all very friendly like, and they wear their own clothes."

He found the square where the unmarked bus was parked. He watched the first batch of prisoners troop out and separate into twos or threes and spend an hour in the town before they reassembled. There were three weekly shifts bringing the men into Shropwith, and the third group included Peter Harrington. Lomax followed him, taking every care not to be seen by the man who was walking with him. He was dressed in casual sweater and jeans, but everything about his walk and build and the proprietary way he steered Harrington toward the shops marked him as a prison officer. Lomax timed their arrival and departure.

After a few days he moved from the motel into a little guest house, explaining that he was a salesman, and left after two nights. He checked into the main hotel in the town, and put a call through to Davina.

"I've got the timetable," he said. "It's going to be easier than I thought."

"Thank God for that." Her voice sounded anxious. "Can you talk about it?"

"Not really," he answered. "I just wanted you to know there won't be any heavy stuff, so you needn't worry. How are you, sweetheart? Missing me?"

"Yes," she said. "I am. When are you coming back?"

"At the end of the week. I just want to make sure I've got the pattern right. What have you been doing with yourself?"

"Working," Davina answered. "Earning Tony's salary for the first time."

There was a pause and then Lomax said, "You won't have to go on doing that for much longer anyway. I'll see you on Saturday. God bless, darling."

Davina hung up as the line cleared. No heavy stuff. She felt so relieved when he said that. He never exaggerated and he never lied. The most truthful man she had ever met, Davina thought, and smiled. Not tactful, either. She did miss him; the little flat was lonely and the evenings dragged without him. She had prepared their tiny spare bedroom. The bed was made up, ready for Peter Harrington. The last place the police would look for him would be in an SIS flat.

She closed the door as the phone rang again. It was Humphrey Grant. He sounded brisk and unfriendly. "I'd like to see you and Major Lomax," he said.

"What for?" Davina countered. Lomax had said he'd be back by Saturday. She had to stall Grant for the rest of the week.

"We've got a problem," Grant said. "Harrington."

"That's not our problem anymore," she answered. "I told you, I've pulled out."

"I know." He sounded angry. "I know that's what you've done. But as a result of your damned recommendation, he's been moved to an open prison, and the Chief wants to know why. You and Major Lomax are going to do some explaining."

"It's nothing to do with Colin," she countered. "You know that."

"He went with you the last time you saw Harrington," Grant snapped back. "Without authorization. So he can come and explain that too."

"What you're saying is the Chief wants to see me," Davina said. "Why doesn't he ring me up himself?"

"Because the whole damned thing has blown up in my face." Humphrey's voice rose. "Your brother-in-law has been stirring up trouble. I'll say this on my own account: you've handled the whole thing disgracefully badly!"

"Anything else before I ring off?" she asked.

"Yes. Get in touch with the Chief. He wants a meeting and I'm going to be there too." The line clicked off.

Davina lit a cigarette. "The whole damned thing has blown up in my face." John Kidson had been stirring up trouble. Lomax had to be covered while he was away. She could go and see Sir James and brazen it out without him. And if he was going to attack her, then she had a weapon to loose off at him in return. And at Kidson and Humphrey Grant. She felt suddenly very angry. She was so deep in her thoughts that she jumped when the doorbell rang. She hesitated, then went to the door and opened it. Tony Walden stood outside.

"Good Lord!" she said.

"Can I come in?"

"Well, yes, of course. Is anything wrong?"

He smiled at her and said, "Does it have to be? Can't I just drop in for a friendly drink—or will your friend throw me out?" He was in the little hallway, half-turned away from her. She saw there was no smile on his face. He looked strained and tired.

"Colin's not here," Davina said. "Come in and I'll give us both a drink."

He sat crouched forward, his hands between his knees, looking at her as she got a whiskey for him and a glass of wine for herself. "I should have brought some champagne," he said.

"What are we celebrating?" she said.

"I always drink champagne when I lose," Tony Walden answered quietly. "Whiskey will have to do tonight."

She sat beside him. "Tony, what's happened—what do you mean, lose?"

"My account with the prince," he said.

"Oh, no—oh, I am sorry. It meant such a lot to you." She reached out and touched his arm.

He looked at her and the smile flickered briefly. "You're a very sweet woman, aren't you—you really mind for me."

"Well, of course I mind," she said crossly. "What do you expect? But tell me what happened. What went wrong?"

"That," he said slowly, "is the part that matters. I could have lost it anytime. I explained it to you—you can't count on anything with the Arabs until the contract is in your pocket and you're on your way home. But this was different. I got a message this morning saying the prince had decided to employ another agency."

"Without any explanation? I can't believe it!"

"I could," he said. "But there was something in the way it was done that made me very uneasy, something hostile—and they're a polite people. He's a polite man who prides himself on his Western manners. I have a contact there, Davina. Obviously, one had to have someone inside to help in these things. It costs money, but then . . . so I got onto them and they told me what had happened. I lost the contract for the agency because it was pointed out to the prince that he was doing business with a Jew."

"Oh, my God. That's sickening!"

"What's sickening," he said softly, "is that it was done deliberately. Somebody cut my throat. And it wasn't one of my rivals. My contact was certain of it. It was done in a semiofficial way, he said. The prince knew perfectly well that I was Jewish, but once it was made public, he had no choice. Who would hate me enough to do that?"

"I've no idea," Davina said. "Tony, I'm so sorry. Will you be able to find out? Isn't there anything you can do?"

"Nothing," he said. "But it's a bad precedent. We have a lot of Middle East clients. If it gets about that I am *persona non grata*, my American colleagues won't waste much time. Who would want to ruin me, Davina?"

"I don't know," she said. "I have no way of knowing. You said it was semiofficial. Why don't you go straight to the Foreign Office and ask them to look into this! They might be able to find out who it was—after all, business is vitally important to us in that part of the world. I'll think of someone for you to go and see."

"I know most of them," he said. "I could make a fuss, but I think it might do more harm than good. I'm not exactly part of the Establishment, Davina. One naturalized English Polish Jew isn't going to find a lot of allies in Whitehall."

"Don't," she said. "It makes me sick!"

"I'm right, aren't I?"

She looked at him and said, "Yes, I'm afraid you are."

"I couldn't face going home," he said. "I was busy all day, and I could stop thinking about this because of the other work to be done, but when I left the office, I couldn't go home."

"That's very sad," said Davina. "Are you sure? Won't your wife be just as upset as you are?"

"My wife will be upset because I've lost a lot of money. She thinks making money is the only thing that matters in my business. She won't realize how much I care about the other side of it. The stab is in the back. That's why I can't tell her tonight. I don't think I'll say anything about it at all. Do you have any more whiskey?"

"Plenty. Colin drinks nothing else. Give me your glass."

"I couldn't think of a better place to go than here," he remarked. "I took a chance on your Army friend being here and kicking me out. I just needed to tell you what had happened."

She came back and sat beside him. "He's away for a few days," she said. "Hadn't you better ring up your home?"

"To say what?" Tony Walden asked her. There was a moment's silence between them. Oh, you bloody fool, Davina said to herself. It's just because he looks as if he's been kicked in the teeth, and you know that feeling. . . .

"To say you won't be home for dinner. I'll make you something here if you like."

He said quietly, "I'd like that very much."

Only three men would be needed to pick up Peter Harrington. One would drive the car out of Shropwith toward Ashton, where a van would be waiting and Harrington and his rescuer transferred. They would then proceed directly to Manchester Airport and catch the flight to Dublin. The plan was timed to get Harrington on the five-o'clock plane to Dublin, where he would be conveyed to a safe house. The leader of the expedition was experienced at what Borisov's people called "removals." He had removed numerous people, many against their will, and he planned meticulously on a tight schedule. He chose his own team. He paid them and they dispersed until required again. Nobody asked any questions or ever saw the others except when they were operating. The leader was known simply as Sam. He had a Liverpool accent and the indeterminate coloring found in many Celtic people. Sandy hair and pale eyes, poor teeth overcrowding a narrow mouth. He had a thin, super-fit body and reactions with fist and feet that betrayed his specialized army training in the Marine Commandos. He had been dishonorably discharged after a five-year sentence for theft. His connections with the underworld were without prejudice. He organized kidnapping, blackmail, and murder impartially for anyone prepared to pay. He ran a small garage and repair shop in West London, and lived with his wife and four children in a pleasant detached house around the corner from the garage. He didn't speak with a Liverpool accent at home.

He had spent three weeks outside Shropwith monitoring the prison routine and the weekly trips to the town. He mapped out a route and drove it himself to see how it worked. Two weeks before he intended removing Peter Harrington, he went through the complete routine himself, driving out of the town while the prison bus was still parked in the square, transferring to the van near Ashton, and catching the Dublin plane. He flew back to London the next morning and sent a report that everyting was ready.

The only thing he couldn't do was alert the subject. A telephone call to Stephen Wood's home took care of that. "Oh, dear," he said to his wife when he had taken the call, "I'll have to make a trip up to see one of my chaps next week. It'll be overnight, I'm afraid."

"Not any trouble, I hope," his wife said anxiously. She admired her husband's dedication to what he called his "chaps."

He said, "He's been asking to see me. That was the governor on the phone just now. Poor fellow's in hospital; they don't like the look of him."

"Where is he?" she asked. "One of your regulars, dear?" She knew the men whom he had visited over a period by name and always asked about them.

"Davies," he said, "in for robbery with violence. He used to be at the Scrubs and they moved him up to Walton. Always in trouble, I'm afraid. Still, if he's asked for me, I've got to go. I'm sorry, it's going to spoil our evening with the parents. Wednesday is the only time I can spare."

"Doesn't matter, dear," she said. "I'll explain it to them. We'll go over another day." He always referred to his old mother and father as "the parents." His wife shared his concern for elderly people, young children, and the criminal outcasts of society. She would never have admitted to herself that canceling an evening spent with her in-laws was a relief.

He traveled up to Shropwith on the morning train. Visiting hours were not till seven in the evening after supper. He spent a pleasant day wandering around the attractive old town, visited the church, which had a fine Norman tower, and browsed happily around the small museum, which had an interesting collection of local artifacts. He never missed an opportunity to see something historic when he went to a new place. At seven o'clock he drove into Shropwith and presented his card and identity papers.

Peter Harrington was watching television when he got the message that a Mr. Wood had come to see him. He knocked over a mug of coffee in his excitement. The trusty on duty insisted that he wipe it up before he went to reception to see his visitor.

Stephen Wood stayed for an hour. He talked away, shelling platitudes like peas while Harrington fidgeted and squirmed, waiting for the book to be passed. How was he getting on? He certainly looked well, hadn't he put on a bit of weight? You want to watch that, you know—Easter and Christmas were the worst times, he found; they always eat so much over the holidays, what with the children and the parents coming over—was he still doing carpentry? He hadn't forgotten his promise to make him something as a memento, had he? He treasured several things his chaps had given him over the years. Harrington stared at him in anguish, mumbling replies. No book. But he had something in a paper bag. As he got up to leave, he pushed it to Harrington.

"All that talk about watching your weight," he said, "and here I am bringing you chocolates." He laughed his ghastly hearty laugh, haha, haha, and it seemed to Harrington that everyone in reception and their visitors paused to look up when they heard it. He took the blue box with the roses painted on it.

"Thanks very much," he said. "Thanks, I like these." He stood up, so eager to get rid of the man that he banged his knee on the edge of the table. "Very nice of you to come," he said.

"Oh, no trouble at all. I had to come up this way to see an aunt who's feeling a bit poorly. Still, she's near eighty-two, so I suppose you've got to expect these little setbacks, haven't you? If I'm up this way again, I'll pop in. Glad to see you looking well and settling in. It *is* a good billet here, isn't it?"

"Oh, yes," Harrington said loudly. "I think it's fine. Good-bye, then."

"Bye-bye," Stephen Wood said. He shook hands. "See you sometime."

Harrington didn't open the box till he went to bed. He stripped off the cellophane wrapping and lifted the lid. The message was on the strip of paper that gave the packer's number. "Wednesday, 19th, 1:45 at the supermarket entrance." He screwed the paper into a tiny ball and swallowed it. Then he began to eat the chocolates.

He'd met James White. . . . Davina woke with a start; she'd been dozing, sleeping lightly and half-waking in the hours before dawn, when the pulse is low and the subconscious exerts itself. Walden had fallen asleep in the sitting room, and she had left him there and gone to bed. He had met James White at dinner a fortnight or so ago. He didn't say it in connection with anything, but mentioned the old man's persistent questions about her and his evident hostility to her working for Walden. "He was a snide bastard," Tony Walden recalled. "I got the feeling he was furious you'd left him and come to the agency. He did nothing but needle me till I was rude back."

And Davina had said she hoped he was *very* rude. The warning didn't go off at the time; it fizzed and ignited in her mind at four in the morning, and she woke with a violent start. Who would have wrecked Walden's contract with the prince—she could think of only one person malignant enough and powerful enough to do it. And she knew it was James White in the moment of full awareness when she switched on the light. He had shipwrecked the Arlington Agency. But why? Why take such a serious step against a man because he didn't like him? Or because he had employed a former colleague? That was it, of course. Something connected with her had motivated White into a particularly ruthless and vicious action against a man he had met only once. "The bastard," she said out loud, and threw back the bedclothes. "He did it—of course he was the one!"

She opened the door and went into the sitting room. She hadn't expected to find Tony Walden there still. The light was on and he was reading. He had taken off his shoes and his jacket. He sat under the little pool of light in the dark room and dropped the book as she came in.

"I looked in on you to say good-bye, but you were asleep and I didn't like to wake you. You don't mind if I'm still here, do you?"

"No," Davina said. "I'll make us some coffee. I've got something to tell you, Tony. I've just had an idea why you lost that contract."

He came into the little kitchen after her; she felt him come up behind her and half-turned around. He took her in his arms and kissed her. "Thank you for tonight," he said.

Davina didn't push him away; she said simply, "Don't do this, Tony. It isn't fair."

"Fair to the major?" he asked her.

"Fair to me," she answered.

"I'd like to make love to you," Walden said.

"I'm sorry, no."

He nodded and let her go. "I'll try again," he said. "I like you so much."

"You may feel differently after I tell you what I think has happened," Davina warned him. "You're just overwrought and tired, and you'd kick yourself when you saw me in the office next time. Let me make the coffee."

"I need you," Walden said. "I need you just as much as your Army friend. Probably more. Nothing you tell me is going to change that. Let's have the coffee, then. I like to sit in a kitchen; ours looks like a spaceship, it's got so many gadgets. I'm glad you're not angry, anyway."

"I'm not," Davina said. "And you know it."

"Why would he do it?" Tony Walden asked. "For Christ's sake, why go out to kill me? It doesn't make sense."

"It does to me," Davina answered. "I know James White. What he did was done for a definite motive, and I'm terribly afraid that I'm the cause of it. And that is why I'm going to make it my business to put it right."

He shook his head. "You can't do anything," he said. "He's a very powerful man, and a dangerous one. You mustn't do anything foolish, it's not your fault."

"It's my responsibility," she maintained. "Bloody Humphrey got you into this to cover up for me, and I'm not going to let you suffer. You said yourself you could be pushed out by the Americans. Everything you've built up in the agency could be wrecked because of this. James White is not going to get away with it. I'm going to see him. He's asked to see me, as it happens, and I'm going to give him the shock of his life."

She was flushed with anger; a very determined jaw, he noticed, her eyes were bright with indignation. He wondered how he had ever thought that his two blond vacant wives were beautiful.

"What do you mean to this man?" he asked her. "Is it only professional, this feud he has with you?"

"He let my husband die," she said suddenly. There was a moment's silence.

"I didn't know you had been married. Can you tell me about it?" Tony Walden asked her.

"He was a Russian," Davina answered. "He came over to the West. I won't go into details, but he was a very important catch for us. He gave us everything he knew; it wouldn't be an exaggeration, Tony, to say that he saved the Middle East from a Soviet takeover. I loved him," she added simply. "We went to Australia and got married out there. He was given a safe post and a new identity. We were promised nothing could happen, he'd never be found. That was James White's responsibility. He didn't give a damn after he milked Ivan dry. So they put a bomb in his car and killed him. I was pregnant and I lost the baby."

"Oh, God," Walden muttered. "What a story—I'm sorry." He looked upset, and she thought for a moment there were tears in his eyes. She knew there were when he blew his nose and cleared his throat.

"Tony," she said gently, "I shouldn't have told you. It was a long time ago. But I've never let that swine forget it. I went back to work for one reason only: to fight the KGB and the man who planned Ivan's death. In spite of James White, not because of him. I let him know that, too. And then I left, just when he thought I'd come meekly back into the team and would do as I was told again. That's what riled him. He didn't want me to walk out. It hurt his rotten pride. He likes to move people about like checkers; he hasn't any feelings and he doesn't consider anyone else should have any. I'm the one person who's spat in his eye, and he can't accept it. So he went for you because you'd made it possible for me to leave and be independent. He's going to wish he hadn't. Now, why don't you have a bath and think of a good excuse before you go home?"

"I don't have to think of one," Walden said. "I often spend nights away from home. My wife doesn't worry so long as she has everything she wants."

Sir James White took the call himself when he heard Davina's name.

"Good morning." He sounded surprised. "How nice to hear from you."

"Humphrey said you wanted to see me," she said. "I've called to make an appointment."

"I'm glad you've been so prompt," he said. "When can you spare time from your new job?"

"I have the most understanding boss in the world," Davina said. "All I have to do is ask."

"In that case, would tomorrow at three be convenient? And Major Lomax could call too."

"I don't make appointments for other people," Davina retorted.

"You must fix that up with him. I'll be in the office at three tomorrow."

James White heard the line clear, and he smiled. He could imagine how angry she was; he knew that voice so well, and the sharp turn of phrase when she was ready to do battle. He had given the first jerk on the string and brought Humphrey spinning on the end of it. Now Davina was feeling the pull. As for John Kidson. . . . His eyes hooded for a moment. Kidson hadn't needed motivating. His own ambition had done that. Ambition and disquiet. Only a worried man sets things in motion because he fears inaction more than he values patience. Worried and aggressive. Very unlike the John Kidson who had worked with him for so many years. Davina had been to the office; she'd used a forged pass, and her so-called job with the Arlington Agency was nothing but a cover. Was she, he had demanded of Sir James, working with official blessing? Or was she doing something without authorization, and if so, shouldn't she be stopped?

Kidson had been very abrupt, obviously suspicious that in some way his sister-in-law was acting against him. The brigadier's little hint about her succeeding him had sunk in. The family connection wouldn't stop Kidson fighting her for what he wanted. It hadn't stopped her, either. He was sorry he had delayed the meeting by a day. It was something he was really looking forward to. To seeing his three colleagues ranged against each other and throwing his wicked pointed questions at them. Humphrey was already pinned like a moth against a board, wriggling and exclaiming. His connection with Peter Harrington's move to an open prison hadn't been difficult to uncover as soon as Sir James heard of the Home Office decision.

Davina's part in it would be interesting. So would her explanation for that visit to the office, which he had also checked out as soon as Kidson accused her. There was the name in the night book. Miss Burgess. It had been too simple to check on the former secretary and discover that she was working in Johannesburg in a very sensitive position in the British consulate.

Tomorrow at three o'clock. He could hardly wait.

CHAPTER 5

THE MAN known as Sam sent for his team. They arrived by train, stayed at two different boardinghouses in the same street, and met their leader in the bar of the hotel. Lomax was having a drink by himself when they came in. It was early and the place hadn't filled up. He noticed them out of habit; he looked at people because he had been trained to observe and to register anything unusual. There was nothing out of the ordinary about the three men except the way they avoided each other till they were standing at the bar. Lomax had finished his whiskey. He'd decided to have a sandwich and go to the cinema—there was a good western showing at the Classic in the square. He hated his evenings; they were lonely, and time crept by. The bar was filling up. He shouldered his way through to order another drink, and because he was curious, he ended up alongside the three who had caught his attention. A sandy-haired, foxy-faced man in his late thirties. Very hard and fit when you got close to him. Lomax said, "Double Black and White, please."

"Okay, see you tomorrow." He heard the muttered comment, spoken in a broad Scouse accent that grated on him. The group had broken up, leaving the bar one after the other; the foxy one was the last to go. He paused to put ten pence into the fruit machine, played it without success, and then disappeared into the street. Lomax had the feeling that he'd delayed on purpose. He took his drink back with a ham sandwich. Several residents smiled at him, one asked him to join them. He couldn't refuse, though it was the last thing he wanted. He didn't like the brief scenario he'd seen played out in the bar. He didn't like the man with the pale eyes and sandy hair; there was something wrong about him. He moved the way Lomax had been taught, lightly on the balls of his feet, ready to spin into action if anything happened.

He didn't enjoy the film, and left before it ended. The next day was Wednesday; he was making his last check on the rota of prisoners going into the town. He planned then to go over his chosen route and get back to London the following evening. He'd be a day earlier than he'd told Davina.

It was market day and the square was full of stalls selling everything from household goods to fruit and vegetables and ready-made clothes. The atmosphere was busy and cheerful. Lomax paused by a stall selling handmade silver jewelry. He wanted to buy Davina a present. He chose a silver friendship ring, with two clasped hands below a little heart. He hoped it would fit. He saw the bus round the corner and take up its position. He lingered, pretending to examine the shoes on a nearby stall. "Real leather," the owner declared. "Soles and uppers, real genuine leather."

He saw Peter Harrington get out of the bus, and immediately Lomax moved out of view, leaving the vendor of plastic shoes in mid-sentence. Harrington was dressed in civilian clothes—a nondescript sports coat that hung on him, and an open-necked shirt with a handkerchief tucked inside the collar. He looked gray-faced and taut with nerves. Lomax edged around behind the group, keeping a good distance. Harrington and his companion separated from the rest. The prison officer again, the same man he had seen with him before. He saw Harrington check his watch and say something to his companion, who laughed. They went through the market, paused by several stalls, bought nothing, and moved on. Lomax followed, as he would follow on the designated date nine days later, with his backup team in place.

"What's over there?" Harrington asked. It was only one-fifteen, and he had half an hour to kill.

"Secondhand books, bric-a-brac. Lots of rubbish, really," the officer said. "Do you want to take a look?"

"Why not?" Harrington agreed. "I might find a couple of paper-backs—what do they cost?"

"Five pence, ten pence. All right, we'll have a wander and see what there is." Harrington had eighty pence in his pocket. He wasted time picking up little china knickknacks and bits of broken paste jewelry out of a bowl that had a card saying everything ten pence, and finally, glimpsing his watch, bought a tattered secondhand book on walking through Wales. "I'd like to go to the supermarket," he suggested. "Get some of those biscuits they have on special offer. Hope they're not all gone."

"Let's go and see then," the officer said. "But we'll have to hurry up."

"I only want the biscuits," Harrington said quickly. He managed a pathetic smile. "I haven't got enough money left to buy anything else."

Lomax saw them change direction, and followed, well hidden behind a stream of people. He pushed through a bit closer as they reached the entrance, and at the same moment he saw the man with the fox's face.

It happened so quickly that Peter Harrington couldn't have said what separated him from the officer. He didn't even see the man who drove straight into his guard, one elbow ramming him in the stomach, followed by a chop on the back of his neck. Harrington felt a grip on his arm that rushed him to one side. He was gasping for breath, shocked by the speed of the incident, being hustled down a side street till he almost fell over his own stumbling feet. A car door was opened and he was literally heaved into the back and the man who jumped in after him pushed him down onto the floor and the car was in gear and moving off. Behind them, Lomax had fought his way after them, just in time to see the green Cortina drive away and get its number. He didn't waste a moment. He turned and ran, dodging through the crowds, back to where his own car was parked. He swore as he unlocked it, cursing the caution that was costing him time, cursing himself for being too far away to interfere when the snatch took place.

Harrington was gone, under his nose. Picked up and speeding out of the town while the prison officer was lying unconscious on the ground and the alarm hadn't even been raised. Davina had been right. Albatross had set Harrington up for a rescue. The bloody opposition had got in first.

Harrington had started to shake. Crouched down on the floor of the car, he felt sick; a rug had been thrown over him and he lifted it and peered up into the face of the man who had rescued him. He'd been very rough, and Harrington's nerves threatened to relieve themselves in tears. "I'm going to be sick if I stay down here," he said.

The pale eyes glanced downward and then searched either side of the car. They were on the open road toward Ashton and there was nothing in sight. "Okay," he said. "Sit up for a minute. But duck down if I say so."

Harrington scrambled up, breathless and awkward. He launched himself in the seat, sliding down to show as little as possible if a car passed. "My Christ," he said, "that was quick. You certainly moved fast!"

Sam nodded. "I never hang about," he said. "Listen, I'm not to talk to you, understand? I've got a job to do, but apart from that, I don't want to know about you, see?"

"I was only going to say thanks," Harrington mumbled.

"Okay, you've said it. Now keep your mouth shut, and if I give you a shove, get down!"

"Where are we going?" Harrington insisted. "I want to know."

Sam glanced briefly at him and said, "Shut up." He turned to look out of the rear window. There were two cars and a transport truck behind them. They were well clear of Shropwith and the van waiting to pick them up was pulled into a rest stop six miles ahead. Harrington was huddled into the corner. His shakes were passing; a sense of euphoria was growing in him, and a longing to talk and talk to the grim bastard on the other side. "Have you got a cigarette?" he ventured.

The other felt in his pocket, dropped a packet and a cheap lighter in his lap. He didn't speak. Harrington drew in the smoke. He was out. They'd kept their word. Out, and on his way. He began to grin as he smoked. What an organization—they never let their own people down! They said they'd look after them, and by Christ, they did. And he'd given nothing away. Nothing but a fucking code name, which wouldn't mean anything. Albatross. Flap, flap, Miss Davina Graham, that's all you'll ever know about him now. He didn't realize that he was giggling to himself aloud. The man glanced at him and made a face as he turned away, keeping observations on either side.

Bloody nut case, sniggering away. Stir crazy, as they used to say in the old James Cagney films. It wasn't going to be a fun trip all the way to Dublin. He reached out and took his cigarettes and lighter back.

Harrington was unprepared for the push he got. "Down," was snarled at him, and he crumpled onto the floor. A white Fiat was coming up in the rear; it flashed past them while Harrington crouched down.

"You stay put," Sam said. "We haven't far to go." Harrington felt like arguing, but he decided not to. He was free. Free. That was all that mattered.

"She's late," Humphrey Grant remarked.

"Not everyone is as punctual as you are, my dear fellow," Sir James White remarked. "I remember when you used to come down from Cambridge, with Philip, you were always down for breakfast on the dot. He had no idea of time, poor boy."

Grant didn't answer. He didn't like the reference to his friendship with the Whites' only son, now dead. He preferred to forget the time at university, and Sir James hadn't mentioned it for years. He was in a dangerous mood; Grant recognized the playful manner. The more jocular the Chief became, the more deadly was the blow in preparation. He turned away and stared moodily out of the window. He had seldom felt more insecure, almost naked under those chilly blue eyes. Once, he thought bitterly, I turned to him as a father. What a fool I was to think he could be trusted. How little I realized the barriers that lay ahead, the long lonely years of concealment, the loss of my identity, the morass of lies I've waded through—the sacrifice of my whole life. And it all began at Cambridge when I made friends with his son.

He turned, hearing the door open, but it was only Kidson. Once they had been on familiar terms, colleagues working closely, respecting their different talents for the job. Now there was coolness, suspicion between them. The succession to James White hung between them like a jewel to be snatched or a weapon to be seized. He and Kidson were not friends any longer.

"Good afternoon," Kidson said. "Good afternoon, Chief." He paused and then said, "I thought Davina was coming."

"She is," Sir James said. "The traffic must be bad. She'll be here any moment."

He lit a Sub Rosa cigarette. Grant wondered whether he came close in order to inflict the smoke upon him, knowing how he disliked it. There was a glint of cruelty in his smile, and the white eyebrows were arched in question. "Quite a conference, all three of you together. It will be like old times having Davina with us. And here she is!"

They all turned as she came into the office. Head up, chin slightly forward, she wore her battle colors flying.

"Good afternoon," she said collectively.

"I said the traffic must be bad," Sir James remarked, "to make you so late."

"It was perfectly clear, thank you. First of all, I've taken time off from my office, so I'd like to get down to business as soon as possible. You wanted to see me?" She spoke to James White.

Her rudeness was rewarded; the smile disappeared and he said acidly, openly irritated, "We are all busy, and you have kept us waiting. I think it best if we sit down." He took his place behind the big mahogany desk and Kidson and Grant disposed themselves in the armchairs. Davina remained on her feet. She shifted a large brown envelope under one arm.

"Davina," he said, "what are you doing visiting Peter Harrington?"

"Carrying out instructions," she said flatly. Kidson looked up quickly and stared at her.

"Whose instructions, may I ask? You had left the Service."

"I left the Service in order to carry them out," she answered. "And that is all I am going to say."

"Humphrey," James White said, "you initiated Peter Harrington's transfer to an open prison. And Davina visited him with authorization from you. Is that correct?"

Grant looked down at his thin hands, folded like claws in his lap. "Yes," he answered, "it is."

Davina didn't glance toward him. She wasn't going to incriminate him; he could rely on that at least.

"John"—James White turned to Kidson—"John, I think you have something to say."

Kidson didn't hesitate. His manner was accusatory when he began. "I saw Davina coming out of Anne's Yard one evening a month ago. I can give you the exact date. April 20 at eight-forty-five. I was curious, knowing she'd resigned from the Service and apparently wanted nothing to do with it or anyone in it. She'd given me that impression when I'd seen her a couple of weeks before, *en famille*. I inquired about it from the security staff the next morning. A woman answering her description had been into the building, signed the night book with the name of Iris Burgess, who used to work here, and produced a pass made out in that name. We've checked it through, and Iris Burgess is in Johannesburg."

"Did you in fact come into the building on a forged pass, Davina?"

She moved the brown envelope from under her arm and held it like a shield in front of her. "Yes," she said flatly, "I did."

"On instructions?" The question was asked gently.

"At my request," she countered.

"And who issued you with a forged pass?"

She shook her head.

"I did," Humphrey Grant spoke up. "And I gave her the key to the filing room." There was a blanket of silence on them then. Nobody moved or said anything. They waited for James White to speak.

"You and Davina acted in secret. You must have an explanation for what amounts to a gross breach of conduct on both your parts. I should like to hear it."

Davina had been waiting for the moment. Before Humphrey could say anything, she stepped up to the desk and laid the brown envelope in front of Sir James.

"The explanation is in there," she said. "Confidential files that have been tampered with over a period of fifteen years. Vital connecting information has been subtracted in order to conceal what I was trying to find." She glanced at Humphrey Grant. He masked his surprise a second too late. Kidson had turned a dull red that faded. Only James White remained unmoved.

"And what are you trying to find?" he asked.

"Albatross." She dropped the name like a grenade among them. "And I just want to give you all notice that I'm damned near to doing it. Good afternoon to you." She walked to the door without a look at any of them, opened it, and closed it firmly after her.

It was Kidson who exploded. "Who the hell does she think she is? Chief, have her stopped! Bring her back here—she can't say something like that and just bloody well walk out!"

Sir James didn't move. "Humphrey," he said quietly. "I think she surprised you as much as John or me. You didn't know about the files, did you?"

Grant's cadaverous head came up. "She asked to see them," he said. "She said they held no evidence." He took a handkerchief out of his pocket and wiped his nose. "She actually resigned from the investigation after she'd seen them."

"Which meant she didn't trust you," Kidson pointed out.

"She didn't trust you either, John, or me," Sir James remarked. "Albatross. The code name for a person or an operation—why did you set out to do this behind our backs, Humphrey? I think you should explain that before we go any further."

Grant cleared his throat. Momentarily shaken, he had recovered himself, and he met John Kidson's challenge first. "After Mexico, I got a report from Major Lomax. It was a confidential report compiled by a man who didn't expect to live beyond six months. He didn't show it to Davina, he gave it to me. It was very alarming. As a newcomer to the Service, he had seen what people like us had overlooked. A series of sinister connections pointing to a traitor working at the highest level. Which meant that one of us, even you, Chief, could be a Russian agent. I would point out," he said sourly, "that Lomax chose to come to me with his suspicions. I in turn recruited Davina as the one person trustworthy and able enough to uncover the mole.

"Her resignation was part of the cover. She went to see Harrington, who confirmed that there was a Russian agent inside the Service and had been for years. He gave her the name Albatross. He was dealing for freedom, and he gave nothing else. Part of that deal was to move him from the Scrubs as a prelude to exchange or rescue. I initiated it before Davina threw the whole thing up, saying she couldn't find anything. I was furious and amazed at the time. After all, I had taken a considerable risk to try to find the traitor."

"You had indeed," James White murmured. "What interests me is that Davina evidently didn't trust you after reading those files. I'm not being unpleasant, Humphrey, just stating a fact. She decided to go out on her own. Which meant that you had joined us as a possible suspect. And she certainly hasn't shown confidence in *you*, John. You'd think she'd have gone to you as a brother-in-law as soon as Humphrey mentioned this."

"Not," Kidson said angrily, "if it was suggested to her that I could be Albatross."

"Are you implying that I accused you?" Humphrey's voice rose.

"I don't know what you did," Kidson answered. "But whatever it was, it backfired in your face. She found enough to suspect you and withhold the information about the files. And, incidentally, you got Harrington out of a top-security jail. Was that before or after Davina pretended to drop the case?"

Humphrey turned his back on him and spoke to James White. "A move was the first part of the deal with Harrington. I instructed the Home Office accordingly—usually, as you know, these things take time. However, on this occasion they moved fast, and Harrington was in Shropwith before I had a chance to cancel. But I was at fault, I admit it."

"Wouldn't plain bloody 'negligent' be nearer the truth?" Kidson snapped.

"That's enough!" James White cut across them as both men were on their feet confronting each other. "Calm down, John. You too, Humphrey. We are all suspect, according to our colleague. And one of us is about to be exposed, if she told the truth just now. We can sit here and wait for Davina Graham to explode her time bomb under us, or we can investigate for ourselves. I think our first move is to get Peter Harrington back into a safe place, and the second is to study these files and see what Davina found." He exclaimed in annoyance as the telephone rang. "I told Phyllis not to put through any calls," he said. He listened for a minute or two and then said sharply, "Good God—when did it happen?" Kidson and Humphrey looked up.

Sir James replaced the receiver. "Well," he said. "That alters everything. Harrington has escaped!"

John Kidson closed the file and stood up. "You certainly ballsed it up, didn't you, Humphrey?" he said slowly. "Without him, I doubt Davina or anyone else will find Albatross. I'll take these along, Chief, and study them properly."

When he had gone, Humphrey stood up. He unwound his long thin body carefully, as if a sudden movement might break a limb. "I'm going to do the same," he said. "And I shall pay particular attention to Kidson after the way he's tried to throw suspicion upon me."

Lomax put the car into third gear and pulled out to overtake the Cortina. He could see one head in the backseat, nobody beside the driver. He didn't glance near the car as he roared past it; he saw all that he needed in the rearview mirror as he came in front. It was vital that they shouldn't realize they were being followed; that was why he had overtaken at unnecessary speed. He went a good distance ahead, not troubling to keep the car in his rearview mirror—there was no major intersection within the next few miles. He signaled and pulled into a service station to let the quarry pass him. As he did so, he passed on the inside of a gray van with "Hudson Garden Center" painted on its sides. One of the men he had seen in the hotel at Shropwith was driving it. Lomax didn't stop at the service station. He drove around and through the line of pumps and sped after the van. The Cortina had not caught up, and he was still in front. Now it didn't matter. He knew the significance of that van. Harrington would be changed over to it for the second part of his journey. Lomax hung back, keeping a car between himself and the van, and soon enough he saw the winking left-hand signal light as they approached a small rest stop. A quick backward look assured him that the car with Harrington hidden in it was not in view. They would stick very close to the speed limit with their cargo, no doubt crouching out of sight on the floor at the back.

The gray van had pulled up. Lomax eased into the rest stop. He was acting on moment-to-moment developments. There were two men in the car with Harrington. One man in the van. He had seen only three in conference at the bar; it would be his bad luck if someone else was hidden in the back of the van. He didn't think so, and he got out and walked toward it.

The driver saw him coming. He saw a man in sweater and jeans, lighting a cigarette between cupped hands as he walked. Lomax stopped by the closed window and tapped on it. The driver shouldn't have opened it; his orders were to stay parked in the rest stop and keep his head down till the Cortina arrived. But it looked bloody suspicious if someone knocked on the window with an innocent query and he didn't open it. He wound it down and said, "Yes, mate?"

"Do you have a jack?" Lomax asked. He slipped his hand on the door handle and it yielded. The driver hadn't locked himself in. That was unprofessional, for a start. "I've got a bleeding puncture in the back."

"Sorry, don't carry one." The driver shook his head.

When the door was wrenched open, he was hampered by the wheel. Lomax's fist caught him square on the chin with the first blow, followed by a crack with the heel of the hand across the side of his neck. It wasn't a killer stroke, but the driver collapsed and fell sideways into the passenger seat. Lomax closed the van door, looked around quickly, and saw nothing but traffic passing on its way. At any moment now the Cortina would come into view. He had to take a crazy chance, and do nothing but sit behind the wheel and hope that the foxy men would do what he would have done in his place—make the transfer without coming around to the front to waste time chatting to the driver. He pulled the peaked commercial cap off the unconscious man's head and put it on. The Cortina came in sight of his side mirror. They'd seen his car parked behind. He could tell because they slowed and then speeded up and then signaled left to turn in. They had to keep to the plan. He could imagine Foxy cursing, wondering why the car was empty, assuming the driver was peeing somewhere out of sight. The Cortina drew into the rest stop and stopped behind the van. Lomax stayed absolutely still, watching through the side mirror. He saw the rear door open and the man get out. He went around the other side; Lomax switched to the left-hand side mirror and saw Harrington scramble out of the door, hidden from the road and doubled up. The other walked up, and Lomax lost sight of him. If he came to the driver's door, Lomax wouldn't have a chance to bluff. He opened it and tensed in readiness.

The man called Sam looked back at Peter Harrington; he was bent low behind the shelter of the car. One quick examination of the road showed that there was a hiatus—no cars were in view. He beckoned furiously, and Harrington straightened up and came to the van. The back door was open; Sam bundled Harrington inside and jumped in after him. He pulled the door shut. There was a small window giving a meager light that showed the outline of the driver's head. Sam banged on it twice; the head nodded once, and seconds later the van began to move and swung cautiously out onto the highway. Inside the body of the van, Sam switched on a pocket flashlight. He found a traveling case and shoved it across to Harrington, who was huddled on the floor. "Get into these clothes," he said.

Harrington unpacked the bag by the beam of the flashlight. A dark blue suit, white shirt, dark tie, black shoes. He wondered how they'd known his size, and then remembered the computer room in Dzerzhinsky Square, where every personal detail of every member of the KGB and its servants was on record.

"Where are we going?"

Sam said from behind the flashlight, "Manchester Airport. You're taking a business trip. There's a briefcase in the corner. We'll be there in an hour. What the hell!"

The van was slowing down; he had no means of communicating with the driver except by banging on the little window. He went up to it and rapped sharply on the glass. The head half-turned, a hand came up and pointed left. They were pulling in. Sam let out a string of swear words culled from the Royal Marine Barracks, Portsmouth. The van stopped. Harrington muttered at him in the dim light, "What's the matter, for Christ's sake?"

"Shut your arse!" was the snarled reply. He was at the back door, opening it a crack. He hissed at the figure glimpsed outside, "What the fucking hell are we stopped for—we'll miss the plane!" The back door was opened and Lomax launched himself inside.

It wasn't as easy as dealing with the driver. His opponent was caught off guard, but his reactions were as fast as Lomax's own. The first savage blow caught him in the stomach, but the muscles were rock hard and he didn't jackknife. He lunged with his right foot and caught Lomax on the thigh, missing the groin by a few inches. It was then that Lomax knew that he faced an adversary as well trained as he was. He would have to strike to kill.

He used the old Glaswegian head butt, but with the variation of bringing the skull up at the last moment so it caught the victim's chin. The impact and the angle were faultlessly timed. Sam's neck vertebrae snapped like rotten twigs.

Harrington was locked into the back of the van with the dead man. He crouched on the floor, shaking like a beaten dog. He had cowered away from the flurry of violence that broke out, shielding himself from the lashing fists and feet. When one of them fell, he wasn't sure whether it was his rescuer or the assailant who had burst in on them. He was in semidarkness again and the door was slammed. The van started to move. He couldn't see or find the flashlight. Eventually he found it because it rolled across the narrow floor as the van made a sharp turn to the right. He grabbed and caught it and fumbled with the switch until it shot its yellow beam onto the body of the man with the sandy hair; he lay on his back, and his head lolled to the right as if the neck were stuffed with rags. Harrington knew at once that he was dead. He turned away and retched into the dark corner. Someone else had taken him; the agent of his Soviet master lay broken at his feet. Who in the name of Jesus God was driving him, and where? He shed a few tears, sniffling in misery. The van turned again; he realized that the roar of traffic ebbed and flowed outside. Then it slowed and stopped. Harrington stayed frozen in his corner, waiting for the door to open, for something to tell him what had happened.

When it did, he blinked and cowered. "Get out," Lomax said. "Watch it, or you'll get a bullet." Harrington bent down and scrambled out of the back; he missed the little step and stumbled. Lomax gripped him hard and kept him upright.

"You!" Harrington whispered, his mouth agape.

"Yes, me. Walk to that white car. Get in the front seat, and don't try anything." They had come back to the rest stop where he had transferred to the van. Lomax had seen a sign of consciousness in the driver slumped beside him. It would be some time before he was able to get out and look inside the van. By then Lomax and Peter Harrington would be well on their way. And when he did find his dead companion, he would make the best disposition of both van and corpse for his own safety. Nobody but the KGB would know that the original rescue had changed its direction. Lomax got in beside Harrington. He said without looking at him, "You've got two choices. You can make the best of it, or you can be a bloody fool and find yourself back in jail. Next time it'll be the D wing at Parkhurst. You won't get out of there in a hurry. And I haven't got a gun, so it's up to you."

Harrington said slowly, "Where are you taking me? What is all this?"

"I'm taking you to a safe place, where we're going to sit down and talk about Albatross. And then, much against my judgment, Davina will keep the bargain and let you make contact with your Russian friends. If that doesn't suit you, we'll stop at the nearest police station."

Harrington looked out of the window. He felt weak with defeat. "You know the bloody answer," he muttered. "Let's go on."

Lomax slipped his car into gear and swung back out into the traffic. He left the highway at the next turning. By that time the first roadblocks were being set up on the roads out of Shropwith.

Davina didn't see Walden that afternoon. He wasn't in his office and she didn't intend to whet Frieda Armstrong's curiosity by asking where he was. She worked with furious intensity, wishing that there was more to do. She was still seething with the injustice of what had been done to Walden. One compensation was the look on White's face when she had thrown down her challenge before walking out. It was a bluff, because until they had Peter Harrington safe, she had no hope of tracing Albatross.

One of those three men in the office that morning was a spy and a traitor. Responsible for death and betrayal over years, a Judas who had been bought for . . . What? For money, like his namesake? Or for politics, also like his namesake? If she could find an answer to the motive, she might come closer to the man. Now the files were open to them all, showing the hidden hand at work. Harrington's capacity to help was in the open too. So was her determination to go on alone until she had the mask of Albatross in her hand and the real identity revealed. It could be dangerous; she realized that, and accepted the risk. But it was worth goading them to get a response.

She had a headache by late afternoon. Her work was finished; the office next to hers was empty. She thought of Walden, and pitied the emptiness of his life that he had to seek comfort from a stranger. His sexual approach had not disturbed her. She could cope with that. She loved Colin; promiscuity had no appeal. But there was something vulnerable about Walden that was difficult to ignore. A bold, self-confident, brilliant man, bursting with energy and ideas. And still this loneliness that no one would discern behind the fireworks and the money.

She closed her desk and went down in the elevator. She was on her way to the parking lot at the rear of Arlington Place when she saw the newspaper headline: "TRAITOR ESCAPES." She bought the paper and knew what she was going to read. Peter Harrington had disappeared from the open prison at Shropwith. She folded it up and got into her car to drive home. She and Lomax were too late. The KGB had got to him first.

She let herself into the Marylebone apartment, dropped the keys onto the hall table, and opened the newspaper again. She felt drained and sickened. The living-room door opened and she saw Colin standing there. "Oh, God," she said. "You know what's happened?"

"Yes." He came to her and kissed her lightly. "Come in, darling. We've got a guest."

She pushed past him and saw Peter Harrington sitting on the sofa with a drink in his hand.

"Well, here I am," he said. "Not where I meant to be, but better than where I was. Nice to see you, Davy." He took a swallow from his glass and smiled. "The major's got a heavy hand with the Scotch," he remarked. "First drink I've had in six years. I'm quite pissed already."

Davina stood looking at him, and then she began to laugh as she held out her arms to Colin Lomax.

I'm safe. They got him out in time. I knew they wouldn't fail me. Albatross. He hadn't relished the name, with its connotations of ill omen. But he had carried it long enough to laugh at superstition. He hadn't found it easy even to smile in the last few months when he was alone. Investigation. The dreaded word that he used about others. Knowing how the machinery worked made it worse; he could recall a dozen instances where other men suspected of treachery had been watched and caught out without having any idea that their time had run out. But his wouldn't. He was impregnable now. The danger had blown up like a high wind, and just as suddenly it dropped, and he could go on in calm. His people in Moscow had repaid many years of faithful service by swift action. Harrington would also reap his reward.

Better for Harrington that he didn't get the chance to betray; Moscow wouldn't have forgiven that. Now he would be feted and honored, miserable specimen that he was, and enjoy the status of a hero.

When my turn comes, I won't want that. I shan't slip away to exile. I shall retire and live out the rest of my life in the country I love, which I've served in my own way. I shall die and my obituary will be published in *The Times,* saying what a fine public servant I was and listing my good qualities. And the truth will go to the grave with me. My truth; my beliefs. And the mourners won't know when they stand about and place their wreaths . . . not even the ones I love best will ever know.

Morbidity followed upon relief; he shook it off, impatient with himself for indulging in a death wish that had no bearing on the present time. The strain had been greater than he had realized. It was one thing to set the bloodhounds loose on others. He had enjoyed that aspect of his work. He didn't like them baying at his own heels. That damnable woman. Why hadn't she been killed in Mexico—why had the car bomb in Australia missed her? He stayed very quiet, thinking that if Harrington hadn't been rescued, something would have had to be done about Davina Graham before she got any closer to him.

Now, thankfully, he could put that idea aside. He put the file she had left in his briefcase and set off for home.

Yuri Rudzenko studied the private autopsy report on the dead girl. It had been done the night before she was cremated. Suicide by drugs and alcohol. He noted the contents of the stomach; she had choked to death while unconscious. There were slight marks on her arms, a bruise from a love bite on her throat, made within hours of her death. Some minor lacerations of the scalp, as if she had been held by her hair. They would do that, he mused, to avoid heavy bruising if she struggled. Some discoloration around the nose, indicative of force being used. They had pinched her nostrils to make her open her mouth. Then they poured in the vodka and the pills. He put the grim document aside. The love bite proved that she had been with Borisov. The autopsy also mentioned that she had been in sexual congress that same night. Borisov had slept with her and then left her with his executioners. Rudzenko grimaced in disgust.

He was a sexual prude as well as a political purist. He hated and despised the corruption of the younger generation, the weakness of old comrades like Zerkhov. He saw the corrosion of the iron ideals and selfless dedication to the cause of Marxist Leninism creeping like a poison through Soviet life and into the Eastern-bloc countries. Only East Germany remained unsullied by the moral turpitude that reached a climax in Poland. Religion, that detestable fraud designed to bribe the people with promises of bliss after death—Rudzenko hated all religions. He chafed at the thought of churches open in Russia, even though the congregations were old grandmothers and a few young people led astray. He longed to repress the intransigent Muslims within the Soviet borders, to crush the tiny groups of Baptists who resisted the state and served as a propaganda for the West. He ached to purge the rottenness he saw and restore his country to its old inflexible attitudes where compromise was punished like treason. He had never feared Stalin. He had a clear conscience; only the guilty needed to cower when the Iron Man's eye considered them. Yuri Rudzenko had helped draw up the list for the great Army purge. He had applauded the genocide of the Ukrainians when they refused to accept the strictures of the Five Year Plan. He had witnessed interrogations, trials, and executions with the conviction of a man stamping out the plague.

And he believed that only a return to the past would save Russia and the world from an American victory. Because he saw war as inevitable; it was a necessary part of world revolution. The Great War had produced the Bolshevik triumph. A global war would give birth to a world where the old, sick values were swept away and the stern society of Lenin's vision would encompass the earth.

He pushed the autopsy away. He felt no twinge of compassion for the girl. He'd scarcely known her except as a face in Borisov's office and a source of vital information. He would miss that badly. Her death and her suffering meant nothing to him. Without Natalia he was cut off temporarily from the minds of his enemies.

How had she been discovered? That was what mattered now. He had agents close to Borisov in the KGB. Borisov had men in his own ministry. Everyone surveyed each other; that was understood. But he must know who had denounced Natalia. Borisov would need a new secretary. Rudzenko judged that this time he would choose a man. He consigned the report to the shredding machine in his office. She had been cremated and her ashes scattered. He would never think of Natalia again.

The van containing Sam's body drove into a scrap yard in the East End of London. It was met there by the third member of the team who had driven the green Cortina back after Sam and Harrington had changed over. There was a consultation and a decision made by the evening. The van doors were securely padlocked, and it was driven to a dump in the early hours of the next morning. There a friend arranged its disposal by crane on top of a forty-foot heap of rusting, shattered cars—wrecks from accidents, abandoned breakdowns past repair. It came to rest securely and gently, high up where the weather would strip its paint and the body inside would molder away undetected. The two men went their ways. Without Sam, they decided it was safer never to do a job together again.

"James?" Mary White put down her evening paper as her husband came into the living room from the little hall. They spent two nights a week in London, rather against her will. He declared it too tiring to commute up and down to Kent, and she didn't like leaving him to look after himself. "Have you seen the paper? That wretched man's escaped!"

He came into the room and said mildly, "Yes, dear, I know. I don't rely on the press for information of that kind."

"No need to be sharp with me," his wife retorted. She had never stood any nonsense from her husband, and he liked her all the better for it. "I'm sure it's a blow to you, but it's hardly your responsibility. Have a glass of sherry. I poured one for you."

He helped himself and sat beside her. "It is my responsibility," he said. "That bloody fool Humphrey had Harrington moved to an open prison."

"What? Without telling you?"

He settled into the sofa and sipped his sherry. He looked rather tired suddenly. "He's been engaged in a bit of private snooping," he said quietly. "Very unorthodox. Not like Humphrey at all."

Mary White put her paper aside. She knew instinctively when something serious had happened. "James, what sort of snooping?"

"It seems that evidence was put in front of him that pointed to a mole in the office," he answered. "He decided to take Davina into his confidence and start an investigation on the quiet. Part of it consisted of her seeing Harrington to persuade him to help. In return, a transfer was arranged for him to Shropwith. You can imagine why, of course."

"So he could get away," his wife said. "Of course. And they did this without telling you?"

"Davina resigned, precisely so she could work without my knowledge," he answered. "She got herself into that job with Walden to put us all off the scent. It was all rather clumsy, when you look at it. Humphrey puts in a word to the Home Office about moving Harrington, and it coincides with Davina pretending to Humphrey that she's dropped the whole thing."

"For heaven's sake," Mary interrupted, "why did she do that?"

"Apparently she'd found out enough to think the mole might even be him. Apart from John Kidson and myself, of course."

His wife stared hard at him and then made a little snort of impatience. "What absolute damned rubbish! I've never heard of anything like it. You should get rid of him at once. And put that young woman firmly in her place. How dare they!" She never swore except in moments of extremity, and "damn" was the ultimate.

He smiled at her and said, "Mary dear, there *is* a traitor. I've spent the afternoon looking at the evidence Davina found. There's no possible doubt. Someone has been working against the Service for the last fifteen years or so. Or it's been made to appear so. That did occur to me."

"Tell me how," she said. She had stopped being angry for him. She became worried instead. "I'll get you another sherry," she said, and did so hurriedly.

"Davina got hold of the files of various top-level operations. They stretch back a long time. They've been doctored. Sections are missing, and it's been very skillfully done. You see, she started by photographing, and if she hadn't been as clever or as observant as she is, she wouldn't have seen that the serial numbers on the pages were out of sequence. She wouldn't have discovered the deception from the photographs. The numbers are too high up, away from the script. It took me some time to see it myself."

"Oh, Lord," his wife said after a pause. "How awful. What are you going to do?"

"I'm not sure," he answered. "Harrington's escape has probably slammed the door on the investigation. He gave her the code name Albatross. He obviously knew a lot more. Now he's on his way to Moscow. They lifted him just in time."

"Then doesn't it seem odd that Humphrey fixed it up?" she said quietly.

"Not if you reckon that he and Davina were acting unofficially," he said. "Letting Harrington go would have to be part of any deal they made with him. Only there hasn't been a deal, so far as Humphrey knows. He's in a very bad position, poor chap. No chance of taking over from me after this, I'm afraid." He put down the empty glass. "Nor John Kidson either. He's quite a suspect too, you know. I'm not Albatross." He smiled and added, "I'm glad you didn't actually ask me that, but I'm not. And I don't think Humphrey is either. He's been so incredibly inept over the whole thing. So that leaves Kidson."

She looked at him and said, "Not just Kidson. What about Davina Graham? How do you know it isn't her?"

"I don't," he admitted. "I don't know anything until I've proved it. But the idea had occurred to me. Not very seriously, though. I have a nose for deceit, my dearest, and it's seldom wrong. She is in pursuit, make no mistake. Mostly because she thinks, or rather hopes, that Albatross is me!" He gave a loud chuckle. "She's going to be so disappointed when I find him first."

"Charlie! Where are you?"

Her voice echoed from upstairs. "Here, darling, putting Fergie to bed. Come up." He hurried up the short flight of steps and into the nursery. Charlie had had it decorated in what she described as unisex, suitable for a boy or a girl. Bright primrose yellow with splashes of apple green. It was a charming room that seemed to be sunny on the dullest day. The baby was lying kicking in his cot; Charlie didn't believe in swathing babies in blankets and shawls. Fergus Kidson wore a warm all-over suit called a babygro, and kicked and stretched until he fell asleep. John came up to his wife, put his arm round her, and kissed her.

"Isn't he growing like you?" she said.

"No, my darling, I'm glad to say he isn't. He's the image of you, red hair and all. He's a grand little fellow—look at him smiling!"

"That's wind," Charlie teased him. "You're home early."

"It's been quite a hectic day," he said. "I want to tell you about it. Is Teresa in tonight?" The Belgian student who helped look after Fergus had a busy social life; John sometimes felt that she should pay them for baby-sitting.

"Yes, she is. Are we going out?"

He squeezed her. "I think it might be nice. Let's go and have dinner at that place by the Thames—it's had a good write-up recently. It's a lovely evening, we might be able to sit outside."

"All right, why not?" She loved doing things on the spur of the moment. "I'll go and change into something nice."

He held her a moment longer and said, "You look beautiful just as you are."

Charlie bent down and kissed the baby. "You be a good boy," she admonished, "and go to sleep. You mummy and daddy are going out on the town. Are we celebrating something, darling?"

"Yes," he said, "yes, we are. I'll tell you about it while you're getting dressed."

The restaurant overlooked the Thames; they decided to sit inside instead of under the awning because a slight breeze was blowing in from the river and John was worried that she might get cold. The dinner was excellent; he ordered a good claret and Charlie blossomed to suit his mood. It was nice that so many people stared at her; it made him feel so proud that she belonged to him and that other men could only look and envy. Charlie smiled at him over her coffee cup; she had the most impudent, seductive smile in the world. He longed to take her home to bed.

"So there's nothing to worry about," she said. "Thank goodness, darling. You look a different person tonight."

"I feel it," he admitted. "It's all worked out perfectly. Humphrey's ruined himself, going behind the Chief's back, making such an incredible balls-up that a traitor like Harrington is allowed to escape. And your sister—oh, Charlie, she really put two fingers up to the old man today—talk about abrasive. He'll never let her cross the door again, even if she begged to come back."

"So you believe the way is clear for you now," Charlie said. She could imagine Davina's entrance and exit from his description. She was very different now from the repressed and diffident woman Charlie had been able to put to flight with a single derisory remark.

"I know it is," he said. "It has to be. The other two have wrecked their chances. That leaves me home and dry. You know, I owe it all to you, darling. You made me see how much I wanted that job."

"You were pretty cross to start with," she reminded him. "You told me I hadn't any morals. That was very naughty." She giggled.

"Nor have you," he said. "You're the original Eve. You'd take the apple every time and make the poor idiot of a man eat it with you. I'd fooled myself for years that I had no further to go in the Service. You made me see the truth. I wanted the Chief's job, but I wasn't prepared to fight for it."

"You certainly fought hard from then on," she remarked. "Did you mean to put suspicion on Humphrey—when you hinted he'd let Harrington go to an open prison on purpose?"

Kidson frowned. "I didn't say it deliberately. It just came out. He did get Harrington transferred. Nothing alters that."

Charlie held out her cigarette to be lit. "Do you think he is the mole? I can't take it seriously when they're called that, I keep thinking of those soft, furry things that dig up the garden. Could it be him?"

"We'll never know now," Kidson said. "Harrington was the key; that's why the Russians got him out in such a hurry. Normally they play about with exchanges. The last top agent they sprang out of jail was Blake; that was years ago. I don't honestly think it matters, darling."

Now it was Charlie who frowned. "Doesn't it? Surely a spy matters very much."

He shook his head. "It's not quite like that," he explained. "When someone as high up as Albatross is supposed to be comes under suspicion, they stop operating at once. It's a well-known procedure. Philby went into purdah once he was questioned. He did nothing for two years till he got out of Beirut because the heat was on again. Maclean and Burgess ran for it. Osborn, the old head of the SIS, was generally believed to be sympathetic to the Russians, if not actually working for them. Nothing happened to him. He retired and died in his bed in a nice little Sussex village. It's all done in a gentlemanly fashion, and the rules are understood by everyone."

"I don't think much of them," Charlie said suddenly. "I wouldn't let a person who'd betrayed their country slide out of it and pretend nothing had happened just because they'd stopped."

"Charlie," he admonished her, "you sound like your sister. The trouble with women is, they're naturally bloodthirsty. Men are much more realistic. All right, what would you do, then?" He asked the question half-jokingly.

Charlie's huge gray eyes grew narrow. "I'd shoot them," she said.

Kidson was quite shocked to see that she meant it. "Not hang them?" he inquired.

"All right, hang them. I'm sorry, John, but I can't take such a casual view of someone who turns traitor. Maybe I'm old-fashioned, but that's how I feel. As far as I'm concerned, there's no excuse."

"Well," he said, and shook his head, "isn't it lucky that I'm not Albatross!"

"Don't be silly, darling." She laughed at him. "Let's get the bill. I feel like going to bed early."

For a moment he looked at her and reached under the table, laying his hand possessively upon her knee. "So do I," he said.

When they were alone and he reached out to undress her, she said unexpectedly, "You don't think it's Sir James, do you?"

Kidson came close and unhooked the back of her dress. "I don't know, and frankly, at this moment I don't care. I love you. . . ."

She forgot about the other questions she had meant to ask him and gave herself up to the delights of being loved. He was a remarkably good lover; he was imaginative and exciting and he had taught Charlie that there was as much pleasure in giving as taking when she made love.

She had slept with a great many men, but John Kidson was the only one, including her two previous husbands, who was in full control in bed. She slept, exhausted and happy, with her arms around him and her face pressed against his cheek. He didn't even doze for a long time. His head was as clear as his body was satisifed and weary.

Humphrey Grant didn't want to go back to his flat and sit alone that night. He left the office in Anne's Yard and started to walk through St. James's Park. The lake stretched like silver on his left, ducks planed in and landed, scattering a tiny spray. The flowerbeds were immaculate, dressed for the early summer, and the stands were going up on Horseguards Parade for the Trooping the Color on the Queen's birthday. England, holding fast to her traditions, her ceremonies; unchanged at heart. Was that the secret? Humphrey wondered. To hold fast to things one believed in, to cling to the values, despite criticism and ridicule. To ignore the trends and the upheavals.

He walked slowly, his head thrust forward, a tall, thin man with hunched shoulders, a typical civil servant on his way home from one of the Whitehall ministries. Dark suit, conservative tie, even the unnecessary umbrella carried like a walking stick, briefcase swinging from the left hand. He circled the park and came out by the splendid vulgarity of the Victoria Memorial at the head of the Mall The usual crowd drifted around the palace railings, hoping for what? Protected from the importunities of tourists, the guardsmen stood on sentry duty behind the railing. A policeman ambled by on a large chestnut horse on his way back to the stables in Hyde Park. It was a typical evening in May, when the fine weather was constant and people thronged the streets to walk and sightsee. Humphrey turned down Buckingham Palace Road. He thought of his austere flat and the sandwich supper waiting for him. He watched television sometimes; often he took work home. He read detective stories for relaxation. He lived a solitary life of total self-containment, and he had never rebelled against it before. It was from choice. He didn't need friends. He had his work. For the first time in many years, he turned into a pub off Victoria Street and ordered himself a glass of beer.

"Mind if I sit here?"

He glanced up and saw the young man hesitating by the empty chair at his table.

"No," he said ungraciously. "It's not taken."

"Do you come here a lot?" The boy wanted to talk.

Humphrey decided to gulp his beer and go. "No," he answered.

"I haven't been here before; just come to London. Lonely place, isn't it?"

He didn't want to turn around and engage the boy in conversation, but he did. He was nice-looking, somewhere in the early twenties. He had a lost look, eager for friendship, like a puppy that's strayed. Suddenly Humphrey felt sorry for him. The word "lonely" had struck home. "Yes," he agreed. "All cities are, I think. Where do you come from?"

"Ipswich," the boy said. "I came up here to see if I could get a job. Things are that bad at home." He looked disconsolate for a moment, and then said, "No luck yet, but I keep trying. There must be something."

"Do you have a skill?" Humphrey asked him. There was a lot written and talked about the problem of unemployment for the young. He hadn't appreciated its significance until he saw the look on the boy's face.

"I worked in the building trade at home," he said. "There's nothing doing there, I can tell you. I'd take anything offered; I'm not one of those that wants to pick and choose. . . ."

He had finished his drink. The glass stood empty in front of him, and Humphrey knew that he couldn't afford to buy another one. He got up. "I'm going to get myself a beer. Have one on me." He walked over to the bar, with the boy's look of gratitude following him. Poor little devil, Humphrey thought, waiting to be served. No job, no prospects of getting one either. What the hell made him come to this bloody city? He'll only get caught up in some mess or other. He went back and sat down. "Where are you staying?"

There was an unmistakable hesitation. "With a friend. Here, have a fag . . ."

"No, no." Humphrey's face crinkled in disgust. "I can't stand the things, do you mind?"

" 'Course not," the boy said. "I don't have to smoke. Costs money too." He grinned. "You don't mind me talking to you, do you? I've been walking round all day; it's nice to talk to someone."

Humphrey put down his beer and leaned back a little in the chair. "Yes," he said. "Yes, it is. Have you had anything to eat?"

"Not yet." He shrugged. "Beer fills you up anyway."

"Well, I haven't either," Humphrey said decisively. "Why don't you come and have a bite with me? I've got nothing to do this evening. There's a place down the road."

The boy hesitated, and Humphrey said kindly, "Look, it's my treat. Come on."

They left the pub together, and spent the evening in the Steak House. Humphrey heard about the boy's family, his weeks looking for work at home until he'd come to London in desperation. He didn't whine, the young man, or complain. He had the directness of a child, a simple cheerfulness that Humphrey found touching and admirable. He felt warm being with him. He paid the bill and they stopped in the street outside. The boy shuffled his feet a little and then said, "Thanks very much. That was great. I won't see you again, I suppose?"

Humphrey had known from the moment he sat down. Twenty years I've been alone. Twenty years of killing everything in myself because I was ashamed. And at the end, what has it brought me? He had made a decision once that had changed the course of his life. A decision to live a lie for the rest of his life. Now he made a decision that could change everything, and suddenly he didn't care.

"Look, Ronnie, if you've nowhere to go, why don't you come back with me? I've got a spare bed."

The boy grinned his happy grin; he blushed slightly. "I was hoping you'd say that," he said.

The jeweler's shop in Grafton Street had an apartment above it. The business was established at the beginning of the nineteenth century; it was an old-fashioned family firm. It specialized in fine antique jewelry and select pieces of Irish Georgian silver. The father had died nine years before, and the head of the firm was the eldest son. By origin they were Dutch Jews; in the last generation two sons had married Irish girls and ceased to be Orthodox. Their children had been brought up as Catholics. Dark-haired and olive-skinned, they spoke with a Dublin nasal brogue, and the son who took over after his father's death was an ardent nationalist and contributor to the IRA. His conversion to terrorism was a mixture of resentments and a yearning to belong to the country where he had been born. He had grown up hating the rich Anglo-Irish families who patronized his father and kept him waiting for his money because he was just an old Jew. He hated them for their contempt for the native Irish, his wife included, and the long history of wrongs suffered by the Irish people echoed the sufferings of the Jews. From the fringes of nationalist activism Philip Gold graduated to the Marxism of the Provisionals, and his commitment to them went far beyond contributing money and passing information.

He lent the flat above his shop as a safe house. It was the ideal place to hide a fugitive and many had lain low there while the hunt for them ranged through the poor Republican districts and the homes of open sympathizers. No one would have suspected an address in the smartest shopping street in Dublin; gunmen and bombers on the run had spent time there until they could be slipped out and back across the border. On two separate occasions Gold had driven wanted men openly onto the ferry in his Mercedes, and never raised an eyebrow. The apartment was prepared for another guest. Gold asked no questions. A supply of food and drink and newspapers was bought.

The day of the guest's arrival came and went and there was no ring on the door. Very early the next morning Gold took a telephone call.

"Something's gone wrong. The parcel didn't come last night. I don't know when to expect delivery now."

"Never mind," Gold answered. "I'll take it when it does come. Just let me know."

The Dublin papers carried news items about the escape of a Soviet agent from an open prison. Questions were going to be asked in the House as to why a traitor should have been moved from a top-security jail. Gold read and drew his own conclusions. By the following evening the Dublin contact who was waiting to pick up Harrington informed his Soviet liaison that the link was broken and he couldn't spend another day hanging around the airport. The London end would have to take it up and find out what had happened. It was quite possible that their people had decided to lie low in England before getting to Dublin. It was possible, the official at the Russian embassy agreed. Anything was possible. But not likely, especially as they hadn't sent a message canceling the Irish arrangements. Gold was told to forget about a visit, the watch on the airport was abandoned, and an urgent message went to Stephen Wood.

He arrived at teatime on Sunday to be met by Sam's anxious wife. No, she said, she hadn't seen or heard from her husband since he left a week earlier. Yes, he had some job to do collecting a car in the north, but he always telephoned home, and the last call she had was on Monday, saying he expected to be back by Thursday morning. Since then, not a word. She was thinking of going to the police. . . . Wood reassured her; there was no need to do anything drastic like that, he said. He just wondered whether her husband was at home, but since he was away on a job, he'd call round again. He gave a false name, stayed for tea, and talked on and on about children and education and the effect the hard winter had had on people's gardens, till she thought she was going to scream if he didn't get up and go. When he did, he told her not to worry once again, and suggested that Sam might be very angry if he found she'd gone to the police and made a fuss. . . . As a result, she delayed reporting him missing for another four days.

Wood took the Underground home and telephoned while his wife was in the kitchen getting supper ready.

"The parcel has gone astray. Let head office know." He hung up and went out to help his wife set the table. He was a firm believer in sharing the household activities.

"Now," Davina said, "you've had a good night's sleep and something for the hangover. Let's get down to business."

Peter Harrington looked up at her with reddened eyes. What a cow, he thought, feeling the headache thudding in a distance induced by two aspirins and black coffee. "I still feel pretty shaky," he protested.

"Not as shaky as you'll feel if Colin comes in and finds you've been playing for time," she said quietly. "You haven't got time, Peter."

"What the hell does that mean?" he snarled at her wearily. "More threats? You're a real peach blossom, aren't you—"

"You'll be reported missing by now," Davina said. "Every KGB agent in London will be looking for you. Which is what you're gambling on, isn't it? Only it won't work to your advantage if they do find you."

"And why not?" He sneered at her, risking defiance because Lomax was out of the room.

"Because you won't get out alive," she said quietly. "Colin will see to that. Tell me what I want to know, and I promise to deliver you to your friends."

"Not in a million years," he said. "You'd never do it in a million years. When you've milked me dry, you'll turn me in to the police. I'm saying nothing."

Davina lit a cigarette and handed it to him. He was put off by the gesture and hesitated. "I'll give you an hour to think it over." She spoke quite calmly. "When I come back, either we start serious work on Albatross or I'll pick up the phone and call the police in front of you." She went out and he heard the living-room door lock. He wished he'd gone easy on the whiskey the night before. He felt queasy and his nerves were jumping at every sound. He'd been bluffing, and she knew it. He called her vile names to relieve his feelings.

He puffed on the cigarette, got up, and moved restlessly around the room. He had thought of escape, and dismissed the idea. He had no money, no place to hide. He didn't know where Stephen Wood lived.

His photograph was all over the morning papers. He'd be picked up by the first policeman who took a good look at him. He finished the cigarette, stubbed it out, and then threw it into the grate, where it lay under the electric fire, catching the eye in a very tidy room. It was a stupid, petty gesture, but it was his last act of defiance, and he knew it. Albatross. Very well, he'd give the bitch the information. Enough to let her find the quarry for herself. At least he could hold back the clue he'd worked out for himself. She could make the final deduction if she was sharp enough. He decided to act positively, to assert himself and drop the passive role of prisoner. He went to the door and called her, using the nickname he knew she hated. "Davy!"

She came into the little hall. "Yes?"

"Let's get on with it," Harrington said. "And I could do with some more coffee."

He talked into the tape; his headache had gone, and he felt relaxed, almost confident. Indecision was the curse of the imprisoned. Now that he had made up his mind, his spirits rose. He began to enjoy himself, threading through the maze that protected Albatross. "I joined in sixty-three," he said. "And I changed sides ten years later. He was well-established then. The impression I got in Switzerland was that he had been in place for a long time. Which brings us to the previous head of SIS, old man Osborn. He was a definite sympathizer, one of those remnants from the war when the idea of Russia being our ally clung on long after the Cold War started. I don't think he actually dealt with the opposition, but you could help as much by shutting your eyes to things or just not taking action when you knew you should. . . . I think he was a kind of fellow traveler rather than an active double agent. That's when I think Albatross got in."

"With Osborn's knowledge?" Davina interposed. "You realize you're putting the Chief in the clear for a start."

"Yes, I know I am," Harrington answered. "But you mustn't let your personal prejudices influence you, Davy dear. Much as you'd like it to be him, I don't believe it is. I think Albatross was introduced in Osborn's time. A nice, liberal-minded chap . . . could have been a bit on the queer side." He paused. "Humphrey joined too late for that, didn't he?" he said. "How about your brother-in-law, Kidson? Wasn't he a bright young man from university who went to the Foreign Office?"

"Yes," Davina said. "He was. But you're basing all this on no evidence at all, just a personal opinion."

That's right. But you can check it out, can't you? You've got the details of Humphrey's enrollment, and the Chief's—see if I've missed anything."

"When do you see Albatross showing his hand for the first time?"

"When Sasanov defected. Earlier on there are indications, principally the loss of our Rumanian network in seventy-one. Humphrey had a hand there, so did Kidson. Humphrey recruited a Rumanian exile and sent him back in. Kidson debriefed him when he came home. The Chief decided to chance him a second time. He was arrested after a tip-off, and the whole clutch of our agents were picked up. I see Albatross at work there. But"—he shrugged— "it could be any one of the three. Sasanov was different. That's where we can identify a kind of handwriting. We all have our signatures in this job, don't we, Davy? I could tell your work anywhere. I got my instructions in the States: get yourself recalled in disgrace. I did, if you remember."

"I remember," Davina answered.

"Well, who decided I should be transferred to Personnel? I know it's one step towards early retirement, a total career dead end, but it also brought me smack into contact with you. Which was what I was waiting for. Who decided to bring me to London instead of sticking me in some backwater out of the way or kicking me out altogether—which is what should have happened. That's Albatross. You find out who recommended that posting—not who *authorized* it, but who recommended it. That will be your first big pointer."

"Supposing they're one and the same person?"

"The Chief again, eh?" He grinned maliciously at her. "You could be right. But it could just as well be Humphrey or Kidson who put in the word. The Chief didn't make all the minor decisions, and what to do with a drunk who'd made an ass of himself could easily have been left to either of the other two. And then, we have our friend Spencer-Barr. My replacement in Washington."

Davina looked at him. "What's he got to do with it?"

"Why didn't he get the minder's job with Sasanov? Have you ever really asked yourself that?"

"No," she admitted. "The Chief made the decision. He felt a woman would suit Ivan better. He gave me the job. Which knocks the first hole in your other theories, doesn't it? If that appointment has a bearing, then it was James White and no one else. Humphrey was dead against my doing it. I don't think John Kidson was even consulted."

"You don't know," Harrington pointed out.

"The fact remains that Spencer-Barr was working for the CIA. If Albatross suspected that, he'd have moved heaven and earth to stop him getting his hands on Sasanov. And he wouldn't have exposed him, either; double dealing between the Allies is always good for the opposition."

The tape finished and Davina changed it for a new one. "I can't understand you, Peter," she said. "You talk about the opposition as if you hadn't been part of them. You were an officer in the KGB. Yet you talk as if you were on the other side."

"If you want an answer to that," he said, "don't switch on the tape. I'm not on any side but my own. They paid and I delivered."

"I see." She reached out to press the record switch.

"No, you don't," Harrington snapped. "You don't see anything. You think everything in life is black and white, don't you? The good guys against the baddies, like an old western where the outlaws always wore black. You're a clever little piece, I'm not denying that, but you've never got rid of the *Girl's Own* attitude to life. You think that because I went over to Moscow, I must be a Communist? Some high ideals burn in this ignoble frame, isn't that it?"

"No, it isn't," she said coldly. "There's nothing in you, Peter, but a mess of selfishness and greed. I wondered how you saw yourself, that was all. Not one of them, that's obvious. Not one of us either. A sort of nonperson. Shall I switch on now?"

"Go to hell," he snarled at her.

The tape whirred and for a while there was silence. A nonperson. That had stung, as she intended it should. Make the bastard angry now and again, Lomax had advised her. He'll let something slip if he's off guard. . . . "Right," she started briskly. "Apart from Spencer-Barr, what else? The fire that was meant to kill us both? That was your doing alone, wasn't it?"

He nodded, still seething. "I pinpointed where you were hiding. The action group did the rest. Albatross wouldn't have risked meddling with that one. But he meddled with something else." He paused, and Davina waited.

"I think," he said, "that where he really showed his hand was in Australia. If you want to find him, Davy dear, look for whoever pinned the flag on the map for you and Ivan."

She had blushed a little; Harrington knew that he had scored. She didn't like references to that. Didn't want to talk about the night the car blew up and Ivan Sasanov died in her arms. . . . "You mean that Albatross told them where we were?" she asked him.

"No other way they could have found you," Harrington insisted. "You were shopped from home. I can see the way your mind's working; who knew besides the Chief?"

"Nobody," Davina said flatly. "The files prove that. Nobody knew, not Humphrey, and not John either. Only the Chief." She paused and then said in a low voice, "He'd hardly tip them off, because of the risk to himself if anything went wrong. I accused him of not looking after Ivan; in fact, he did as much as possible, certainly from the London end, to keep us hidden."

"So you take one step near him and another back," Harrington pointed out. "You say he protected you from the London end—what about security in Australia?"

"Nothing," she said bitterly. "Not a bloody thing. That's why I've held him responsible for what happened. We had no guard, no special precautions round the house, nothing! They just moved in when they were ready. And the man who masterminded it was made head of the KGB as a reward!"

"That I didn't know," Harrington remarked. "He won't be too pleased about what happened to me—I wonder how long it'll take him to pick up the trail?"

"Let's hope it's long enough to get this sorted out," Davina answered. "Australia—you think someone knew besides the Chief?"

"They either knew, in which case White waited till he thought it was safe and then tipped them off, or someone else found out. An interesting problem, isn't it?"

"Yes," Davina said slowly. "You've given me the best incentive in the world for finding out. I'll play this back and we'll see if we've missed anything."

The news reached Borisov as he was about to leave his office. Harrington had disappeared en route for Manchester Airport. So had his companion. The other men involved had gone to ground. Efforts were being made to find them. Results would be telexed through to Moscow within the next twenty-four hours, if possible. Borisov telephoned his wife. He would not be home till late, he said. The whine at the other end made him wince. How late—and how did she really know he was working? He slammed the phone down. The ache for Natalia waited like an attacker in the shadows. He didn't think of her death, or the reason for it. He remembered nothing but the warmth of her body and the skill of her lovemaking; above all, the sense of sharing his work with her. He longed for the companionship even more than sex. Sex he could and did command, but it left him empty and lonely when the women had gone. His hatred for Rudzenko had a deeper motive than before. He owed Rudzenko for sending him Natalia, for giving him happiness, and then, because she was corrupt, forcing him to cut her out like a cancer. . . .

He sent a series of coded telexes to the embassy in London. The instructions were brief: find the men who had helped their agent carry out the operation. They must be questioned. Put an immediate watch on Davina Graham. Alert Albatross. Report progress on the plan to substitute the replacement. He added an angry postscript to the senior KGB officer in the London embassy, expressing his displeasure at the slowness of their reaction. If Harrington was not recovered and British intelligence had frustrated the escape, Borisov would hold the officer personally responsible. After he had sent the telexes, he called for his new secretary. A man this time, a young lieutenant who had been in the service since he became head of the KGB. No danger of a Rudzenko spy here. But not Natalia either. Sometimes, when he was working late, he thought he heard her voice or the soft step approaching his chair. He didn't believe in ghosts or in any aspect of the supernatural. But she haunted him. Rudzenko would put another spy in her place; Borisov was waiting for that move. Perhaps one already there would somehow slip into promotion. . . .

But not Alexei. Alexei was his man. He was not a good secretary, but he had other skills. One day they would be called upon. But till then there was nothing he could do but go home. When the present crisis was over, and the larger crisis that the autumn promised had been resolved, he would get a divorce. That hope made his return to the luxurious Moscow apartment easier to bear.

Sam's two recruits were found the following day, one in the morning and the second a few hours later. They were found, not by the KGB, but by the underworld. It was a simple method of detection. Word went to the gang bosses of Sam's neighborhood that his men had to be dug out, or serious consequences for the drugs and prostitution and burglaries they controlled would follow. Nobody asked questions; past experiences proved that the threat came from a quarter capable of carrying it out. Their own people found Sam's men, and the questioning was done by them with an observer in the background. It took only a little violence to extract the truth. Both men supplied the details as clearly as the agony of a broken arm and a shin cracked in three places would permit. The snatch had gone wrong, Sam had been killed, and the quarry spirited away. They were held in the basement room of a derelict house in Hackney while the dump of wrecked cars was found and someone persuaded the crane driver to lower him to the van. The rotting corpse was smelled before they opened the door. The crane brought him back to ground level. Nothing was said. The men in the basement knew too much. The observer watched while they were shot in the head. The information was passed through from the embassy to Moscow. And with it went a rough description of the man who had knocked out the driver of the van and taken his place. It went into the computer at Lubyanka offices in Dzerzhinsky Square. The computer came up with several possible identities. Three were of known international agents; one of them was British; two were actual Soviet citizens who were not in Europe, least of all London; and the one which the computer suggested, without being able positively to identify from the few details, was Major Colin Lomax.

Colin kept in the background. He saw Harrington once or twice, but at Davina's insistence he stayed away from the apartment when they were working together. He made a date with his old SAS comrade and once more they met in the pub where the plan to pull Harrington out of Shropwith had been discussed. Captain Fraser didn't ask for reasons when Lomax telephoned originally and canceled the arrangements. He saw the newspaper reports and decided to wait. A convicted Soviet spy had escaped from the very place his old friend Lomax had mentioned as the venue for his plan. Someone had got there first. Bad luck for Lomax. He wasn't the kind to take being outmaneuvered with a good grace. When they met that evening, Fraser was surprised at how cheerful his friend seemed for someone who had had his quarry grabbed under his nose. They drank and chatted for a while, and then he said, "No names, no pack drill, but any connection between that business up in Lancashire and your little caper?"

"No," Colin said, and didn't pretend to be telling the truth. "No connection, Jim."

"Glad to hear it," the captain said. "Wouldn't want to be mixed up in a mess like that. If you should need any help, though . . ."

"I'll let you know." Lomax nodded. "One for the road, then I must be off." He brought the drinks back. He seemed miles away from the crowded bar.

Fraser didn't interrupt him. He had always been a taciturn man who didn't talk unless he had something to say that mattered. Lomax emptied his glass. "I might be interested in a security guard keeping an eye on a friend of mine," he said. "Two chaps, like the ones you had in mind before. I'll get in touch. How much notice do you need?"

"Just a phone call," the captain answered. "I'll see you get the same two. They're very good."

"They might need to be," Lomax answered.

He left the pub first, leaving Fraser to down the whiskey and leave later. He had parked his car some two side streets away; he drove home carefully, concentrating on speed or traffic dodging. Davina was making progress; she'd put quite a picture together in the two days of grace they'd had so far. A long-established Soviet operator, moving only when absolutely necessary and then always covered by the contingency of his two colleagues. Elusive, shadowy, all the fictional spy clichés came to mind, and they were apt. But with something more. A desperate cunning that made him very dangerous. There was no face, only a blur came to mind with the name Albatross. Harrington had believed he had told the KGB where Davina and Sasanov were living. A new identity, a new name, a post in a university in western Australia. Light-miles from Europe or the States, the recognized havens of defectors. The killers had trailed them and set their trap. A few moments' delay had saved Davina from dying with him. Albatross had scented them out.

Lomax put the car in the lock-up garage and went up to the flat. He opened the front door and called for Davina. She came out of the kitchen. He thought she looked tired and strained. He jerked his head toward the sitting room. "Is he in there?"

She nodded. "I've just given him a drink. I could do with one myself. Come and sit down, Colin love, will you? Break it up for me a bit. He's been getting on my nerves."

He kissed her and she leaned against him and sighed. "He keeps on harping," she murmured, "on and on about Australia. I don't know whether he's doing it to get at me or because he thinks it really holds the key."

Lomax kissed her again. The bastard, he said to himself. The snide bastard, opening up that wound. . . . "You go and have a bath or lie down for a bit, sweetheart. You look weary. I'll entertain our friend in there."

She said quickly, "Colin! Never mind what I just said. Don't get difficult with him, will you—please?"

"My darling," he whispered in her ear, "if I got difficult, I'd break his neck. Go off and take a break. I promise to be as sweet as pie. . . ."

She was running the bath when the phone rang. She picked it up and said, "Hold on a minute," and went back into the bathroom to turn off the taps.

"Davina . . ."

She heard Tony Walden's voice repeating her name. "Tony? Hello, sorry about that, I couldn't hear—"

"Why haven't you come into the office? I've been in New York and Frieda said you hadn't been in for two days. You're not ill, are you?"

"I'm never ill." She laughed. "Just busy, that's all. Do you need me?"

There was a pause. "You know I need you. I'm in a call box over the road."

"What? What on earth are you doing there?"

"I was coming in when I saw your major turn up. And I saw something else . . . Hell, I'm running out of money—"

She heard the coin go in and his voice come back. "That's my last five pence. Listen, I've got to tell you something—can I come up and see you?"

"No," Davina said quickly. "No, better not. I'll come out. Wait in the phone box."

No time for a bath now. There was an urgency in Walden's voice that made her hurry. She put her head around the door. The television was on and Lomax was sitting quietly reading the newspaper while Harrington watched the news. "I'm going out for a bit," she said. "I won't be long." She ran down the stairs and out into the street. The phone booth was on the other side of the road. Walden wasn't in it. She said "Damn!" and looked around for him.

A taxi pulled up at the curb, and he opened the door and said, "Davina!" She got in and the cab drove off.

"Tony, what the devil is all this about?"

He glanced back out of the rear window. "That foxed them," he said.

She could have shaken him. "Foxed who?" she demanded.

He leaned forward and closed the glass partition so that the driver couldn't hear. "The two men who have been watching your apartment building," he said quietly. "One of them followed your major friend. I saw him. The other joined up with him. That's why I telephoned you, to warn you."

She couldn't help herself. She went pale. "Oh, my God. Are you sure?"

"The man following your friend got into a stationary blue car parked a few yards up the road by the entrance to your building. There was another man in the car. They didn't drive off. I was curious, so I hung about. I drove round the block and parked myself. Just before I telephoned, they changed over. The blue car moved off and a grocer's van came straight into the spot and stayed there. So I phoned you. You've gone very white, Davina. What's going on?"

"Nothing I can talk about," she said. She looked out of the back window. "There's a cream van behind us," she said. "Is that the one?"

"No . . ." he said. "So whoever is keeping surveillance, it's on the building; obviously they don't have instructions to follow you."

"But you say there was a tail on Colin . . ."

"I'm afraid so," he said. He leaned forward, opened the glass panel, and said, "The Ritz Hotel, please," and shut it again. "I have a room there. I use it sometimes. We can talk." He reached out and took her hand. She tried to pull away, but he held tighter and she would have had to struggle. "You're cold," he said. "Stop being a fool and let me hold your hand. You're mixed up in something nasty, aren't you? I thought my car was too distinctive, so I picked up the taxi instead. Good idea, wasn't it?"

"Good ideas are your business," Davina said. "For God's sake, don't start fancying yourself as a spy! I've got enough trouble without worrying about you."

"I'd like you to worry about me," he said. "Here we are. My favorite hotel."

She hurried through the famous ground-floor lobby, followed Walden into an elevator, and came out on the third floor. He produced a tagged key and opened a door marked "Suite A." It was a charming room, decorated in pale blue, with elegant furniture and fresh flowers.

Inside Davina looked around and said, " 'Room' is hardly the word. What do you do in here?"

Walden was taking glasses out of a cupboard stocked with drinks. "I entertain," he said. "Wine for you, or something stronger?"

"Stronger," she answered. "Entertain clients?"

"Ladies." Walden handed her a brandy. "And sometimes clients who don't want anyone to know they're employing the agency; a suite at the Ritz makes them feel secure. Beautiful view, isn't it?"

"Lovely," she agreed. The park spread out under the windows; they might have been in a grand country house surrounded by a vast acreage. "Tony, you're *certain* that blue car was a stakeout?"

It was almost an appeal, but he only nodded and said, "Absolutely certain. And in case you think I'm playing at spies, as you call it, I'll remind you that I knew a little about escape routes from East Germany. I'm not a professional like you, my dear, but I'm not an amateur either. The building is being watched, and Major Lomax was followed home. You'd better tell me why, or I can't help you."

"I don't need any help," she said. "Nor does Colin; he can look after himself."

"I'm sure he can," Walden said. "I'm not thinking about him. Davina, why don't you trust me? I could be very useful. I've got money, facilities, anything you need. Tell me one thing: who do you think is doing it?"

She sat down and sipped her brandy. She needed it. Only two days, and the flat was already being watched. He waited and the silence lengthened. She looked up at him. He was right. He could call up the sort of backing that they lacked. Transport, a private plane, money. The suite at the Ritz. She made up her mind in that split second.

"The Russians," she said. "You read about the double agent Peter Harrington escaping from prison last week—we've got him in the flat."

"Holy Christ!" He jerked out of his chair. "You mean you got him out of prison?"

"No, the KGB organized that. Colin grabbed him from them. That's why what you've told me is so desperately serious. It means they either suspect he's there, or they know it. Whichever, they'll move in on us soon."

He watched her closely, a deep frown drawing the thick dark brows together. "You've no official backing."

It was a statement, and she didn't hesitate. "None. Not even Humphrey, so I'd be glad if you'd keep this quiet if he starts nosing around."

The frown didn't lift. "Why not? I understood you were in the Service, working under a cover. That's why I provided the job."

"I was, and I am," Davina answered. "You asked me to trust you a minute ago. I could do with a little trust on your part. I didn't have to tell you. I don't have to explain any more, and I'm not going to."

He held up his hand. "Good enough. Thank you for taking me into your confidence. It sounds so dangerous and crazy that I almost wish you hadn't. What can I do to help?"

Davina sat back; she felt steadier now, and she was thinking at top speed. "I know what you can do, but I have to say something to you first. You're right about the danger. The KGB want Harrington. My feeling is they'll take a chance that he's hidden in Marylebone and break into the flat. If he gets killed in the process, that'll be too bad. All they want to do is shut his mouth. What I need is to get him out of there and somewhere where they won't find him. Not for a week at least. Will you let me bring him here?"

"What a brilliant idea! Nobody will think of the Ritz. . . . You're a genius, Davina. And quick to see the main chance. You'd better work for me properly after all this is over."

He lit a cigarette and gave it to her. "I'll be starting my own agency," he said. "My trip to the States decided that."

For the moment she forgot Harrington and the menace of the watchers in the street. "You've resigned? I am so sorry."

He shrugged. "The loss of that Arab connection was too big to explain away. They wanted my head on a platter, and I gave it to them before they had the chance to cut it off. I feel rather relieved. But never mind that. That's what I came round to the flat to tell you."

"Thank God you did," Davina said. "Tony, I'd better get back. I'll call Colin first."

"Where are you?" Lomax asked.

"I'm with Tony Walden. Hello . . . Colin? I thought we'd got cut off—I said I'm with Tony. You'll never guess where . . . Never mind . . . No, of course I'm not!" Walden heard the sharp tone of her voice and smiled a little. Jealous, he thought She doesn't like that. "I'm coming back right away. What's Harrington doing? For God's sake don't let him drink too much—he can't hold it—and pack some things for him and for us. Yes, I said pack . . . I'll tell you when I get there." She hung up, and when she turned, Walden saw there was a little color in her face. He wondered what Lomax had asked that put it there.

"Tony, I think we should get him over here tonight. There's no point in waiting. But you'll have to help. And I've got to warn you that it could be dangerous for you."

He said lightly, "I'm not worried. Just panic-stricken, that's all. I can use a gun, by the way."

"You won't need one," she said. "All you'll need is an overcoat and a hat. Something distinctive. Do you keep any clothes here?"

"Only pajamas," he said. "Just for appearance' sake. I can get a coat and a hat from home. What do I have to do?"

"Come to the flat in an hour," she said. "Wear the coat and the hat. We'll take it from there. I'll get back now. And thanks." She came up to him and kissed him on the cheek. "I'll make it up to you about the agency. I promise." Then she was gone.

CHAPTER 6

"I'VE CLEANED up for you," the boy called Ronnie said. "And I got some sausages and stuff for supper."

Humphrey looked around at the bleak little living room. It was spotlessly tidy, as it had been when he left for the office that morning. Ronnie stood waiting for approval.

"It looks very nice," Humphrey said. "Thanks for getting the shopping for me. It's a nuisance buying food on my way home. Usually I don't bother," he admitted.

"I'll cook up something," Ronnie offered eagerly. "I'm not too bad at it, used to help Mum when we were all at home. You sit down. Like a drink?"

Humphrey nodded. He looked at the smiling young face and felt a sense of warmth and comfort he had never known. Such a genuinely nice boy, grateful for everything, anxious to please. He had never had anyone to look after him before.

"That would be nice, Ronnie. Sherry please—and have one with me. Thanks. Now, tell me, did you go to the job center today?"

"I went as soon as I'd tidied up," was the answer. "There was a job as a washer-up in a café up Pimlico way. I saw the manageress, but she was a right old cow. The pay was twenty quid a week, for six nights, seven till twelve o'clock."

Humphrey said sharply, "You didn't take it, I hope?"

The boy looked awkward. "Well, I did, starting tomorrow. I can't sponge off you much longer."

Humphrey said firmly, "Don't be ridiculous. Twenty pounds a week wouldn't feed you, let alone anything else. It's slave labor, that's all. Besides, if you worked in the evenings, we'd never see each other."

Ronnie glanced up at him; he looked shy. "No, we wouldn't. I did think about that. What shall I do about it, then?"

Humphrey finished his sherry. Ronnie was on his feet at once to get him a refill. "You go back to the center tomorrow," he said, "and tell them that the job was quite unsuitable. And don't worry. Something will turn up so long as you keep going. And you know you're welcome to stay here as long as you like."

He had the most infectious, guileless grin. It spread over his face and made Humphrey smile a little too. "You're good to me," he said. "I was dreading that job. She was such an old bag, that woman. . . ."

"Forget it," Humphrey advised. "You don't want to work for someone like that anyway, whatever they pay you. After all"—he said it quite casually—"if you want pocket money while you're looking for something, I can manage that. You keep the flat tidy, see to the shopping and that sort of thing. . . " He didn't look at the boy. He didn't want him to see the anxiety behind the offer. He didn't understand how he could mind so much about Ronnie getting a job and going to live somewhere else.

But he did. He didn't care if he never found work, so long as he stayed in the flat and gave him something to look forward to when he came home.

For someone so young, Ronnie showed natural tact. "I'd have to earn it," he said gently. "I wouldn't just take money from you. I'd look after everything for you. I'll get the supper, then. . . ." He went out to the tiny kitchen. Humphrey heard him whistling. Normally he would have winced at the silly tuneless little noise. But it was comforting. It showed that the boy was happy. A voice called through, "How d'you like your bangers done?"

"Nice and brown," Humphrey called back. He picked up the evening paper and settled down to read. He thought the warm feeling inside him was two glasses of Tio Pepe, but it wasn't. It was something new in his experience. He wasn't lonely.

They had finished their supper and Ronnie asked him if he minded having the television on. Humphrey hated television unless he watched a serious program. He took refuge from the dreadful inanities of a family quiz game behind the newspaper, and the boy kept the sound down so as not to disturb him. It merged into a meaningless mumble and Humphrey didn't notice it. Then the telephone rang. Ronnie jumped up. "Shall I answer it?"

Humphrey put his paper down. "No," he said after a moment. "I'll take it. Turn the volume down, will you?" Ronnie switched the set off.

The call was from Sir James White. It was brief. "I've just had a call from the duty officer. Telex from our people in Moscow. They haven't got Harrington. On the best authority, yes."

Humphrey Grant said slowly, "Then who has?"

James White snapped the answer. "That's what we want to know. I've got my own idea. Come back to the office at eight-thirty. Kidson's coming in. We'd better have a meeting and get to grips with this at once." The line cleared and Humphrey hung up.

The boy said, "Anything the matter? You look like you've had bad news—"

"I've got to go out," Humphrey said. "I won't be back till late, I think."

"Doesn't matter," Ronnie said simply. "I'll wait up."

John Kidson and his wife were due to have dinner with friends when the Chief's message came through. He always left a number where he could be contacted if he was not at home. He came back after taking the call, and apologized. "I'm terribly sorry, some silly nonsense has blown up at the office. I've got to go in."

His hostess said, "Oh, poor you—don't tell me someone has invaded the Isle of Wight!"

There was a general laugh. Kidson was known to all their friends as an undersecretary at the Foreign Office. Only Charlie knew that something far from trivial summoned him back at that hour. She got up, excusing herself for a moment, and came out to the hall with him. "What's happened?"

"I can't talk now," he snapped irritably. "I've got to go."

"Darling . . ." Charlie wasn't used to being brushed aside. "Surely you can tell me. . . ."

Her husband scowled at her. "Ask your bloody sister." He pushed past her and hurried out into the street.

They met in Humphrey's office. The building was opened up, the duty officer who had once complained to Kidson that nothing ever happened was told to get in touch with the Foreign Minister's deputy. The Minister was in Canada; his deputy was difficult to contact because he was en route to Edinburgh for a family wedding. The Chief expressed his impatience, and the duty officer described it afterward as being like standing under a tap dripping vitriol.

The telex from British intelligence in Moscow had come direct through the embassy. Harrington had been rescued by the KGB, but there had been an outside intervention en route. Harrington had vanished. There was no question about the authenticity of their information. It came via a highly placed informant in the Soviet Foreign Ministry. The man in question had deliberately leaked this information to his British counterpart. "Why?" Humphrey asked quickly.

"Because there is an internal power struggle going on," White said. "The hard-liners headed by Rudzenko against the Chairman Zerkhov and Igor Borisov. The object of the leak is to discredit the KGB leadership. They're hoping we'll catch Harrington and make their balls-up public."

"This is Graham and Lomax," Kidson broke in. "They've got Harrington, and she's pumping him for information about Albatross."

James White eyed him thoughtfully. "That's a serious statement, John. Do you know something Humphrey and I don't?"

"No, of course not," Kidson answered sharply. He seemed more on edge than Humphrey. White, as usual, remained icy calm. "It's obvious, that's all. She said she was going to get Albatross, and Harrington is the one who'll help her do it!"

"I agree." Humphrey said it quietly. "Although it seems a very complicated operation. One man on his own certainly couldn't have got Harrington away from the KGB removers. That's my only doubt. There must be an organization behind it. Someone is helping them, if we're right and it is Davina and Lomax. Chief?"

"There's a simple way to find out, before we start bringing in the Foreign Minister. Since Fuller's on his way to Edinburgh, we've got a few hours to act on our own. But not more. I've got to make this information known, and that will mean a full-scale search for Harrington. I think"—he looked from Humphrey to Kidson—"we'd like to find him ourselves."

"We have to find him," Kidson said. "And if I'm right and those two have taken the law into their own hands and kept a convicted traitor in hiding, something has got to be done about them!"

"Don't worry about that," James White assured him. "Just let me have the proof. Now, what I suggest we do is this. . . ."

"You told him?" Lomax said. "You told Walden about *him?*" He jerked his head toward the closed door. "For Christ's sake, Davina!" He was taut with anger.

She faced him without backing down, but her own temper and nerves were fraying. "I don't think you've taken in what I said," she retorted. "We're being watched. You were tailed back here!"

"According to that bloody fool who knows how to sell Tampax and soap," Lomax exploded. "What does he know about staking out a place? Or following someone? The whole thing's ridiculous. Do you imagine I wouldn't have spotted it if they were after me?"

"Well, you didn't," she snapped at him. "And I believe Tony. That van was parked out here when I got back. Anyway, I've made the arrangements and I want them carried out. I'm going to tell Harrington now."

He came and caught her by the arm. "Just a minute," he said, and his voice was deceptively quiet. "You're not giving orders to me."

She stood still and prized his fingers away from her arm. "Colin," she said, "you're letting personal feelings get in the way of the job. What you said on the phone proves it. He wasn't chatting me up. He was telling me that we were likely to be jumped at any moment.

You're jealous and you're behaving like a fool. I'm taking Harrington out of here, and you can't stop me." She opened the door to the living room and went inside.

Harrington was twitching with nerves. He chewed on his lip and twisted his hands in and out while she talked. "If you don't do it," she said, "they'll come in here and arrest you."

"How long have they been watching?" he demanded. "Why the hell didn't you think of this and take me somewhere else?"

"Because I thought the Chief would believe you'd got away to Russia," she said. "Obviously he suspects you haven't. But he isn't sure—that's why our people are keeping a watch and haven't acted yet. But they will, Peter, and we'll all be in it. You've got to do what I tell you. I've got to trust you to go out of here and take the taxi waiting for you. You've got to trust me to know what's best."

He started to swear under his breath. "Christ almighty, why didn't I stay in the Scrubs? Why did I ever let you talk me into any of this?"

"If that's how you feel," Davina gambled, "all you've got to do is walk out of here and give yourself up to the boys in the grocery van parked outside. There's the door. Nobody's going to stop you."

It was a gamble, and she took it knowing that the watchers outside were KGB men. If he had been the old Peter Harrington of six years ago, she wouldn't have got away with the lie. He would have seen through the deception as soon as he was alone in the street, and guessed that his friends were in the waiting van. But his nerve and his judgment had suffered during those six years. He wasn't the same man who had gone into Russia with her and played the game of secrets with subtlety and skill. He was bemused and shaken, and she had succeeded in panicking him. "There's the doorbell now," she said. "Make up your mind."

She heard voices in the hall and went out quickly. Tony Walden stood there, with Lomax looming in the background. Walden wore a fawn vicuña overcoat and a broad-brimmed brown hat. His face was difficult to see at close quarters.

"Fancy dress," Lomax said. "Is that what she told you to wear?"

Walden didn't answer him. He said to Davina, "Will this do? You said to find something distinctive. The taxi's waiting."

She didn't waste time. "Right. Give me the coat and hat. Go into the bedroom; I don't want Harrington to see you. And thanks, Tony. You've been a marvel."

"The key of Suite A is in the pocket," he said as he went inside and closed the door.

Lomax came up to her. "Don't do this," he said. "Harrington could run for it."

"The major's right." Tony Walden came out of the bedroom. "Look, I don't care if he sees me or not. What the hell?" He shrugged. "I left my car here, remember—I'll go down and I'll follow that cab to the Ritz. If he tries anything, I'll stop him."

"How?" Colin's sarcasm was savage. "You're playing out of league, Walden. Why don't you just go home to your wife and leave this to us?"

Walden looked around at him. "I will—when he's safely installed in the hotel and one of you comes to take over. And don't worry about the league. I learn the rules very quickly." He went out of the front door, a figure quite different from the American type that came in. Bareheaded, wearing a dark suit—looking years older.

Davina and Lomax didn't speak; she brushed past him. She was shaking with temper, and the temper itself was fueled by extreme nervous tension. She came to Harrington and held out the coat and hat. "Put these on. Go straight downstairs and get into the taxi that's parked outside the front door. Tell him to take you to the Ritz Hotel. The key of your room is in the coat pocket."

"The Ritz?" Harrington was struggling into the coat. He pulled on the hat and tugged the brim down. "The Ritz—have you gone out of your tiny bleeding mind?"

"Get out of here!" Davina shouted at him.

He left the flat in a shuffling run and she pulled the front door closed after him. She ran to the living-room window and looked out, standing to the side in case she was seen. Below, a man in a brown hat and a fawn coat took a few steps across the pavement and the taxi driver leaned out and opened the cab door for him. He got inside and it drove away. She didn't move, although she knew that Lomax was beside her. When Walden's blue Mercedes slid into sight following the taxi, she gave a sigh of relief and turned away from the window. There was a heavy silence between them. She lit a cigarette and sat down. Lomax poured a drink and after a pause said, "Do you want one?"

"No, I had a brandy already. Why don't you go out and buy cigarettes or something and see if that van is still there?"

"Why don't you stop telling me what to do? If it wasn't for me, you wouldn't have the bastard here in the first place. I don't hear anything about that."

"I'm telling you," she retorted, "because you're so screwed up and you can't apparently think straight." She swung around in the chair and said angrily, "I'm not having an affair with Tony Walden! Now, will you go and see if they're still outside!"

"If you're not," Colin Lomax said, "it's not for the want of him trying. I'll go."

She heard the front door bang and said, "Oh, goddamn it all," to herself, and then looked at her watch. It would take twenty minutes to get from Marylebone to the Ritz if the traffic was bad. It shouldn't be; they ought to be there soon.

"And I've got to get there," she said out loud. "We've both got to get out of here without being followed. I can't think of a way . . . I can't think of anything more for the moment. Colin?" She heard the sound of him in the outer hall. The door opened.

"Good evening, Davina."

She got up and saw that there were two men behind Sir James White. John Kidson and Humphrey Grant. And Lomax in the background.

"We were passing," the Chief said amiably, "and we thought we'd drop in. I do hope it isn't inconvenient?"

"Who the hell are you?" Harrington demanded. He had suffered a terrible fright when Walden caught up with him in the hotel lobby and took him by the arm. His smile hadn't reassured Harrington, nor had the murmured assurance that he was a friend and coming up to the suite with him. For a moment Harrington stood rooted, undecided whether to pull free and run for it, not knowing whether the man was a friend or SIS.

"You're wearing my hat and coat," Walden said. "The lift's over there."

When they were in the suite, Harrington mastered himself enough to ask the question "Who the hell are *you?*"

"I'm a friend of Davina's," Walden said pleasantly. "Take the things off and make yourself at home. Want something to drink? I could do with a vodka myself."

After a moment Harrington said sulkily, "Scotch and soda." He wandered over to the window and looked out on the splendid view of the park. "Well," he said, "this is better than that little dump in Marylebone."

"Glad you like it." Walden handed him his drink. "Have you had anything to eat?"

Harrington shook his head. "No. I could do with something. Christ, what a performance! I'm bloody shaking like a leaf." He sat down, watching Walden go to the house phone and ask for room service.

"Any preference?" he inquired. "Will you leave it to me?"

"Steak," Harrington muttered. "I haven't had a steak in years. . . . Do you have any cigarettes?"

Walden pointed to a big ivory box on the coffee table. "In there. Help yourself." There were mentholated filter-tipped and Balkan Sobranie, along with some Ritz book matches printed with the suite number.

Harrington took out the black cigarette in its distinctive gold holder. "Haven't seen one of these for a long time either," he remarked. "I used to smoke them. Whoever stays here does themselves bloody well. Is it you?"

"I come here now and again," Walden admitted. "Go into the bedroom, will you, when the floor waiter comes?"

Harrington grinned nastily. "He won't be surprised at dinner for two, eh? Sobranies are popular with the gays, aren't they? Who do you bring up here—women, or are you one of 'those'?"

"You needn't worry," Walden said smoothly. "Whichever I fancy, it certainly isn't you. So into the bedroom, please."

He didn't raise his voice, but Harrington quickly did as he was told. He came out when Walden called him. A beautifully laid table had been set for them, and the smell of food turned his stomach into a knot with greed. They didn't talk; Harrington gobbled the food and gulped down the wine. He saw Walden look at his watch. Davina and Lomax should have come by now. But they had to dodge the watchers outside. . . . Walden didn't break the silence; he let Harrington finish the last scrap of dessert and start on the cheese. They were very late. It was dark outside. Perhaps that was what they needed. He could stay the night with Harrington if need be. . . .

"You're edgy," Peter Harrington remarked. He looked bloated and his eyes had a slight glaze over them from the amount of wine he'd drunk. There was a mean little smile on his mouth. "Anything gone wrong with our lovely friends? He's a right thug, isn't he? But she likes that type, I suppose. . . . I fancied her a bit once, but she didn't tip me a wink. Not rough and tough enough for her." He laughed unpleasantly.

"If you say another word like that," Walden said quietly, "I'll knock your teeth in. I am not a violent man, so don't make me do it. Back into the bedroom while I get this cleared away!"

Harrington lurched as he stood up. At the bedroom door he paused. "Oh, pardon me." He sneered. "You're boyfriend number two. How was I to know?" He shut the door.

When the table was cleared and the floor waiter had gone, Walden went to the bedroom. Harrington was stretched out on the double bed asleep. Tony Walden looked at his watch again. Eleven-thirty. In God's name, where were they?

"You know we can't hold them," James White said. "We haven't a scrap of evidence!"

Kidson was pacing up and down the office. "There was the spare bed," he insisted. "It had been used. We know they've got him hidden away somewhere!"

"Why don't you calm down," Humphrey said icily. "Harrington wasn't there, and there's no proof he ever was. Lomax said he slept in the spare bedroom. Who's to say he didn't? I think we should let them go, Chief, before we make damned fools of ourselves."

James White gave a slight yawn, as if he were more bored than weary. "I agree with you," he said. "We did look rather foolish, didn't we, when we searched the flat? I think you jumped to a conclusion, John. It's put me in a difficult position."

Kidson stopped walking up and down. He swung around on James White. "You and Humphrey thought the same," he insisted. "And you still do. What's awkward is that she's outwitted us. Put a tail on them. That'll lead us to Peter Harrington, I stake my life on it!"

"Humphrey," the Chief said. "Go down and offer to send Davina and Colin home in one of our cars. That's the least we can do. And try to make peace, there's a good chap. I'm going home to bed. John, would you be kind enough to drop me off?"

"You know what you can do with your car?" Lomax said.

Humphrey's gaunt face didn't register anything but a chilly politeness. He said to Davina, "The Chief sends his apologies. It was all a very unfortunate mistake. He'll find a way to make it up to you. Do let us run you home."

"No, thanks," Davina answered. "We'll pick up a taxi. And tell Sir James from me not to apologize. Let's go, Colin." She pushed past Humphrey and walked out.

In the little cul-de-sac they paused, and both glanced back at the house; the lights were going out.

"No tail so far," Colin muttered. "This is our chance. We separate. You make for the Ritz. I'll join you later." He didn't wait for her to answer. He sped down the narrow passageway and emerged briefly into the light of a streetlamp in Birdcage Walk.

Davina slipped out after him and turned quickly to the left. She walked briskly for about twenty-five yards and then flattened herself against the railings of the Guards Barracks. Nobody came out of the mouth of the cul-de-sac. She didn't hurry; she made her way to the top of Birdcage Walk and headed for Victoria Station. There she joined a small queue for late taxis and picked one up in a few minutes. It was close to midnight when the night porter admitted her to the Ritz and phoned up to Suite A. A very relieved Tony Walden came down in the elevator to meet her.

The watchers outside the Marylebone flat had gone. There was nothing for them to do after they went in and picked the lock of the apartment. The two they were surveilling had left with three other men; lights were out and there was nobody to see them break in. The search took only a few minutes. The van drove away and later that night the telex went out from the Soviet embassy in Kensington

Palace Gardens that Harrington was not in the custody of the suspected British agents. Further instructions were requested, and the team went to their quarters in the embassy and slept for the rest of the night.

Colin Lomax didn't go to Marylebone. He doubled back through the park and slipped up the Mall toward Trafalgar Square. From there he dived down into the Underground. He got out at Euston Station and slipped into a phone booth. It had been vandalized. He had to go into the station itself before he could find a telephone in working order. He dialed, and the number rang for some time before a sleepy voice answered.

"Fraser, it's me, Lomax. Can you give me a bed for the night? Thanks very much. I'll explain when I see you."

He walked the short distance to Temple Road, and disappeared inside the house where his ex-colleague lived with his wife and children. He didn't give much of an explanation; he had to stay clear of home for a few days. Fraser accepted what was said, offered a glass of beer, and within twenty minutes all the lights were out and his sleepy wife couldn't be bothered to hear what had happened till the morning. Her husband ran the kind of business where people turned up in the middle of the night, and the phone was never switched off.

Albatross couldn't sleep. He had pretended to be tired to avoid being asked questions. Harrington was not in Russia. He wasn't safe after all. He couldn't reach his KGB contact till the morning. Why hadn't they let him know? For years now he had sunned himself in other men's trust of him, forgetting that one day it might turn to suspicion. Why hadn't Borisov warned him that the danger hadn't been removed? Was he abandoned, then? The thought filled him with such panic that he slipped out of bed and crept away to the bathroom, where he locked the door. His reflection gazed back at him, hollow-eyed, cold with cunning and fear. He wasn't going to be caught. He wasn't going to run if he could help it. If his own people were hanging back, he would act to protect himself.

"I don't think you should stay here alone," Tony Walden said. "He's a nasty piece of work."

"What's he been saying?" Davina asked him.

Walden shrugged. "Nothing specific, but he was drunk when he went to bed, and I think he might be difficult if he knew you were alone here."

She shook her head. "I know him, don't worry. He's got a filthy tongue, but that's as far as it goes. He won't try anything." She spoke her thoughts aloud. "I've got to get information out of him!"

"What information?" Walden asked her.

She was haggard with exhaustion. She looked up at him. He'd saved the situation for them that night. Without him, James White would have scooped them up, and her last hope of finding Albatross would have gone. Damn Colin for his stupid jealousy. He'd have to give Tony Walden credit for his coolness and initiative, however much he resented him. . . .

"I can't tell you," she said. "I'm sorry, Tony, don't for God's sake think I wouldn't like to, but it's better not. Not yet, anyway. You've been such a help—I can't thank you enough."

"I was there at the right moment in the right place," he said. "That's luck, my darling, nothing to do with me."

She couldn't let the word go unchallenged. Lomax's accusation lingered. "Don't call me 'darling,' " she said.

"All right, if you don't like it. I don't say it to everyone."

"I know," she answered. "That's why I don't want you saying it to me. I've told you, I'm committed already."

He took a Balkan Sobranie out of the box and offered it to her. "Try one of these. They're strong but not harsh."

She lit it and after a moment said, "I like it. I don't think I've ever tried one before."

"Your friend Harrington was very scornful about them," Walden said. "He said gays smoked these."

"Typical bitchery," she said wearily. "He used to smoke them himself. Take no notice."

"I didn't. You're not committed to Lomax for life, you know."

"I didn't say I was," she countered. "You're the one who's married, Tony."

He smiled. "Would that stop you—if there was no major?"

"Yes, I think it would. Look, it's two-thirty. I've got to get some sleep. I'm going to go hell for leather at Harrington tomorrow. We just don't have much time left. I wonder where Colin went?" She answered her own question. "I expect he's gone to ground somewhere for the night. He'll contact me in the morning." She yawned and stood up. "Tony, good night. I'm going to curl up on the sofa here; let him have the bed tonight. And thank you. Thank you for everything."

He didn't come near her; she was glad, because she knew she would have let him hold her. "I'll call tomorrow," he said. "I've arranged with the manager. You're to have anything you want. Good night."

She kicked off her shoes and settled into the big sofa. She had drifted into sleep within a few minutes. She dreamed fitfully and anxiously of being caught in twisting passageways without an exit, of driving a car and finding there were no brakes, and of seeing herself naked in Walden's arms.

She woke soon after six A.M. Harrington was still asleep in his clothes when she opened the bedroom door. "Wake up!" she said loudly. "Breakfast is ready, and we've got a lot of work to do."

He sat up, rubbing his eyes, muttered, "Christ . . . what's the time?" and focused on her. He remembered where he was, he remembered going into the room and stretching out on the bed, and nothing until then. "You don't have to stand there like a bloody wardress," he said. "I'm going to have a bath first. Where's the boyfriend?"

"Colin will be round soon," Davina answered. He had not yet telephoned, but it was early.

Harrington grinned. There was a rim of dried spittle around his mouth. "I didn't mean him. I meant your rich Jewish friend. See you in a minute, Davy."

She heard him laughing before he turned on the bath taps and the water blotted out the sound.

"Darling," Charlie said, "I meant to tell you—Mummy phoned and asked if we'd like to go down to Marchwood for the weekend. I thought it would be nice to get away." She didn't mention the evening before. She'd been asleep when he came in. He looked very tired that morning.

Charlie was glad she had accepted the invitation to go down to Marchwood with the baby. She felt that a change would relieve the tension and give John a chance to relax. He seemed miles away as they sat over breakfast; she had to repeat the remark about the weekend, and he said guiltily, "Sorry, sweetheart, I wasn't thinking. Yes, why don't we go? I'd like to get out of London. I love Marchwood too. And you." He pulled her close to him and kissed her. God, did he love her. He had so much to fight for now.

"Mummy wanted Davina to come too," Charlie said casually. "She couldn't find her. She wasn't in her office, and there's no reply at the flat." Kidson sat very still. "I didn't press it because of what you said last night. 'Your bloody sister.' What's she done, darling?"

He managed a tired laugh. "Nothing really, just caused a flap that interrupted our evening. I didn't mean to say that, I'm sorry. She's not my favorite person at the moment, as you know."

Charlie turned to look at him. "You said she was out of the running for the job," she reminded him. "That hasn't changed, has it?"

"No, no," he said hastily. "She's made a proper mess of her chances. The trouble is, I'm afraid she may make a mess of mine too."

Charlie disengaged herself and said, "How? Can't you stop her?"

Kidson said slowly, "I could, if I knew where to find her. Apparently she's disappeared. The truth is, she's poking around still, trying to find something to discredit me. It would suit her purpose to leave suspicion in the air about the traitor. With herself in the role of avenging angel, of course." He scowled at his clasped hands.

Charlie saw the look of anxiety and felt very angry. She seldom lost her temper or gave herself lines by looking cross. It was very important not to frown, if one didn't want that ugly line between the brows. Crow's-feet from laughter were attractive in middle age. You got bags under the eyes from crying. She had made it a rule all her life to laugh and smile as much as possible. But there was her husband, whom she loved, looking miserable and harassed, and her sister Davina was to blame. Antagonism flared up in her; it had lain dormant over the past few years because she was so happy she could afford to forget how badly she had treated her sister. She insisted to herself and everyone else that she felt no guilt for stealing Davina's fiancé and marrying him. It was all so long ago, and she'd been married twice since then . . . but the guilt remained, and with it the accompanying element of hatred for the person wronged. "I'm fed up with Davina trying to hurt you, John," she said suddenly. "If I find out where she is, would it help?"

He looked at her, and the bright eyes, flashing with anger, surprised him. "Why, yes, darling. Yes, of course it would . . . but how can you?" How indeed, when someone as experienced as Davina Graham had gone to ground, could an innocent like Charlie flush her out?

"You leave it to me," his wife said firmly. "I'll find her."

"Now," Davina said, "let's recap what we've done so far. We've got a probable date of entry into the Service. Around 1958 to 1960. We base that on two factors. One, the removal of data from the files two years after those dates, and two, the remark made by the agent who recruited you, indicating that there was a penetration in the office itself, right?"

Harrington said, "So far, yes. So if those assumptions are correct, Humphrey and the Chief are in the clear. Leaving your brother-in-law. How's the family going to like that?"

"Keep to the point," Davina snapped at him. "You can be bitchy afterward if it helps you. Certainly those two facts put both of them out as suspects. But mightn't the person who altered those files have that precise intention in mind? That he'd avoid suspicion by backdating to a treason that never took place? We can't ignore that."

"My contact didn't have that motive," Harrington countered. "All right, he could have been encouraging me; come-on-old-boy-you're-not-the-only-one-feathering-your-nest sort of thing. But I don't think so."

"What we're working against," Davina said slowly, "is the fact that we've got a series of clues in those files which may not be clues at all. The time that Albatross entered the Service is the key to his identity. And it's pointing a damn sight too obviously at one person."

"You're taking one thing for granted, aren't you?" Harrington said. "People have been subverted *after* they joined, not necessarily before. You're basing everything on the Cambridge connection, recruiting among the undergraduates destined for places in the Establishment. That happened, but not to me, for instance. I was dead straight for years. Then something came along and I switched sides. Albatross could have done the same."

Davina lit a cigarette; her throat was dry from smoking the Sobranies. "All along the line we have situations where any one of the three suspects could be Albatross. From the Rumanian fiasco to Sasanov and your recall. And his death." She hated saying it.

Harrington's voice was smug. "I told you, that's where the pointer really lies. You've got to be a brave girl, Davy, and look into that if you want to find him."

She didn't look at him; she couldn't have borne the satisfaction in his face. "You're right, she said at last. "I don't know where to start, that's the trouble."

Harrington watched her. By Christ, he thought, she's never got over that. The soldier boy hasn't made up for Ivan. And never will. Poor Davy. The bitch; serves her right.

"I'd start," he suggested gently, "with the people who knew you were in Australia. And go on from there."

To her relief, the phone rang. A terse voice at the other end said, "Davina . . . Colin here."

She could imagine the awkward stubbornness that went with that tone, and in spite of everything she smiled. "Hello, darling. I won't talk over the phone. Are you coming over?"

There was no doubt about the reply. "Right away. Everything all right?"

"Fine," she said.

There was a second's pause; then, "Sorry about last night." He was hopeless about apologizing, especially when he was in the wrong.

"And so you should be," she said gently. "Don't be an idiot. Hurry up; ask for Suite A, and they've got my name." She turned back to Harrington. Be a brave girl and look into the most painful time of her life. She was going to take him up on that jibe, but she thanked God that Colin Lomax would be with her.

* * *

"Mr. Walden"—Frieda Armstrong's voice came through with a slightly querulous note that put him on his guard—"there's a Mrs. Kidson asking to speak to you. She says she's Miss Graham's sister."

Tony Walden hesitated. He remembered the beautiful redhead only too well.

"Tell her Miss Graham will call her later," he said.

"I did," Frieda said, "but she still wants to speak to you. She said it was urgent. Apparently she can't contact Miss Graham."

"All right, put her on," Walden said.

She did have an attractive voice. It sounded as if she had just heard a good joke and was going to share it. "I am sorry to be a nuisance," Charlie said. "Do you remember me? I came into the office a little while ago . . ."

His reply was instinctive. "How could I possibly forget? What can I do for you, Mrs. Kidson?"

"I'm trying to get hold of Davina. Our mother's not terribly well and I've been ringing the flat, but no answer. Is she away on a job?"

"Yes," said Walden cheerfully. "As a matter of fact, she is. But I'm expecting her to call any minute. I'll tell her to get in touch with you at once. I hope it's nothing serious?"

"Oh, no, it's only that she gets a bit tired, her heart's a little tricky, you know . . . she just wants to see Davina and she couldn't find her and started to worry and get pains. Tell Davy to ring me at home as soon as she can, would you? That *is* kind." And because it was second nature to Charlie to flirt with any man, even at a distance, she added, "And I hope I'll see you next time I come to the office."

"And I hope you'll let me give you lunch," was his reply.

He put the phone down and thought for a moment. Something about that call didn't sound quite right. From apparent urgency it petered out into a rather feeble excuse about Davina's mother having tried in vain to find her. . . . Walden asked for an outside line and dialed the Ritz. It was Colin Lomax who answered. Walden set out to be diplomatic. Always disarm an enemy if possible. "How's everything?"

Lomax answered briskly, "It's okay."

"I didn't stay with Davina," Walden explained, as if he owed

Lomax the explanation. "She said she'd be quite all right alone. I'm glad you're with her; I don't like your friend very much."

Lomax said, "I don't either." And then, because he knew Davina was listening, he added, "Thanks for what you did last night."

"No problem." Walden sounded friendly. "I'd like a word with her."

Lomax said, "Hold on; I'll get her."

Davina listened without interrupting him. Lomax hovered in the background, wondering what Walden was saying that held her attention so closely. At the end she said, "Thanks, Tony. That was a lot of nonsense—she's trying to find me. I'll ring her right away." She turned to Lomax. "Charlie," she said. "She's been on to Tony with some feeble story about Mother not being well and worried because she couldn't get an answer from the flat. Tony said he didn't believe a word of it."

"He's becoming quite the expert, isn't he? And just how well does he know Charlie to tell whether she was making it up or not?"

Davina looked at him; she took a deep breath. "Colin. Colin, for God's sake, what's got into you?"

"I don't trust him," Lomax said flatly. "I don't trust him with you, and I don't trust him generally. And not just because I'm jealous; I'd see him off in two seconds flat if he started any bloody funny stuff." He scowled and dug both hands into his pockets, rocking on the balls of his feet. Davina knew him so well that she understood the body language; the sheathed hands contradicting the fighting stance. He was jealous, that was all. The only mistrust he had of Tony Walden was concerned with his fear of losing her. It didn't make her love him; for the first time in their relationship she suffered a loss of respect for the man she respected above all.

"There's no point in arguing," she said after a pause. "I'm going to ring Charlie and see what she wants."

Her sister was bright and amiable on the telephone. "No, Davy, there's nothing wrong with Mummy—I made it all a bit dramatic because I thought your darling boss might be annoyed with me for ringing up. He couldn't have been sweeter. John and I are going to Marchwood this weekend, and Mummy said it was ages since she'd seen you and Colin. Why don't you both come down?"

Davina smiled at the invitation. Charlie knew how to charm, how to glide over the obvious. Davina's parents never invited her and Colin at the same time as their favorite daughter and their only grandchild. The idea of a cozy family weekend was Charlie's, and she could wind both parents around her finger if she chose. "I don't think Colin can come down," Davina said slowly. She held up one hand to stop him interrupting. "He's got some regimental reunion this weekend. But I could come down for a night. I'd better ring them, hadn't I?" To make sure I'm welcome. I wasn't always wanted, though they like me better now. It was you, Charlie, they longed to see, however you neglected them. . . . She was surprised and angered with herself for feeling bitter after all the years. For forgetting how they had nursed her after Australia, how they had taken Colin in and cared for him when they came back from Mexico. Did the wounds of childhood never really heal? She knew why she was walking into whatever trap Charlie was setting for her. She knew why Charlie was doing it. Be a brave girl, the jeering voice of Harrington echoed in her mind. Go back and find out about Australia. She would have to go to Marchwood for a start.

"I'll ring Mummy," Charlie said helpfully. "When will you come?"

"Tomorrow evening," Davina said. "When I get back to London." She rang off before her sister could ask her where she was.

She left Harrington alone with Colin Lomax; she shut herself into the luxurious bedroom, where Walden brought his girlfriends, and started the tape. Her own voice murmured dates and reflections culled from the files she'd photographed. There was a reference to herself and Sasanov having been settled in a safe place. No mention was made of Australia, and the section was not one of those that had been interfered with; the record of where the Soviet defector and his wife were living was not kept in the confidential files. Possibly only the impenetrable coding devised by the computer and registered in its twin at the Foreign Office held the information. And that information was available only to the Chief and the Foreign Minister and through them to the Prime Minister, should it be requested. James White again. However she circled around the question mark of Albatross, she came back to the same person. Lomax suspected John

Kidson; Harrington veered among all three at times. She herself tried to be impartial, but the clues had one factor in common. The means of wrecking SIS intelligence operations like the one in Rumania, of leading the KGB assassin to Ivan Sasanov, of turning the Plumed Serpent in Mexico into a setback instead of a disaster for the Soviet Union, were only available to one man at all times—Sir James White.

"You're walking into it with Kidson," Lomax protested. "He wants to get hold of you, and he's put Charlie up to it!"

She couldn't resist the retort. "You mean you agree with Tony? I thought you dismissed the whole idea!"

"I've changed my mind," he said obstinately. "I don't give a damn whether he's right or wrong, though you seem to. All I'm thinking about is your safety. Why did you say I couldn't go with you? Couldn't you even ask me?" He stood with his back to the bedroom window, blocking the view of the sunny park—a broad-shouldered, aggressive figure who seemed to Davina more of an opponent than a colleague.

"And who is going to look after Harrington?" she said.

"Walden," he snapped at her. "If he wants to play bloody secret agents, he can come back here and mind that bastard while we go down to Marchwood!"

"Harrington's not his responsibility," she said coldly. "He's ours. If anything happened and the opposition found out where he was and came after him, Walden wouldn't stand a chance. You can't insult him one minute, Colin, and then make use of him the next. You'll have to stay here, and I'll go home for tomorrow night. That should give me time to ask a few questions and see if anything comes out."

"What the hell could your family possibly know that would help?" he demanded.

"I'm not sure," Davina answered. "But they knew where we were. They were the only ones who did, apart from James White. I'm going to start there. Charlie's given me the excuse." She turned to go out of the room. The tension between them crackled like static electricity. She had started by being angry with Lomax; now, suddenly, she felt saddened and confused. She wanted to get away from him, even to rejoin Harrington, rather than see the antagonism in his face and the hurt hiding behind it.

In the middle of all this, she said to herself, what the hell is happening to us? There was no answer, and she spent the rest of the day with Harrington, going over the same ground, parrying the mean little jibes that relieved his overwrought state, feeling as she did so that she was making no progress at all. The time seemed to creep by; seldom had a day lasted so long. The confinement of the suite got on her nerves until she felt that she and not Harrington was the prisoner. By five-thirty she felt that unless she got out for a walk she would turn on Harrington and the background figure of Lomax and scream at them both. The park was green and the evening soft in the aftermath of a warm June day. She walked along the pathways down toward the Mall, and then, remembering the risk of being seen and followed, turned back and kept to the smaller routes. There was a big hillock toward the end of the park leading to Hyde Park Corner and the majestic outline of the Quadriga on top of the triumphal arch at its head. She walked up the hillock and sat down on a seat. Two children were playing nearby; one of them rolled down the steep slope, shrieking with excitement. A beautiful evening, with people strolling at leisure. She had seldom felt more alone.

It didn't help to realize that the person she most wanted with her at that moment was no longer Colin Lomax.

Friday afternoon; James White finished his meeting at the Foreign Office at just after three-thirty-five and decided that he had better go to the office for an hour before leaving for his home in Kent. The meeting had been a difficult one; the Minister's deputy had come back early from Scotland, cutting the wedding celebration short, and was in a sour mood. The information that Harrington was not in Soviet hands actually pleased nobody. Having escaped, he could surface eventually in Moscow and make a minor nuisance of himself by giving interviews. He had no new information to impart except a firsthand account of life in a British prison. He had obviously warned of the danger to Albatross and his escape had been planned in consequence. His presence in England, in the hands of an unknown organization, posed different problems, none of them easy to solve. A leak would embarrass the government and its security services. If Harrington hadn't got to Russia, how had he not been recaptured? This question was asked in a most aggressive way by the Foreign Office official named Fuller, and Sir James parried it with his genial smile and a nonanswer. He gave the impression that he knew, but couldn't say, exactly where the missing traitor was, and that he was not in the least worried. No mention was made of a suspected Soviet agent with the code name of a large seabird associated with ill luck. That, as Sir James and Humphrey Grant agreed beforehand, might never have to be revealed.

They came back to Anne's Yard together. Kidson was called in. They held a brief conference before breaking up for the weekend.

"How was the meeting?" Kidson asked.

"Difficult, but we coped," James White said. "Didn't we, Humphrey? Abrasive little man, Mr. Fuller. I must have a word with the Minister about him. No news of Davina?"

"She's going down to Marchwood tonight," Kidson said. There was a silence.

"They haven't been back to the flat. Our people have been on duty since last night. There's no other stakeout on the place either. We should have a tail put on her as soon as she gets down," he added. "That should lead somewhere."

"You still believe that she and Lomax have Harrington, don't you?" White said.

Kidson's jaw clenched. Humphrey said nothing; he watched first one, then the other with his pale eyes. "I'm certain of it," Kidson said. "Certain Lomax is guarding him. He's not coming; some bullshit about a regimental reunion."

"Which you checked," the Chief said.

"Of course. No such thing."

"She must be expecting this." Humphrey said it in a mumble, as if he were talking to himself. "Why is she putting herself on the line, John?"

"Maybe she thinks she's got away with it, maybe she imagines she can bluff it out with me in some way," he answered. "But she's surfaced, and that's what we wanted."

"You are taking this very seriously, aren't you?" said James White. "Shouldn't you have consulted first with Humphrey and me?"

"You happened to be at Whitehall," Kidson retorted. He looked at his watch. "I'll miss my train if I don't get off," he said.

"You go from Waterloo," Humphrey remarked. "I hate that station, it's always so crowded. I'll be in the flat, Chief, if anything blows up."

"I'll be at home," Sir James said. "And John will be doing sterling work at Marchwood. Have a good weekend, both of you." He gave them his empty smile, and they went out. He didn't leave for some time. He stayed at his desk and made notes on a pad, which he then fed into the shredder. There was a grim expression on his face until he left his room and passed through the outer office. The duty officer was given instructions which took all the fun out of his plans for the weekend.

Then Sir James got into his car in the underground garage attached to the third building down from the Office, and took a circuitous route out of central London. He did not head in the direction of Kent.

CHAPTER 7

CAPTAIN GRAHAM and his wife were having tea in the garden. The June roses were in their full glory, complemented by the rich scent of Mrs. Graham's favorite shrub, philadelphus. The graceful drooping white blossom, known as mock orange because of its sweet fragrance, framed the mellow red brick of the terrace of the old Queen Anne house. It was a peaceful scene, almost stagey in its Englishness: the elderly couple enjoying a quiet tea in their splendid garden under the shelter of their gracious early-eighteenth-century house. Tony Walden's copywriters would have loved it.

"I do think it's a pity," Captain Graham said.

His wife reproved him in her mild way; it was even milder than usual because she agreed with him. "You mustn't say that, darling. Davina's got as much right to come down as Charlie. We haven't seen her for ages."

"That's my point," he said crisply. "She spend months down here with Colin and then they both take off into the blue without a word. She leaves the Service and takes up with some bloody advertising agency, and they don't bother to come near us. Now, because presumably it suits her, she decides to come when Charlie and the family are coming. It also makes a lot of extra work for you!"

"I don't mind that," Betty Graham said. "And she's only staying tonight. It's a shame Colin isn't coming too."

The captain sighed impatiently. "It's not that I'm not fond of her," he said. "But everything she does disappoints, doesn't it? She finally meets a really good chap like Colin, but she won't marry him and settle down. Charlie was always supposed to be the fly-by-night—if you ask me, it's Davina who won't accept responsibility."

Betty didn't argue. She had long ago come to terms with her husband's blind preference for their younger daughter. He had nothing in common with Davina—to be honest, neither had she, except a sense of kindly duty.

They were both victims of Charlie's gaiety and charm, proud of her beauty and tolerant of her behavior. Two marriages and a succession of love affairs were all forgiven now that she was settled and they had a delightful grandson they could spoil.

Not so the elder daughter. Always reserved, difficult; independent, yet a reproach to them both because she had been given so little love while Charlie had so much. The reproach was even more irritating because they had reason to admire Davina and be proud of her achievements. After Sasanov's death, the trio had come close for quite a time, only to drift again with absence. And because the basic incompatibility couldn't be rationalized. They had hoped sincerely that she would marry Colin Lomax, with whom the captain felt very much at home. Now he wasn't even coming with her as a compensation.

"Charlie said they'd be here by six," Betty Graham said. "She wasn't sure about Davina."

"In time for dinner, I hope," he grumbled. "I hate being late for dinner."

"You hate being late for anything," his wife reminded him. "And Davina is just like you; she's *very* punctual. Stop grouching about it, Fergus, and bring the tray."

She got up and after a pause he gathered the crockery and took the tray into the kitchen after her. He was very much the master in his own house, but he recognized when his wife was losing patience. He was helping her wash up when the dogs started barking. They hurried out to the front of the house expecting to see Kidson's red Volvo parked in the forecourt. Instead, it was Davina who came up the steps to meet them.

* * *

The senior KGB officer at the London embassy was ostensibly the second secretary to the trade councillor. He was a highly experienced and successful ranking colonel who had served in Toronto and for a brief period in Tehran during the Shah's reign. He was thirty-eight years old, spoke five languages fluently, and had been posted to London as promotion. Borisov had galvanized him. His predecessor had used the criminal element when violence was necessary. The colonel sent in a bitterly accusatory report in defense of his own competence, urging that in future only Soviet agents be employed. His surveillance team had found nothing; not only that, but they had lost their quarry. He couldn't blame the former occupant for that. A second team arrived at the Marylebone flat and they reported hastily that there was an SIS stakeout in place. The colonel found this satisfying. Both intelligence services were looking for the same thing. In other words, Harrington had gone astray, but SIS had not recaptured him. . The colonel sent a hasty telex to Moscow. Harrington would be found. And when he was, what were the instructions for Albatross? The colonel settled down to wait for a reply from Borisov and for the news of where Harrington was being hidden. He didn't doubt that it would reach him in time.

The time difference between Moscow and London was two hours. Igor Borisov received the report from London at one o'clock; he read it and out of habit buzzed his secretary.

Natalia always came in and brought him the late-morning glass of tea. He would tell her if something important had arisen. It was usually the time they arranged to be together for the evening. The young officer Alexei came into the room and advanced to the desk. Borisov looked up and frowned. Reflex prepared him to see Natalia. The hard, square-featured face of his chosen Praetorian guard loomed over him, not speaking until spoken to. Borisov cleared away the phantom, smiled at Alexei, said in his firm but friendly way, "I have a telex to send to London. It's highly confidential and I want you to transmit it, Alexei."

"Thank you, Comrade General. Is it on tape?"

"No," Borisov said. "You must carry this in your head. Listen and repeat it to me, and when you've sent it, destroy the copy. And sit down—you don't need to be so formal. I've told you that before."

The young man shifted awkwardly. He wasn't used to the general's odd desire for familiarity. There had been a woman in the job before. A woman said to have committed suicide. He closed his mind immediately, as he'd been trained to do. What was done was never thought about again. She might haunt the general and send him groping for human contact with a subordinate like himself, but he, Alexei, didn't think about her. He had poured the vodka down her throat, but he couldn't have described her face.

"The message," Borisov said, "is to go to Albatross."

Ten minutes later Alexei was in the huge coding section located in the first level underground. He took possession of a Type A machine and turned the general's message into the top-security code for transmission to London.

In his office, Igor Borisov reflected quietly. He had made an important discovery aside from the information his colonel had sent with such relief from London. Harrington was not in the hands of the SIS. The fact they were looking for him and watching Davina Graham might give the man in the embassy a temporary respite, but it posed one question that only Borisov had seen. How did British intelligence know that Harrington had not reached his Soviet haven? A Soviet agent had witnessed the execution of the only two witnesses who might have given James White's people information.

How had they known the rescue had failed? From Dublin—because Harrington hadn't arrived? Borisov doubted that. All Dublin knew was that Harrington hadn't gone there. They'd received no further information. Whoever had leaked the failure to the SIS had done so from Moscow itself.

He drew abstracts on a little pad while he was thinking. Lines and interlocking angles, with a sudden whirl of circles superimposed . . . and then a face took shape.

A narrow face with heavy brows and a drooping Albanian mustache, eyes that were only pinpoints, a mouth turned down like a thin trap. Making him kill Natalia was not enough. Now he was passing information to the enemy in his efforts to discredit the KGB and its director. Borisov drew a line from the left-hand corner of the face, bisecting it. The lines continued until the ugly caricature looked as if it had been slashed to ribbons. Then Borisov ripped off the top two pages, mindful of an imprint from heavy pen marks, and fed them into the shredder. The necessity angered him. Treachery was everywhere. His jotting pad could be examined, evidence sneaked to his enemies. Even the vital instructions contained in that telex couldn't be risked through the ordinary office system. No tape, no record; nothing but the memory of Alexei could be trusted. He had no doubt about that. The sooner he could carry out his promise to President Zerkhov, the sooner he would set about the organization of the KGB's huge internal structure and purge it of the extremists. A purge so thorough and so merciless that they would die in admiration.

"Leave the Scotch alone," Lomax said quietly. "You've had enough."

Harrington glared at him. The television offered little; time was dragging; he felt restless and uneasy with Lomax, his look of contempt the only communication during hours of silence. He had helped himself to two large drinks and they were taking a hold on him. He felt aggressive and brave, eager to do battle with his guardian. In words, of course. Harrington felt confident in his ability to goad and wound "This is going to be a jolly evening," he remarked. He tipped another measure in as Lomax raised himself from the chair. "I get rid of smiling Davy, and I'm left here with you glowering at me like a bloody ogre! If I feel like getting pissed, I will!" He slumped down on the sofa, nursing the glass, watching Lomax with a sneer as he locked the cupboard and put the key in his pocket. "Why didn't boyfriend number two take over?" Harrington demanded. "He was better company than you." He saw Lomax stiffen, and thought gleefully: I've scored a hit there . . . he doesn't like that. . . .

"Why don't you shut up?" Colin said. He looked down at Harrington and gently he began to rock on his heels. "If you're going to talk, why don't you make it interesting? About Albatross, for instance?"

"I've told Davy all I can." Harrington spoke with mock sincerity. "It's up to her now."

Lomax said slowly, "I think you know more than that. I think you've been holding out on her. Why don't you open your heart to me, friend?"

Harrington sobered suddenly. Fear made him choke on his whiskey. Lomax wouldn't really start playing rough—not in a place like this . . . he wouldn't come at him and use those clenched fists. They *were* clenched, and he was moving. Harrington dropped the drink and started up.

Lomax reached him and put a hand on his chest. "Sit down," he said, and pushed.

Harrington took a gamble. He was soaked with the spilled whiskey and the sweat was oozing out of him, but his wits worked as they always did when personal danger threatened. "You're doing this because I said that about the boyfriend," he accused. "I can't tell you anything, and you know it. You just want an excuse to beat me up."

"I don't need an excuse," Lomax answered in a level voice. "I think you've sent Davina into a dicey situation. If you come clean with me, I can get her out of it. That's all I want. Who do *you* think is Albatross, Harrington?"

Play for time, Harrington told himself. Don't, for Christ's sake, provoke him any more. Why did you say that about the boyfriend, you bleeding idiot? "I think it's the Chief," he said. "But I haven't said so to Davy. That's who she hopes it is, and she'll never find out if she goes in with her mind made up." Lomax turned very slowly and sat opposite him. Harrington didn't let his breath out in a gasp of relief; he coughed instead.

"Why him?" Lomax asked.

"Because he was the only one who knew where she and Sasanov were hiding in Australia. That's the key to it. But she's got to get proof. And I can't give it to her."

"She thinks she's going to get it at her home," Lomax said. "Which could put her in danger if you're wrong, Harrington. If it's Kidson, she's completely unprotected, and he's in the house. Having got her to go down there."

"If you suspect him," Harrington countered, "then why not that old poof, Humphrey? He had the same opportunities in many ways as either of them. But he didn't have the information about Australia, any more than Kidson."

"For Christ's sake"—Lomax suddenly sprang up—"of course he knew—he was bloody well married to her sister! That's how Kidson found out! He probably married her to get it."

"Not according to the files," Harrington protested; he sounded uncertain. "Don't run away with yourself. . . ."

Lomax turned around to him. "I'm going to leave you here," he said. "With a couple of chaps to look after you." He saw Harrington's look of alarm and dismissed it. "You needn't worry; they won't hurt you, and you'll be a lot safer with them around than the fellow last night. He wouldn't know what to do if the SIS came calling, but these boys would." He went into the bedroom and telephoned Fraser. An hour later the former SAS sergeant and the ex-Marine commander were settled in front of the TV with Harrington bunched up on the sofa between them. They were genial, and chatted to him about the programs, and on Lomax's instructions let him have another whiskey. The floor waiter who brought in trays of sandwiches and bottles of lager managed to conceal his astonishment. These days, the most extraordinary people came to the hotel.

"The garden's looking lovely," Davina remarked.

"Yes," Betty Graham said, "it's a lot of work, you know, but it's so satisfying when things grow. You look a little tired, Davina—are you working hard?"

"Quite hard," she answered, "but it's very interesting."

"I'm not clear what you actually *do,*" Captain Graham said.

"I look after some of the clients; I explain the advertising layouts to them, and I collate the ideas and information for my boss on some of the bigger campaigns."

"You mean like the awful television adverts?" her father said grumpily. "They always come in the middle of something interesting."

Betty Graham stepped in quickly. "How's Colin? We're so sorry he didn't come with you."

Davina repeated the lie about a regimental reunion.

"Is he really a hundred percent now?" The captain showed some warmth when he asked about Lomax. A splendid type. Davina did look tired; time she hurried up, or she'd lose him.

"He's very well," she said. "He's working very hard getting himself fit. He sends his love." Then she added, "What time is Charlie arriving?"

"Any minute," her father answered brightly.

"I'd better go and do something about dinner." Betty Graham got up and immediately Davina followed her out. She had never been close to her mother as a child; now that she needed to talk to her about something that was so important and so personal, she hesitated. She didn't know how to approach her. Mother darling, you remember how we used to write to each other when we were in Australia. Did you ever tell anyone we were there? Did Charlie know, or John? She could imagine the look of surprise on her mother's handsome face, the raised eyebrows at the suggestion that she might have been careless or indiscreet and that Ivan Sasanov died because of it. . . . And she could hear the pleasant voice inquiring why she asked such an extraordinary question. Surely she *knew* they never mentioned anything to a living soul? And wasn't it a little morbid, said more gently this time, to look back on the past when she had a fine man like Colin in love with her and a new life ahead? It would be so sensible and calm and well meant; she would hear it and want to scream at her mother, to take her by the shoulders and shake the complacency out of her.

They were in the kitchen. Davina took over the salad and began preparing it. She felt stiff and tongue-tied, and her resentment was growing.

"Davina," her mother said quietly, "what's the matter? You seem so worried. Do tell me about it."

It was so unexpected that tears came into her eyes. Mother and daughter looked at each other for a moment. Davina felt herself blush. She had forgotten how kind and supportive her parents had been when she came back from Australia; she had been judging in terms of the past.

"Mother," she said, "I've got to ask you something. It's going to sound awful. Promise you won't mind?"

"No, of course I won't," Betty Graham answered. "Ask anything you want."

Davina bit her lip for a moment; it was a habit she had picked up in Mexico, and Lomax always teased her when she did it. "You never told anyone Ivan and I were in Australia, did you?"

"No," her mother said firmly. "Your father and I knew that both your lives depended upon it. We never said a word to anyone."

Davina asked the worst question. "Not even to Charlie?"

Betty Graham shook her head. "Least of all Charlie," she said with a little smile. "She'd never keep a secret. Certainly not from John."

"Oh, thank God." Davina gave a long sigh of relief.

"Why are you asking, Davina dear? What's happened to bring this up again?"

"I can't explain, I'm sorry. But it was important to be sure." She came close to her mother and kissed her.

Betty Graham held her daughter gently by the arms and said, "You're not really in advertising, are you, darling? This is something to do with your old work, isn't it?"

"Yes, Mummy, it is. Bless you, you're far too clever to be fooled."

"I'm not clever at all," she said. "It's not anything dangerous, I hope."

"No, don't worry about that."

"And you've got Colin to look after you. That's a blessing."

"I'm glad to hear you say so, Mrs. Graham." They stepped back as Lomax came into the room. He walked up to Davina and kissed her. "You heard your mother," he said, "so you needn't look like that. I hope you don't mind my bursting in, Mrs. Graham?"

"Not in the least," she said happily. "But what about your regimental reunion?"

"I decided to give it a miss. Charlie and John have just driven up."

Mrs. Graham said, "Oh, I must go and see them. Davina, don't worry about the salad, I'll make it later. . . ." She hurried out, and Davina and Lomax were alone.

"Who's with Harrington?" She didn't mean to sound abrupt, but he stiffened.

"Two very competent members of my old regiment," he answered, forgetting the ex-marine. "He's in good hands, don't worry. I didn't think you were, so I decided to come down. From what I heard, your mother knows something's up."

Davina nodded. The exchange was becoming more awkward between them. She didn't know what to do to break the barrier that had sprung up as soon as he came into the kitchen. "She guessed," she said. "Anyway, she answered the main question. She and my father never said a word about Australia to Charlie or anyone else."

"That's why I came down," Lomax said. "Because I thought Kidson would have been the one person in a position to find out."

"He couldn't have done," Davina said. "We're on the wrong track, Colin. John had nothing to do with setting Ivan up. We'd better go out and say hello."

She turned and walked past him; he caught her by the arm. There was real pain in his expression as she looked up at him. "Don't be like this with me," he said. "I love you. Don't let this happen between us."

She should have responded. She should have turned to him and put her arms around him. She didn't, and she couldn't say why. "Colin, let's talk about it later. I've got too much on my mind at the moment. Later, please?"

"All right." He let her go. As he did so, he knew for certain that he had lost her. Moments later, they were gathered on the sunny terrace behind the house, with Charlie holding court and her parents cooing over their little grandson.

"Ronnie, you're sure you'll be all right?"

The boy said, "Of course. Don't you worry about me. I'll settle in with the telly; if you've got anything to go to the launderette, I'll take it along with my things."

Humphrey shook his head. "I use a laundry."

Ronnie showed his excellent teeth in a cheery grin. "Well, you won't need to in the future," he said. "I'll do it for you. I like ironing; it's peaceful." He hesitated for a moment and then said, "What happens if someone rings up? What do I say?"

Humphrey patted him on the shoulder. "You say you're a friend staying here and take a message," he told him. "I'll give you a call myself, just to see you're not too lonely. I'll be back on Sunday anyway. Take care."

"You too," Ronnie said, and went out into the little hallway to see him off.

"Well, this *is* a surprise." Captain Graham was in a jovial mood; his irritability with Davina had disappeared when Charlie and his grandson arrived. He was genuinely delighted to see Lomax, fond of John, his son-in-law, and mellowed by the harmony that flowed between his wife and his elder daughter. He hadn't heard her call

Betty by the childhood "Mummy" since she'd come back widowed from the tragedy in Australia.

And then an unexpected figure appeared through the wrought-iron garden gate, flanked by the house Labradors, who recognized and welcomed him. Sir James White advanced upon the family group, the last of the evening sunlight turning his white hair into a halo. He radiated good humor, kissed Betty Graham, shook his old friend's hand, and said expansively, "I was passing this way and I couldn't resist dropping in. And how nice to find everyone gathered together. Davina, my dear girl, how are you?"

Kidson had changed color. Lomax was watching him closely, and he saw the light tan fade and then deepen as he reddened. He hadn't been expecting to see his chief. He watched Davina square her shoulders slightly as Sir James came up to her.

"I'm very well," she said coolly. "I suppose we'll see Humphrey next?"

"Is he coming too?" exclaimed her mother. "Why didn't he telephone? We'd love to see him, of course."

"Oh, I doubt you will." The Chief chuckled. "It's only your daughter's sense of humor, my dear Betty. It's always been a little wry. Charlie, as beautiful as ever—come and give an old man a kiss."

"There's nothing old about you," Charlie declared, and responded handsomely with an embrace.

"Ah, but there is," he insisted. There was a drink in his hand by then, and they were sitting around watching the day die. "I'm retiring soon, you know. Going out to grass at last." He looked across at John Kidson and chuckled again. "Making way for someone younger."

"You'll stay for dinner," Betty Graham said. "What a pity Mary isn't with you."

"She won't leave the house at weekends," he explained. "She says two nights a week in London are bad enough. She can't wait for me to give up, you know."

He can't stop harping on it, Kidson thought. "Goading" would be a better word. Goading me, because I'm the only bloody candidate left. But it isn't going to make any difference. That's why he came down, to spike my guns with Davina, to stop me getting to Harrington before he does. But he won't succeed. Kidson busied himself pouring drinks. Betty Graham retired into the house and Charlie followed with the baby. Davina sat between her father and Lomax.

The Chief offered her a cigarette. He seldom shared his precious Sub Rosas with anyone. "No, thanks," she said curtly. "I prefer these." She'd filled an empty packet with the Balkan Sobranies.

He said quizzically, "That's a new foible, Davina. I've never seen you smoke those things before."

"It's not a foible," she answered. "I happen to like them. You like Sub Rosa."

"I do," he agreed. "I also think it's rather amusing, all things considered. Not many people see the joke. Let me give you a light."

"I've got one here," Davina said. She didn't want to take anything from him, not even a match. John couldn't have known about Australia. Nor Humphrey. It was the smiling Judas sitting close who had set the KGB killer on their trail when he felt it was safe. And then she remembered her bitter accusation, thrown at him face to face, in this very garden only a year before. "You milked him dry and then you didn't give a damn what happened to him. . . ." There was something wrong with that, surely. Surely Albatross would have shut Ivan's mouth long before he'd told enough to wreck the Soviet strategy in the Middle East. She got up and said, "Excuse me, I'll go and help Mother."

Lomax and the captain stayed behind with John Kidson to play audience to the fizz and sparkle of Sir James White's conversation.

Humphrey took the six-fifteen from Waterloo. The train was packed, and he was forced to buy a first-class ticket to be sure of a seat. Normally frugal, he resented the extra cost, but he didn't want to be jostled and talked to on the journey. He wanted to stay unnoticed. It was stuffy and the carriage was crammed. Luckily he had found a place in a nonsmoker. He hunched his long body down into the corner seat and raised an evening newspaper as a shield between himself and the rest of the travelers. He didn't read a word of the middle pages: theater, the arts, some rather waspish book reviews, a three-column feature on women's fashions with photographs of beautiful girls made ugly by bizarre hairstyles and unwearable clothes. He thought for a while about Ronnie, and his mouth twitched into a meager smile. He grew more and more endearing as their friendship went on. So young, and so naive, yet with the directness of his Suffolk background and the affectionate nature of a grateful puppy, he brought out tender feelings which Humphrey didn't know he possessed. He made him smile with his constant cheerfulness. He had brought a warmth and brightness into Humphrey's life. From an act of impulsive kindness, he told himself, happiness flowed for him at last. They were of a kind, and yet so different. The world beyond would see them and not ever know them as they truly were in human terms. He didn't care if Ronnie never got a job. He wanted him to stay cozy and waiting in the flat.

And then he thought about Davina. She had fooled him; he was sure of that. The look of contempt was so clear in her eyes when she refused the offer of a car and dismissed the insincere apology. She knew where Peter Harrington was. And Peter Harrington would lead her to Albatross. Kidson had rushed in with his own plan, using his family connection. He must be a fool indeed if he thought that Humphrey intended to stay quiet and leave him a clear field. But Humphrey's way was unobtrusive, silent. He hadn't been an operative for many years; for so long now, his work had been behind a desk, leaning over James White's shoulders. But he hadn't forgotten. He would join the family gathering, but they wouldn't know it. He got out at Salisbury, which was the farther station, and was met by the car he had hired before he left London.

"Come in," Charlie called out. "Oh, Davy . . ." Davina came into her sister's room and shut the door. It was the double guest room, a comfortable, chintzy bedroom that she remembered being reserved for her parents' friends when she was a child. Now it belonged to Charlie and John, and the baby slept in a portable fold-up bed in the corner.

"Wasn't it a good dinner?" Charlie inquired, turning back to the mirror with a lipstick in her hand. "Mum is a marvelous cook; I'll never be as good."

"She's good at everything she does," Davina said. She perched on the edge of the bed. "She doesn't make a fuss about it, that's all. Why did you suddenly suggest that I come down this weekend?"

Charlie wasn't easily caught off guard. "Mum said she hadn't seen you for ages."

Davina swung one foot backward and forward clear of the floor and stared at it for a second before looking at her sister and saying, "Don't lie, Charlie. They never have us together. John wanted to get in touch with me, didn't he?"

Charlie finished making her mouth red and put the lipstick away. "Why don't you ask him instead of me?" she suggested.

"Because I wanted to let you know what you are meddling with," Davina answered.

"I do know," Charlie snapped suddenly. "I know you're trying to bitch up John's chances of taking over when Sir James retires. What the hell are you doing, Davina? Why don't you just get on with your own mess of a life and leave him alone?"

"That's what he would like," Davina said. "He, and Sir James, and Humphrey. They'd all like me to leave them alone, but one of them has a very special reason. And I'm going to find out which one it is. You know about that part of it too, do you?"

Charlie came up to her. "I know," she said loudly, "that John is not a Russian spy. That's what you're trying to suggest, isn't it?"

"I'm going to prove it, one way or another," Davina said. She took out a black cigarette and lit it. It was the last match.

Charlie's pale skin had flushed an angry red. She glared down at her sister. "I've been sorry for you," she said. "Everything always went so wrong for you, didn't it? Poor Davy, couldn't keep her man, her wicked sister ran away with him. You've traded on that for years. Then you lose your husband. And what did we all do? We rallied round. No one was more sympathetic than John. Who rushed out to Mexico when you were in trouble? John. And what do you do, you hard-faced cow, but try to wreck his career just to justify some half-baked theory you've cooked up. Why don't you face it—whoever you sleep with, you're just as twisted and frustrated as you ever were!"

"Give John a message, will you?" Davina got up. "Tell him I'll have Albatross by tomorrow evening. Good night, Charlie. You shouldn't shout like that, you've woken the baby."

As she opened the door, she came face to face with Kidson. "Charlie and I," she said, "were just having a chat."

When she came into the drawing room, Sir James got up. There was no one else in the room. Her father put his head through the doorway and said, "The coffee's on its way—what will you have, James, brandy or Cointreau?"

"Nothing, my dear chap. I have to drive back, and it's quite a way."

"Davina? Something for you?"

"No, thanks, Father."

"Right, won't be a minute."

She didn't sit down, and Sir James lowered himself into the big sofa, taking the corner seat. "Well," he said, "I wonder why Humphrey hasn't turned up to join the happy group?"

"He was never very sociable. He thinks he'll find Harrington another way. How do you think you'll find him, Chief?"

"I think you'll tell me where he is," Sir James replied quietly, "when you realize that I'm not the person you're looking for."

Davina looked into the cold blue eyes. There wasn't a flicker in them. No nerves. She had to give him credit for an arctic coolness. Just that emptiness that made her feel that she was talking to someone who was not quite human. "I'll give you all the information you want by tomorrow evening," she said. "You may not thank me for it."

"Perhaps not," he admitted. "I shall be distressed to find that someone I trusted was a traitor. You are that near to Albatross? Clever girl. How is Mr. Anthony Walden? We met, you know, at a dinner party. He insisted upon being called Tony. Such a pity, with a fine Christian name."

Davina held herself in check. "He's a Jew," she said.

White smiled at her. "I know. He said so."

Davina sat down in one of her mother's upright chairs. The exquisite needlework was Mrs. Graham's hobby. She smoothed her light silk skirt, crossed one leg, showing a fine ankle and narrow foot. White watched the measured movement, waiting.

"You ruined him with the prince, didn't you?"

There was the tiniest reaction: the glass-blue eyes opened a fraction, and then there was a deprecating little smile under his mustache. "My dear Davina, you must think I'm very powerful indeed to accuse me of ruining anybody."

"But you did do it, didn't you? Why?"

He shrugged slightly. "How strange—you're as prickly about him as he was about you. Don't tell me you're growing tired of our admirable Colin?"

"I'm tired of you hurting people," Davina said quietly. "You haven't even got the decency to tell me why you did it."

"I'll tell you that," he countered, "when you tell me who Albatross is. And incidentally, where I can find Peter Harrington. It's becoming an embarrassment in the office, you know. I can't let you have much longer. Still—" He turned as Captain Graham came in with a tray of coffee. His wife, Charlie and John were in the background. "Still, you did say by tomorrow evening. I'll have to hold you to that. Ah, my dear Fergus, what a splendid dinner. I've just got time for one cup to keep me awake, and then I must be on my way home. It's been such fun to be all together again. I must get you all to come to Kent." He looked from Davina to the Grahams and then briefly his smile encompassed Kidson and Charlie. It glanced over Lomax like a passing spear. "One big happy family, aren't we?"

Humphrey had parked his car on some high ground in a sheltering belt of trees. He could stay awake without any difficulty. He had a thermos of hot sweet coffee and some chocolate; he also had binoculars and night glasses, so that his watch on Marchwood wasn't impeded by night or day. He had seen James White's car arrive and the lights in the house twinkling from room to room. He could imagine it inside. The fine paneled drawing room, with its French windows leading out onto the garden. The dining room. Ancestors and a coaching scene over the fireplace. A warm red-walled room, where good food and wine lulled the guests, with Captain Graham at the head of the table, a perfect English gentleman playing host. Humphrey knew the house so well he could monitor the movements by what window was lit, ending with the fanlight over the elegant portico.

Someone was leaving. The night glasses showed him Sir James White as the car turned out of the drive onto the road. Heading in the direction of Kent, by the long route. That left Davina and Colin Lomax in the house with Kidson. He must be preening himself, Humphrey thought with animus, thinking that he had outwitted his rival, poor Humphrey with his caricature of a face and lanky body. The perpetual second-in-command. Kidson would learn how foolish it was to underestimate him. Robespierre had hardly been a comic figure to his contemporaries.

He sipped his coffee and nibbled at the chocolate bar. He checked through the night glasses, although he didn't expect any activity until morning. But the lights were still on, and until the last one snapped out, he stayed on the alert. And that alertness was rewarded when half an hour after James White left, at a few minutes past eleven, Davina Graham's car came down the drive and took the road to London. He saw her and Lomax clearly through the night glasses. Humphrey didn't waste time. His car was quickly on its way down the grassy slope and onto the narrow side road while Davina's taillights twinkled in the distance. He picked up the car on the Andover road. There was almost no traffic and although Humphrey trailed far behind, he was able to keep it in view as it sped along the empty highway and into central London.

Davina took the route through Gloucester Road and turned into a side street. There were two sleazy hotels on the left-hand side, with an inscription in Arabic lit up in the window. Humphrey turned into a cul-de-sac and got out. He watched from the corner as she and Lomax got out and went into the second hotel. He waited for twenty minutes. How ingenious. What a clever place to choose. A dingy semiboardinghouse that catered to the lower level of Middle Eastern visitor. Little English would be spoken and less notice of who came and went. Very clever of you, Davina, but not quite clever enough. Humphrey's face was set and the thin mouth turned down. From being ugly he became cruel-looking. He started the car up and drove quietly back to his flat. He came in without making any noise; he didn't want to startle Ronnie. He closed the living-room door and went to the telephone.

James White didn't trouble to be quiet when he reached home. It was very late, but he knew his wife would be awake and waiting. He put his car in the garage, paused in the garden to admire its pleasing aspect in the moonlight, and marched up the steps to the front door with a sprightly gait. He whistled going into the kitchen. He made two cups of tea and placed a cookie jauntily in each saucer. Mary White was reading in bed when he came up. She saw the triumphant gleam in his eyes. She loved him deeply, but she was a woman who didn't believe that one human being had the right to probe too deeply into another, however close they were. There was too much she would rather not know; his work and how he conducted it were not her business.

"Well," she greeted him, putting aside the book and taking off her spectacles, "you must have enjoyed yourself, dear. What a good idea to bring up some tea. How did you know I'd be awake?"

"Because you always are, till I come to bed," he retorted. "Everybody at Marchwood sent their love and said they were sorry you didn't come."

"I would have done," she said, "if you'd given me the chance."

He patted her arm affectionately. "Not this time," he said. "It was all done on the spur of the moment. And well worthwhile."

"Tell me," his wife said, "who was there besides Betty and Fergus?"

"John and Charlie, Davina and her friend Major Lomax. All very well, and pretending to like each other as usual. There's no gathering in the world so full of tension as a family's get-together," he remarked, eating a cookie. "These are very good. I like the crunchy bits."

"You're a terrible cynic," Mary said. "I wonder what people say about us."

He laughed his gleeful little chuckle. "Exactly the same, I should think. Those Whites seem such a devoted couple, but did you notice . . . ? Come, Mary dear, when Philip was alive, we were often at odds with him and each other. Remember poor Humphrey sitting in the corner trying to pretend he wasn't there. What an awkward fellow he was, even then. . . . He hasn't changed, either. Nor have his problems."

"How could they?" she said. "He never faced up to them except that one time when he came to you."

"And I helped him," James White maintained. "So I'm not entirely cynical. Be fair."

"Nonsense," Mary retorted. "You made the poor man work for you, that's all. You *are* looking smug. I'm not going to ask about it because I'm dying to get to sleep, but did you get what you wanted?"

Her husband got up and stretched a little. "Yes, my dear, I think I did. Good Lord, look at the time!"

John Kidson was undressing slowly. "You shouldn't have had a row," he said. "I don't want to make bad blood between you."

Charlie sat down on the bed; her pale pink nightdress was slit provocatively to the thigh. "Darling, we've already been over this, why bring it up again? There's always been bad blood," she said. "I mistook a truce for something more. I thought she'd stopped hating me till I realized what she was trying to do to you. I told her what I thought of her, and I don't regret a word! John, did you find out anything? Was it any help bringing her down here?"

He came and sat with her, one arm around her waist. "Of course it was," he said gently. "She didn't know it, but she told me a good deal. I'm not a fool, you know. She's got so arrogant lately that she doesn't reckon other people anymore. That's the first sign of losing your grip."

Charlie leaned against him. She felt like making love. "And do you think it'll be all right—she hasn't hurt your chance of getting the job, has she?"

"No," said John Kidson, "I'd say that she's done quite the opposite."

"Sir James was throwing out pretty broad hints," Charlie murmured. She slid both arms around him. "It'll be all right," she repeated. "He was so sweet to me tonight. I know you're going to get it."

Kidson didn't answer. He kissed his beautiful wife and tried to match her eagerness, but he felt cold and drained. Desire faltered and died, and for the first time since they were married, he disappointed her. His mind was obsessed by something very different.

"Do you think we were followed?"

Lomax hesitated. "There was a Ford Escort I noticed at the flyover—it was some way behind, but still there when we turned down here." He went to the window overlooking the street and inched the curtain back. "Can't see anyone at the moment, but maybe the hotel management are due for a surprise visit."

"What a depressing place," Davina said. There was a pervasive smell of cooking and human bodies. The room was clean but furnished in cheap, garish colors, and it smelled as stuffy as the rest of the hotel.

She looked at her watch. "Have another look," she suggested.

Lomax went back to the window. "Nothing, no cars coming down at all." If a car drove through more than once, it was certain to be the "tail" keeping an eye on the place.

"I think we can go," Davina said. "We've been here an hour."

"No point in waiting for the visitors, if they arrive," Lomax remarked.

It was one in the morning and the streets were empty; a distant car hooted forlornly like a lonely owl.

Lomax drove; they spent most of the journey in silence. "If Humphrey stayed away it could put him in the clear," Davina said suddenly. "If nothing happens at the hotel, it means he didn't have us followed. Which leaves the Chief and John."

"That narrows it, certainly," Lomax agreed. "But what happens if they don't react either? Then what do we do?"

She snapped at him, irritable because he was voicing her own doubts, "I haven't any idea! Keep plugging at Harrington."

"I told you I thought it was a very risky scheme," Lomax said quietly. "But I've gone along with it. I'd feel a lot happier if I went back to the Ritz."

"If you did," she countered, "Albatross would know it's a setup. He wouldn't move. You've got to stay put, and so have I. You said your friend Fraser's men would know what to do."

"They'll keep Harrington locked away," he said. "And they're on full alert. That should be enough. But I still don't like it. And what's your friend Walden going to say about his end?"

"He'll understand," she answered, wishing he would stop pointing out the risk of failure when she knew it so well herself.

"Maybe . . ." Lomax turned off the highway and the car sped down the Andover road. "Maybe, but will his wife?"

She didn't answer. Three clues, and only one of them led to Harrington. Three colleagues, one of whom would send, not the Special Branch to arrest the missing traitor, but the KGB to rescue him. And thereby reveal himself. They turned into the drive and went into the house by the back door, which was never locked.

They crept upstairs and separated on the landing. Lomax looked down at her. She couldn't see his face in the semidark. "Get your head down and try to sleep," he said.

"I will." She felt thankful that he didn't try to come in with her. "Good night, Colin."

The room had been hers since childhood, and nothing had changed in it. The same furniture, the same china animals as ornaments. In the narrow bed, she and Ivan Sasanov had made love for the first time. Colin Lomax was right. It was both risky and uncertain, but she had no alternative but to gamble and hope to win. She didn't expect to sleep at all, but she did, and without dreaming.

It was a glorious summer morning when her mother knocked on the door and called out, "Davina? It's half-past eight. Are you coming down to breakfast?"

John Kidson suggested a walk after breakfast. He had brought Charlie's upstairs on a tray; she never came down until late. He said to Davina, "I'd like a chance to talk to you. Let's wander up through the wood, shall we?"

She saw Lomax glance up suspiciously and signaled him to stay behind. "Why not?" she agreed. "It's such a lovely morning." They reached the fields behind the house and walked through a little belt of trees that didn't really constitute a wood. As they came out, the splendid panorama of Salisbury Plain unfolded before them.

"This always gives me a thrill," John Kidson said. "It comes on you as such a surprise when you leave the trees."

Davina said quietly, "What did you want to say to me, John?"

He took her arm and they began to walk slowly along the edge of the wood. "It's about you and Charlie," he said. "I couldn't help hearing you quarreling last night. I don't want this to happen, Davina. We've worked together for years, and we've always got along.

You and she had your differences long before I met her. I don't want them flaring up again because of me."

"I didn't realize she was so ambitious for you," Davina answered. "She wants you to take over from the Chief. And you want it too, don't you?"

He didn't quite hide the flash of hostility when he answered, "Of course I do. I'm the only person *to* step into the job. I mentioned it to Charlie, and I did say you weren't exactly helping. But I didn't expect her to fly at you the way she did. I wish you'd stop all this private snooping and let the Service deal with this Albatross business in its own way."

Davina stopped and disengaged her arm from what had started out as a friendly clasp. "You mean let the bastard that helped to kill my husband cover up for himself? Not a chance, John."

"So the motive for all this is personal, after all," he challenged her. "Not just the selfless patriotic bit. Why don't you leave the past where it belongs? Nothing's going to bring the dead back to life. Why don't you get on with your new job and make up your mind about Colin? I'm really talking as a friend now. I don't suppose you'll believe me, but it's true. I'm looking after my own end, and I'm pretty confident. You're out there punching on your own. You know where a convicted criminal is hiding; that could put you in a very awkward spot—we all know you've got him holed up somewhere. You say you're going to produce Albatross like a rabbit out of a hat—I don't believe you can. The bluff's going to be called, Davina. Think about it, and if you need any help, I'm here and I'm genuinely anxious for you."

She walked on briskly, keeping step with him. They turned back into the shelter of the trees and started down toward the house. "Thanks," she said briefly. "I'll bear it in mind. I wouldn't be too confident, if I were you. I'm the one who's going to call the bluff."

The message was sent to Borisov's dacha, where he was spending the weekend with his family. The dacha was the perquisite of the Director of State Security, set in seclusion amid the beautiful pine forests outside Moscow. It was close enough to the splendid house allotted to the President himself; Borisov was able to walk there, accompanied by his guardian Alexei, who came everywhere with him. It was a hot day, very still, and the scent of the pines was sharp in the air. Borisov wore the casual shirt and trousers of the ordinary citizen, his feet in sandals, a dog trotting behind him. He looked a very ordinary man in his late forties or just touching fifty—well-built, pleasant-looking, but unremarkable. He could have been any one of Moscow's citizens enjoying a walk in the woods with a friend. Except that the whole area of Zhukova was reserved for the members of the Politburo and the important officials in the Party. No ordinary Russian was allowed there, and the idyllic landscape of woods and fields bisected by the yellow ribbon of the Moskva River concealed armed men discreetly placed around each dacha.

Borisov was admitted to the private swimming pool where Zerkhov took gentle exercise. The ruler of Russia was wrapped in a big toweling dressing gown, sipping fresh lemonade in the sunshine. Borisov dismissed Alexei. Zerkhov glanced after the retreating figure and said, "Your new secretary. More trustworthy than the previous one? Yes, sit down, Igor Igorovich; have some lemonade. It's very good; my doctor recommends it. You have news for me?"

"We have found Harrington," Borisov said.

"Good," Zerkhov muttered, blinking in the sunshine.

"We have to protect Albatross and get him out as soon as possible," said Borisov. "I've arranged for his replacement."

"And is that all you came to tell me, my son?" the old man asked gently.

"No," Borisov answered, "I wouldn't disturb your little leisure time for that alone. Albatross had some important information he sent on. We have an Albatross of our own."

The old man's head came up, the sleepy look changed to one of piercing intentness. "Where is he, and do we know who?"

"He is in the Foreign Ministry," Borisov said.

There was a moment of silence between them. Zerkhov pressed a hidden bell in the side of his chair. A man appeared at the entrance to the swimming pool. Zerkhov didn't even look at him.

"Bring more lemonade."

"My organization has been penetrated," Borisov went on, his voice a monotone that made the words more threatening. "There are spies in my own offices. One of them passed secret information to the

Foreign Ministry, and the traitor then leaked this information to the British embassy."

"What was the information?" A jug of fresh lemonade tinkling with ice was brought and two glasses poured.

"Information that discredited the KGB." Borisov went on, "Information that put Albatross in danger, and was designed to make us a laughingstock before the Western world. Fortunately, Albatross was able to warn me of the leak and I have taken action. That action will now be implemented."

"Do you have proof of this, Igor Igorovich?"

"Albatross has the proof," Borisov said. "That is one reason why he must be protected and brought out. So that he can tell you himself."

"It was an attack on you," Zerkhov remarked. "Coming from the Foreign Ministry."

"Yes," Borisov admitted. "But a power struggle within the state is one thing, and we both know what is going on. To benefit the enemy in pursuit of advantage in that struggle is treason."

"Which is what we need." The old man spoke thoughtfully.

Borisov said no more. The minutes passed while the most powerful man in the Soviet Union gazed at the sunlight shimmering on the swimming pool and thought about the downfall of his enemies. "Get me the proof," he said at last. "Bring Albatross to me. Then we won't have to wait until the autumn. By the time the Supreme Soviet meets, Poland will have settled because there won't be any provocation coming from us. And the other problem will be settled too. I shall go inside and dress now." He rose slowly to his feet, and Borisov helped him. "We will win," he said. "Russia is not going back into the Dark Ages. Report to me as soon as everything is done."

"I will, Little Father." Borisov walked back to the house with him. He had used the old Russian form of address to the ruler. So his people had called the czar. Zerkhov had not rebuked him.

"Two roast beef and the trimmings, one saddle of lamb likewise. Two pints of light ale and a half-bottle of red wine. The gentleman says you choose something for him."

"I'll speak to the wine waiter," the old man said. "And the light ales are bottled or draft, sir?" His expression was disapproving as he asked the question. The roast rib of beef was especially succulent and tender. Light ale. He sucked his lips in and out in distress. The marine called over his shoulder, "Bottled or draft for you, Bob?"

The reply came back from the sitting room: "Bottled."

"Right, then, two bottled light ales," the younger man said, and firmly closed the door again. He came back into the sitting room.

"No problem?" the other inquired.

"No, nobody hanging about. The old geezer was just like the young one yesterday. Looked as he had done a fart under his nose. Pass us a fag, will you?" They settled down to wait for their lunch to arrive.

One on each side of the door, with the door itself ajar. Harrington could see one of them through the keyhole. The man had his hand in his pocket, casually, not holding the gun too tightly. Much bloody good it would do him, Harrington muttered to himself, and retreated to his own position, a comfortable armchair the other side of the bed.

His stomach knotted with suspense. One o'clock. When would something happen? Was he going to sit this out till the evening? He didn't know how he could stand it. He rapped on the door. "I'd like a Scotch," he called out. "Coming up" was the answer. He took the drink, didn't say thank you, and paced up and down, swigging from the glass. One-thirty. Christ, he wasn't hungry, but he wanted something to eat to pass the time. . . . He heard the rattle of a trolley beyond the locked door.

It opened and the older man brought in his order. "Smells good," he remarked.

Harrington watched him set the tray on the table. He sat down and poured himself a glass of wine from the opened half-bottle. Pommard '75. They'd picked the best. He took the silver lid off the lamb and the vegetables and helped himself.

In the sitting room the two men took it in turns to eat. One stayed on guard behind the door leading into the tiny hall while the other cut into his beef and swallowed his beer.

The floor waiter changed out of his uniform in a broom closet on the landing. It was cramped in the tiny space, with vacuum cleaners for the corridors and the body of the young duty waiter bundled up knees-to-chin in a corner. The maids would get a fright in the morning, he thought, and didn't smile. He had no sense of humor. He slipped into a jacket left hanging behind the door, ripped off the gray wig, and stuffed it into his pocket. He had spent some time in a minor repertory company. He had never got beyond walk-on parts. He had become a better actor since then. When he took the elevator to the main hall, he was a young man in a Continental-style suit, wearing thick spectacles. He crossed the lounge and down the steps into Arlington Street, where he declined the head porter's offer of a taxi with a courteous "No, thank you." He turned left into Piccadilly and disappeared down Green Park Underground station. In the station he went to a pay phone and dailed a number.

"Colin," Captain Graham called out, "phone for you."

Lomax didn't hurry. He didn't look at Davina, and she asked her mother for a second cup of coffee. Lomax wasn't long away. He came back to the drawing room and said, "That was Jim Fraser; he wants us to go to them for drinks and something to eat before the theater."

"That means we'll have to leave early." Davina picked up the cue.

Lomax explained to Betty Graham. "Sorry about this, but we're going to see a play tonight. *Another Country.* Our friends are mad on the theater and they say it's the best thing in years."

"Isn't it all about traitors?" Kidson inquired. "That's what I heard."

"We'll have to make tracks pretty soon." Lomax ignored the remark. "It's a shame to cut the afternoon short." He shrugged and looked apologetic.

"I'll get my things together," Davina said. They didn't hurry or show any signs of urgency. In the hall she whispered, "The Ritz?"

Lomax nodded. "The boys got hold of Fraser."

She saw his face and said, "Colin . . ." and then stopped.

"Harrington's dead," he said. "Cyanide in his wine. They don't mess about, do they?"

She paused at the top of the stairs. "Oh, my God, what have I done?"

"You've found Albatross," he said. "That's what you wanted, wasn't it? You better let me deal with this."

She didn't answer. *They'd killed him.* She had gambled on a rescue. She'd dealt three cards, and one of them had turned out to be the queen of spades for Harrington. She went into her room, threw her clothes into the bag, caught a glimpse of her reflection in the mirror, haggard and white-faced with shock. Now she knew the identity of Albatross. She turned to the door. To find him, she had killed Peter Harrington as surely as if she had put the poison in the wine herself.

"Phone call for you, Humphrey." Ronnie smiled and said, "I'll make us a nice cup of coffee," and went off contentedly into the kitchen.

Humphrey picked up the receiver. He listened quietly and then said, "Sorry about that."

He hung up, and Ronnie's voice called out, "Coffee's ready."

He took a deep breath and composed himself. "Let's have it, then," he said. He slipped an arm around the boy's shoulder as he came into the living room, and took the tray.

"Oh, Lord," Mary White exclaimed, "do we have to go up to London? Whatever it is, can't it wait till Monday?"

James White shook his head. "I'm afraid not, dear. But you don't have to come."

She glanced at him and said quickly, "It's not a top priority, is it?"

"It could be," he said. "We shall have to see."

"I wish we didn't have a telephone," his wife said. "Of course I'll come. Otherwise you'll be in the office till all hours. We'd better stay in the flat."

He came up and kissed her lightly. "I'm going up at once. Why don't you enjoy the rest of the day and come later? I shan't be free until the evening anyway. That's much the best idea." He left quarter of an hour later.

Mary White didn't argue. She realized by the speed with which he revved up and drove away that he was very worried about something.

"Just my luck," John Kidson complained. "They always have a crisis at weekends."

"Such a pity," Fergus Graham said, seeing his darling daughter leaving a day early. "Why don't Charlie and little Fergie stay down? I'll drive them up tomorrow evening."

John Kidson said, "That would be far the best." He came and put his arm around Charlie. "You stay put, my love. What's the point of dragging up to London? I'll be at the office all day tomorrow, I expect, so stay here. I'll phone this evening."

The call had come in the late afternoon. He went upstairs to pick up his razor and pajamas and was on his way toward the highway in less than half an hour. He drove fast and with fierce concentration. He had neglected to kiss his wife good-bye for the first time since they married.

Stephen Wood was sorry about interrupting the plans he and his wife had made for Saturday. He explained that one of his chaps had assaulted a prison officer and he had to drop everything and go to Pentonville and try to see if he could help. A poor subnormal type, he said sympathetically, only able to express himself through violence. His wife clicked her tongue, which was a habit that irritated him, and said of course she knew he had to go, but what a nuisance when they had a nice afternoon at London Zoo planned. Wood had received a telephone call just after one-thirty.

He had spent some time on the phone after that, while she saw their outing being whittled away. His call came first from a public phone at Green Park Underground station. He made its equivalent to a telephone-answering service for a firm of Battersea plumbers. The tapes were monitored day and night for messages like his. Within an hour it had been relayed to the appropriate source in the Moscow embassy and instructions were received for transmission back to Wood. When they came, he had to cancel the trip to the zoo and listen to his wife making the clicking noise of disappointment with her teeth and tongue. One day, albeit very tactfully, he'd mention it to her. . . .

The mission was completed successfully. Albatross was safe. Now the final phase of the operation had to be set in train. Wood was going to be very busy.

Davina went to the Marylebone apartment. It was very quiet inside and she shivered as she went into the living room. She felt cold and sick. She lit the last of the Balkan Sobranies and sat down, staring at the dead face of the television set. She didn't want to go to the Ritz with Colin. She didn't want to see the two men who had failed to safeguard Harrington. She didn't want, above all, to see his body, however sheeted and concealed. When the doorbell rang, she jumped. It rang twice in succession, as if the caller was very impatient. She got up and went into the hall. "Who is it?"

"Me!" Walden said loudly. "Davina, let me in!"

He came through the door so quickly that she hadn't time to speak before he had slammed it and hurried her back into the living room. "I called the Ritz," he said. "Lomax was there and he told me what had happened. Christ, what a mess! You look terrible. Sit down. . . ."

"I feel terrible," she said slowly. He was solicitous immediately, but she shook him off with fierce impatience. "Tony, stop it. I don't need a drink, I don't need cosseting, I'm perfectly all right! Just leave me alone." She turned away and sat down.

Walden didn't move. "It's not your fault," he said. "You tried to protect him. You can't blame yourself."

She raised her head and said quietly, "I used him as a decoy. I set him up. I just didn't reckon they'd kill him. Now, tell me I'm not to blame." She turned away from him again.

Walden sat down beside her. He reached out and took hold of her hand. It trembled slightly. "I don't know the reasons for any of this," he said. "And frankly, I don't care. You shouldn't care either. Look at me for a minute."

She didn't want to, but there was a compulsion not to run away. She had already done that when she fled to Marylebone and left Colin to pick up the pieces of a human life.

He had intense brown eyes, which beamed their message at her. "If he's dead, he deserved to be. He was a traitor, a stinking double agent, working for the worst tyranny on earth. To hell with him. If you set him up, so what? Did you get what you wanted—that's all that matters."

"Yes," Davina said at last, "I got what I wanted. You're in the wrong business, Tony. You should be doing this."

"I know that's not meant to be a compliment," he countered. "But

I'll take it as one. I know the Russians, my darling. You forget, I'm a Pole. I haven't any tears to shed for them or anyone who works for them. Now, pull yourself together. You had a job to do. You've done it. Come here and let me tell you what a wonderful woman you are."

She was in his arms and he was kissing her, fighting down her resistance with outright physical force. Soon she quietened and gave in to him. Neither of them heard Colin Lomax come into the flat. He stood in the doorway and saw her arms around Walden's neck, her mouth enclosed by his, her hand caressing the back of his head. He didn't say anything. He turned and left the flat without either of them knowing he had been there.

"You're early," Sir James White said. The office was filled with evening sunshine; it played on the watercolor of his pink-washed house in Kent hanging over the antique fireplace. He was sitting behind his desk, the smoke of his Sub Rosa cigarette hanging in a blue haze over his head. He looked completely relaxed, and when he saw Davina, he got up and smiled and said, "Do sit down, my dear." She didn't go to the chair he indicated. She walked to the window and looked out over the paved courtyard that fronted a gentleman's eighteenth-century town house.

"I didn't want to keep you waiting," she said at last. "I know you value punctuality like loyalty."

"A value we share, I think," he answered. "You said you would have Albatross by tonight. I believe you've kept your promise."

She looked at him. She seemed remote, withdrawn. He noticed how extremely pale she was. "There were only three people who could have been Albatross," she said. "You, Humphrey, and John. I gave each of you a clue this weekend, but only one of them was genuine. I said I would expose the traitor by tonight, because I wanted to panic him into action. I succeeded. But I had to risk a rescue attempt for Peter Harrington. It had to be for real, and I took the chance that he might actually get away."

"And did he?" James White inquired.

Davina shook her head. "No," she said, "he was murdered instead."

"Ah." He made it a long sound. "Albatross did panic, didn't he? Who is it, Davina?" The cold eyes were fixed upon her; he leaned forward a little, and the voice had lost its gentle tone.

She dropped a box of matches on the desk in front of him. "I left one of these in my sister's bedroom. I left it on the bed. Albatross is my brother-in-law, John Kidson."

The matchbox lay on the desktop; he picked it up. Black and gold with the number of the suite stamped on it beneath the inscription "Ritz Hotel."

James White turned it over and then put it down. "What an ingenious place to hide him. How was it done? Were there other casualties?" He sounded matter-of-fact.

"Poison," she answered. "And a young floor waiter killed. The assassin took his place. There hasn't been any fuss; the management haven't been told. Colin is coping with it."

"Kidson," he murmured. "How could it be? John Kidson. . . ."

"I've been trying to answer that myself," she said. "He married my sister, crept into my family . . . and found out where Ivan and I were living. All he needed was proximity. An Australian stamp, a bit of envelope. My father thought he destroyed my letters. He wouldn't be able to hide them from a professional like John. Oh, God, what a sickening bloody disaster. . . ."

She saw James White pick up the internal telephone. "Get me a glass of brandy somewhere, will you? Yes, of course there is—I know Personnel keeps something for emergencies." He said kindly, "That aspect is distressing for you, I know."

"I never thought Harrington would be killed," she said. "I set him up for them. I find that pretty distressing too."

"Well, you mustn't," he said firmly. "The KGB have saved us a lot of trouble. I needn't remind you of how much pity he showed you when the positions were reversed. Remember that, if you feel guilty. Personally, I think it's the best possible solution to an embarrassing situation. Here's your brandy. Drink that up, it'll make you feel better."

"You've got to arrest him," she said. "He was still at home when we left."

"You think he'd make a run for it? He wouldn't get far."

Davina hesitated. "I'm not sure. Thanks for the brandy, Chief. He thinks he's going to get your job, he's dead set on it. The last thing we talked about was him taking over from you. He was trying to persuade me to drop the investigation. He must have known Peter would be taken care of. Maybe he won't run. Maybe he'll play it by ear and see what happens. He wants the top job—it would be worth the risk."

"It might be as well to let him think he's got away with it," James White said. "We can play for time too. I'll call Marchwood to see if he's still there. Why don't you go home, Davina? I'll let you know developments."

She said, "You know I thought it was you."

He nodded. "Of course you did. I hope you're not too disappointed. By the way, the little subterfuge with the Balkan Sobranie cigarettes wasn't quite up to your usual standard."

"Why not?" She got up, paused. She had forgotten about that. And about Humphrey Grant.

"Because I knew Harrington used to smoke them. Also that your friend Walden was responsible for a big advertising campaign a few months ago. One couldn't escape the advertisements."

"Did you go to Arlington Agency?" she asked him. "I was sure you would."

"No, but we did pay a visit to Walden's flat in Grosvenor Square. He wasn't best pleased."

"You really are a bastard, aren't you?" she said quietly. "You knew perfectly well he wasn't hiding Harrington there."

He looked innocently at her. "I had to make sure," he said. "After all, we've been keeping an eye on his offices, just in case. And it seems that Humphrey did have you followed last night. There was a frightful commotion at some hotel catering for Middle Eastern gentlemen when the Special Branch swooped on them this morning. Do you have your car?"

"No," Davina said. "As a matter of fact, Tony Walden brought me here. He's waiting outside. And he never mentioned anything about this morning!"

"How very thoughtful of him," James White said blandly. "I shall apologize to him in person. Now, I had better get Humphrey to sort out this little mess at the Ritz. While I take my old colleague John

Kidson into my confidence." She stared at him and he said, "Twenty years of treachery. He'll pay for it. You can be sure of that."

There was no report in any of the papers. The first shift of cleaners at the Ritz found nothing but their equipment in the broom closet. Sir James's men had taken control of the situation very quickly. The murdered waiter was found in a West London street after a hit-and-run accident. The occupant of Suite A who died of a heart attack was removed by a back entrance; Fraser's employees went home after signing an undertaking not to mention anything to anyone on pain of prosecution under the Official Secrets Act.

John Kidson joined Humphrey in a meeting at the office very late that Sunday night. Sir James amazed them by bringing out a bottle of whiskey and offering each of them a drink.

"Poor Davina," he said. "I saw her early on. The whole thing failed completely. Borisov's people got to Harrington and took him out. Not out of the country, either." He gave both of them a smug look. "Saved us a lot of trouble," he said. "And put the lady well in her place. She won't set out on her own again. Even if someone was foolish enough to suggest it." For a moment he withered Humphrey and then turned aside.

"And Albatross?" Kidson demanded. "What about that?"

"Nothing," James White answered. "She couldn't solve the puzzle without Harrington. Now I'm afraid it will be up to us to settle it. Internally, as we always do."

"How did they find Harrington?" Humphrey asked slowly. The question hung like a fireball in the air.

"Does it matter?" Kidson said irritably. "She was probably followed—careless in some way. The point is, there's still suspicion. It's got to be cleared up." He looked obstinate, as if he expected to be opposed.

"It will be, in due time," Humphrey said. "We don't want a scandal. Davina would have caused one. We have to keep our troubles to ourselves."

"Spoken like a good member of the Firm." Sir James applauded him. "We won't let Albatross fly away. Let's drink to that."

* * *

John Kidson didn't go to his house that night. He left Anne's Yard with the whiskey numbing his stomach, killing the swirling butterflies that had tormented him throughout the last thirty-six hours. That was his weakness, a stomach that reacted to stress.

He'd brought it off. Harrington was dead and Davina hadn't broken the cover that protected him. She was finished, disgraced—he knew the procedures for internal inquiries within the SIS. He knew how long and difficult it was to track down someone who could protect himself at every turn. He had doctored the files a long time ago; the computer would carry the same errors, when they checked. No scandal. He smiled a little, easing the tension. Too many rivalries from other security sections, always jealous of the funds and privileges allowed the SIS. Philby had done his successor a favor by creating so much bloodletting in the Service. They wouldn't want a repetition. He had time; there was no need to panic now. So much to gain if he kept his nerve. Such an incredible prize to give his friends in Moscow. Head of the Secret Intelligence Service. It was a dizzy prospect and it made him light-headed thinking of what a triumph it would be. What a historic coup against the forces of capitalist society. And as he had always intended, he would take his achievement into a peaceful English churchyard with him, and die respected by the people he had betrayed.

He drove to a pub near the King's Road. It was cheerful and full of young men and women enjoying themselves. There was a freakish element, intent on showing off, painted like Red Indians, with cropped hair dyed rainbow colors. Kidson observed them with disinterest. The young were disillusioned. Their obsession with ugliness was a sign of revolt against the corrupt society they were growing up in. He didn't blame them. As a nineteen-year-old he had felt the same. Dissatisfied, searching for a belief, savagely antifascist with the horrors of the Nazi holocaust peopling his dreams at night. A very clever, introspective young undergraduate, with a history don who sensed the lack of direction in life and his desire to be of use to others.

The process of his political education had been gentle, tactful, and finally so illuminating that it was close to ecstasy. His road to Damascus had been the living room of his tutor's rooms at King's. He had been blind, and with his friend's help, he saw for the first time. That was how he had begun, and he had never once turned back. Never doubted, never faltered under the terrific strain of living a schizophrenic life. Never married until he met Charlotte Graham and fell in love for the first time. Loved and wanted her and found incredible happiness. It was not conflicted with the search for the traitor Ivan Sasanov. The letters were destroyed. Torn up, meticulously burned and flushed away. He had seen the residue of ash in the lavatory at Marchwood. But not the envelopes. Not after the first year. He had found the scraps in the wastebasket and pieced enough together to see the postmark: Perth, Western Australia. It hadn't worried him at all to pass on the information. It didn't change his adoration for his wife or his liking for her family. It didn't stop him being sympathetic to Davina when she came home widowed and having lost her child as well. The two sides of his life were separated by a gulf that could never be crossed. He did his work with enthusiasm and consummate skill. He was recognized as the best in-depth interrogator in the Service, and he had never needed to use threats or force. He delivered his own people without scruple, because he dared not permit himself to fail. Because of his record, promotion and access to top-secret information followed. Indeed, he considered calmly, the end justified the means, even when he trapped Soviet agents and they were sent to jail. He had nothing but contempt for the bought traitor like Peter Harrington. Money would never have influenced Kidson. Nor did personal risk. He believed in his duty to the Soviet ideal; he sacrificed the lives of others for it, and he wouldn't have hesitated to die himself either. But subtlety, not heroics, was his specialty. Harrington might convulse and expire like a stray dog, but Kidson's role was to serve from behind a screen of deep deception and to elude discovery to the very end. He had a drink in the pub and looked at his watch.

He had to meet a contact in that pub just before it closed. He saw the man come in, carrying a garish yellow cardigan over his shoulder, and Kidson went to the bar and bought cigarettes. The man with the cardigan elbowed his way alongside him.

"Just on closing," the barmaid said to the new customer.

"Time for a half of bitter," Stephen Wood insisted. He jogged Kidson's elbow. "Sorry," he mumbled. "Hot today, wasn't it?"

Kidson picked up his cigarettes and his change. He gave the recognition signal. "Makes a change from rain." He moved back to his table, and the man's monotonous voice boomed over the bar, followed by a tuneless haha, haha that grated on Kidson's nerves. He was the emergency exit, the professional bore chatting up the barmaid and slurping back his beer. He had never been contacted before, until Kidson found the matches lying on Charlie's bed. He wouldn't be seen again after they left the pub and he passed Kidson his instructions.

They mingled with the crowd that spilled slowly outdoors.

"You're to make for home," he said. Kidson gasped. "Home" meant Moscow.

"I can't. I'm clear. In line for W.'s job. Tell them."

Wood paused and pulled on the garish cardigan. He buttoned it up. A last group of loiterers went by.

"Brr. Got cold suddenly. Glad I brought this along. No arguments. They were specific. You're to go home. Via Paris. Take your wife. Good night."

Kidson went back to the empty house. Charlie had furnished and decorated it with her special flair. It provided a perfect background for her. Photographs of herself and the baby; their wedding picture, smiling outside the Kensington Register Office. Vases of flowers; she loved flowers and spent a fortune on them. Their bedroom. He felt a lurch of desire and despair. She wouldn't come with him. He knew it. He would lose her and his son if he did what he was ordered. He sat down on the bed. Go home. Take your wife to Paris. That wouldn't be difficult. Charlie would jump at the chance. It wouldn't look suspicious if they went for a weekend together. But he wasn't to stay and bring his long years of work to a sublime conclusion.

He understood what that meant. He went cold and his stomach filled with fluttering wings again. Killing Harrington hadn't been enough. He had never disobeyed. He wouldn't do so now, but he knew that the price was higher than discovery and a life sentence. Charlie wouldn't go to Russia with him.

Charlie believed that anyone who betrayed his country should be shot. He remembered so clearly that conversation in the restaurant by the river. She meant it. She had reminded him of her sister for a moment, and he had been disturbed. Charlie would recoil from him in loathing if she knew what he had done. He would take her to Paris to cover his escape. But he would have to leave her behind. He sat on the bed and hid his face in his hands as he wept.

Lomax had left Humphrey in charge at the Ritz and gone back to the Frasers' for the night. He didn't want to see Davina. He couldn't rid himself of the image of her in Tony Walden's arms. There was nothing platonic in that embrace. It was fiercely sexual. If he hadn't turned and left, he would have attacked Walden. He didn't telephone that night. He sat with his old friend and got rather drunk, talking about the Army and their time in the regiment together.

Fraser had no idea that anything was wrong with him. He apologized over and over for his men's failure to protect Lomax's charge; he became a little maudlin as the drink went down.

Lomax assured him that they had done their job as well as anyone could do. "They're good straightforward blokes," he mumbled. "Send in a couple of heavies, start shooting, and they're the best there is. But not bloody cyanide, not an old waiter with a bottle of cyanide wine . . . they weren't trained to deal with that, Jim, for Christ's sake. Nor was I," he added. He turned to his friend as they went unsteadily upstairs. He looked dull-eyed and miserable; to Fraser he seemed merely drunk.

"It's a stinking job," Lomax said out loud. "Everything about it stinks. And everyone in it. I've had enough. . . ."

The following morning he woke with a headache, but the mild hangover didn't last longer than breakfast. He had made up his mind. He asked Jim Fraser if he'd consider taking on a partner in the security business, and he telephoned Davina to say that he was coming around.

"Why didn't you come back?" she asked him. "I waited up, thinking that you'd telephone. What happened to you?"

She seemed on edge, he thought. Tired, dark rings under the eyes, but totally mistress of herself. She's got over what happened, he thought. With that bastard's help. He had kissed it better for her. And she let him. He felt a wave of hot anger sweep through him, and then quietly die away. And with it died his love for Davina Graham. He felt a sense of loss, as if part of himself had withered up. Pain followed the anger, and regret. There is always one who loves and one who lets himself be loved. He had loved her always; she had reciprocated, but she had never wholly belonged to him.

"I spent the night with Jim Fraser," he said. "I knew you wouldn't be alone."

Davina saw the expression on his face and said in a quiet voice, "You mean Tony? Colin, I'm very sorry. He did call around."

"Don't be." He shrugged slightly. "I knew all along it was going to happen. I told you so, if you remember. He meant to get you, Davina, and he's the kind of man who never gives up. I did come back to the flat yesterday to see if you were all right. He was here, and I didn't like to disturb you." He saw her look down and faintly blush.

"I didn't mean it to happen," she said. "I didn't want it. Please believe me, Colin. I really tried not to . . . I've never believed people can't stop these things. Now I know it's true." She lit a cigarette. They were not Balkan Sobranies.

"Which means you're in love with him," he said. "You like Slavs, don't you? Pity I'm just a Scot. I'll get my clothes packed up. It won't take long."

She came to him and caught hold of his arm. There were tears in her eyes. "I'm so sorry," she said. "I never wanted to hurt you. We've been happy together, we've been through so much. You don't have to go, Colin, love. Give me a little time. . . ."

He looked down at her and shook his head. The endearment wounded him. Colin, love. She had always called him that. He wished she hadn't done so then, when it was over and he was on his way.

"I'm sorry too," he said. "I can't share a woman; you ought to know that. I hoped you'd marry me and get out of all this when we'd wound this last thing up. I really hoped we'd make a life and settle down. I must have been barking mad, Davina. You love what you do; I can see that now. But I hate it. I hate what happened at that hotel yesterday. It makes my bloody skin crawl. But you're part of it. Give me a clean fight, but not this sort of thing. It's not for me, and I'm glad I realize it. Just take care of yourself, won't you."

He bent down and gave her a light kiss on the cheek. He felt the tears that spilled onto it. He went out of the room and didn't look back.

Igor Borisov and his companion took a private flight to Yalta. From there they were met by an official car and driven to the splendid modern dacha with its swimming pool and panoramic views of the Black Sea. The head of the Union of Soviet Socialist Republics greeted them with his wife beside him. They sat down to a lunch served by the swimming pool and there were toasts in the local white wine which was famous for its fruity taste. It was a jovial occasion, marked by informality; Zerkhov made heavy jokes in Russian, and his wife and his guests laughed heartily.

They swam in the luxurious pool, and the hot sunshine blazed down through a screen of palm trees. The setting was idyllic in its beauty, the dacha sculptured in white marble, with a terrace that overlooked the coast. Zerkhov's guest spoke good Russian, but he seemed quiet and ill-at-ease: they did everything to make him feel welcome and honored. His future was assured. A flat in the select block in central Moscow reserved for high-ranking Party members, a small dacha at Zhukova, a job with the Ministry of the Interior, and the companionship of other Englishmen like himself.

John Kidson would also receive a coveted Soviet decoration for his services, but that was being kept as a surprise. By the evening, Madame Zerkhova had retired for a sleep before the final heavy meal, and Borisov took Kidson to the President's private office at the rear of the villa. There they held their conference: an old man running to fat in his lightweight summer suit, his big head sunk into his shoulders like a buffalo at rest; the trim Director of the KGB in white trousers and a stylish cotton sports shirt that had come to Moscow via Rome—Borisov had a liking for Italian clothes, and the Englishman who had taken his wife to Paris and walked out of the hotel the second morning, promising to meet her for lunch at the famous Petit Escargot, and got a plane to West Berlin instead. From West Berlin he had been brought to Moscow, and by that time

Charlie had his message and was on her way back to London. He had asked her to forgive him. And told her what to do if she decided to follow him. He knew beyond hope that he would never get an answer. He carried a snap of her with his baby son taken in the garden at Marchwood. It was already creased and dog-eared from handling.

He was asked by Borisov to explain where London got their information about Harrington. Before he answered, he was aware that this was not a simple question. Both men waited in expectant silence. He told them. Through the British embassy in Moscow, and the leak had come to them direct from the Soviet Foreign Ministry. The leak was officially inspired, with the consent of the Minister. It wasn't through a British security contact. Borisov said nothing. Zerkhov nodded and said, "ah," several times. For twenty years Kidson had been reading other men's minds and motives.

He had accomplished what was wanted. He had given them proof against the hard-liner Rudzenko. He realized suddenly that this was why they had brought him out. His personal testimony was needed. A wave of sick despair engulfed him as he reflected on the motive behind the ruin of his life. He would be the means of putting a rival out of the way. For that, not for his safety, he had been uprooted and would live the rest of his life alone. He was shown to his room, while Borisov and the old man remained behind. Loneliness and isolation closed in upon him as if he were in a prison cell.

"It is all recorded," Zerkhov said. "Now we can move. What will you do, son? No scandal, remember. No division in the Party. The wounds must all be healed before the conference."

"Trust me," Borisov said. "I have the man who will deal with this. And if there are questions afterward, we have the evidence."

Zerkhov sighed. He felt tired, but the guest had to be entertained. "He looks unhappy," he remarked, moving his head to the left, to the door where Kidson had gone out. "His wife should have come. It makes it difficult for men like him when they are alone. What was she like?"

"Red hair," Borisov said. "Very beautiful. They had a little son."

"Find him someone," the old man rumbled. "He needs comfort. And his replacement?"

"He will be told what he must do," Borisov said. "He won't dare to resist when he knows what is at stake. All that we'll need is a little tug on the string now and then to remind him."

"Blackmail," Zerkhov mused. "The price human beings pay for their stupidity."

"Or for love," Borisov said. "I've given him the code name Scorpio. I've changed from birds to the zodiac. I think it's an appropriate choice. Don't worry about our friend. There are many beautiful Russian girls with red hair, if that's what he likes. He'll enjoy his new life with us."

He got up, and the old man looked at him, a brief smile touching his lips. "It's been well done," he said. "All that's left is to get rid of Rudzenko. Then I can sleep in peace, and so can Russia. Dinner is in an hour."

It was a long summer. The fine weather persisted well into autumn, delaying the start of nature's yearly sleep, giving a respite to that part of her which had to die. The leaves didn't fall and the flowers bloomed on past their time. It was mid-October when Davina walked through the narrow passageway off Birdcage Walk and into the cul-de-sac called Anne's Yard. She looked tanned and some years younger than her age, and her entry through the main hall drew glances that were curious as well as complimentary. She went up in the old-fashioned elevator to the second floor and down the corridor to the familiar office, where James White's secretary, Phyllis, got up and welcomed her. "Good morning, Miss Graham. You're looking very well."

"Thank you," Davina said. "We had marvelous weather."

"The Chief is expecting you," Phyllis said, and went back behind her desk.

He was reading the *Telegraph* when she came in, lounging at ease in one of the leather armchairs used by visitors. He put the paper aside and came to meet her. He took her outstretched hand and held it, to her dismay. He saw that she was uneasy, and he laughed. "I may congratulate you, my dear," he said, "but I'm not going to kiss you. I know you wouldn't appreciate it." The frosty eyes were twinkling with amusement. He pointed to his desk. It was a theatrical gesture that annoyed her. "There," he said, "ready and waiting for you. Sit down and see how it feels."

"Sir James," Davina said quietly, "I don't have to behave like an idiot, sitting at the desk. Did you have a good holiday?"

"Excellent," he replied. "Mary and I both loved Spain. She's making noises about buying a flat and escaping the English winter. And I needn't ask how you enjoyed Florida. It obviously suited you. Did you do much sailing?"

"We went round the Keys, which was great fun," she said. "It's a marvelous place for a holiday."

"And you come home relaxed and ready to take up my burden," he said. "What does your friend think of it?"

Davina smiled slightly. "He thinks I'm mad," she said simply. "He offered me three times the salary to stay on with him. Plus trips to Florida and Australia and anywhere else that's going."

"I'm glad you weren't tempted," James White said. "He must be doing very well in his new business."

"He is." She sat down, searched her bag for a cigarette; he gave her a light from a handsome gold Cartier lighter.

"A present from Humphrey and the staff," he said, seeing her look. "Very extravagant of them. Humphrey will be in later to see you. I wanted the first hour to myself. You'll keep Phyllis on, won't you?"

"So long as she wants to stay," Davina answered. "She may not like working for someone else after being with you for so long."

"She'll see you settled in anyway," he said. "She's a very good person and I think you'll get on. How are the family?" He didn't quite look at her as he asked.

Davina shrugged. "Wrapped up in Charlie and the baby," she said quietly. "They still can't make up their minds who is most to blame, me or Kidson."

"I'm sorry about that," he said. "I'll go down and see them if you like."

"It wouldn't do any good." She shook her head. "All they can see is my sister being left flat with the little boy. They wouldn't thank you for saying it was partly my fault for finding Kidson out. But thanks for offering."

"They'll come round," he said. "People always do in the end. You did the right thing. After all, if your sister is so lost without him, she can go to Russia. We won't put any obstacles in the way. She knows that."

Davina glanced up at him. "Can you see Charlie in Moscow? I can't."

"Nor can she." His tone was brisk, dismissing the subject. "She'll find another husband and the whole business will be forgotten. The news on him is satisfactory, by the way. He's drinking himself to death out there. They can't even employ him anymore."

"Why did you let him go?" Davina asked him. "You must have known that taking Charlie to Paris was the first leg of the journey out. Why didn't you stop him?"

James White leaned back, balancing his fingers tip to tip, making an arch with them. "I had to make a choice," he said after a pause. "The sort of choice you'll have to make in the future. A colleague who'd betrayed us, against a political advantage. Not just to us, but to the West in general. I was asked to let Kidson leave."

She stared at him. "Asked? By whom?"

"My opposite number, Igor Borisov. Indirectly, of course. They needed him to provide evidence against a man who had passed us information. Also indirectly. Yuri Rudzenko."

"Who died last month," Davina said slowly.

"Exactly. The enemy of détente, the worst kind of Stalinist fanatic. I thought letting Kidson go and live in Moscow was worth the price of getting rid of him. You would agree, I hope?"

"Yes," she said after a moment. "I would have done the same."

"I know you would," James White said. "I knew you could make the right decisions after Harrington was killed."

She frowned. "I don't see why," she said. "It went wrong. Not the way I planned at all."

He shook his head. "It went *right*," he retorted. "You took a risk and you knew deep down that they might murder Harrington, even if you didn't admit it to yourself. You had to expose Albatross, and you did, by throwing him Harrington as bait. It's that kind of dedication that's needed if you're going to run the Service."

"Ruthlessness," she said slowly. "That's what you mean. That's what Colin couldn't take. He couldn't take what happened to Harrington."

"He couldn't take your responsibility for it," James White said. "Not many men could cope with that. How will it affect your friend? Have you thought about that?"

"Tony and I have a different relationship," Davina answered. "He has his life, his family, and his business. I have my job. We're not going to live in each other's pockets; we'll be together when we can. It'll work out."

"I hope so," he said mildly. "Now . . . Humphrey."

"Yes," she said. "Tell me about him. Is he going to stay on?"

"I persuaded him to do so," James White said. "He was upset, of course. But he's a good chap, you know. Very responsible, very loyal. In the end I convinced him that you couldn't do without him. Nor could you, not for a long time." He said it as a flat statement that she couldn't contradict. "You'll need to get your team together. I've drawn up a list of people you might consider, with comments. There's an outsider from Bristol University. Young man, very bright. You could give him a try as a personal assistant if you like. I can recommend him."

"You seem to have done all my work for me," she said. "You won't be offended if I pick my own PA? I'll see your man, of course."

"I hoped you would," he said. "His name is Johnson. Rather an abrasive type, but with an original mind. I think you'll like him."

"I doubt it," Davina said. "He sounds too much like me." She saw the disarming smile appear.

"You'll mellow, Davina. You'll learn to manipulate people instead of meeting them head-on. It will give me a certain amount of amusement to watch it happen. Be patient with Humphrey; he'll sulk for a time, but he'll never let you down. I'm going to be on my way quite soon. Anything you would like to know? Any help at all?"

She got up. It was an awkward moment for her, and she felt embarrassed. "Tell me," she said suddenly. "Knowing how I felt about you, Chief, why did you recommend me for this job?"

He put his head on one side, regarding her with the twinkle and the empty smile. "Because you're by the far the cleverest of all the candidates," he said. "And I believe in that old cliché about the female being deadlier than the male. You will give Igor Borisov a run for his money. It will be very interesting to see who wins. Good-bye, my dear. I may be out to grass, but I shall hope to keep in touch. Good luck."

He held out his hand and she took it. They shook hands. It was suddenly formal, almost stagey. He went to the door, closed it behind him, and Davina was alone in the office. She stood still for a moment. The room was very quiet; no sound of traffic reached the windows from the distant street. The watercolor of the Whites' house had gone; so had the hunting prints. She wondered what she could put on the walls to replace them. Then she went around and pulled out the chair and sat down at the big mahogany desk.

He looked very glum, Ronnie decided. When the boy was depressed, he used the old-fashioned adjective, although these days he was happier than he had ever been. He didn't like to see Humphrey slumped in his chair, long body twisted up, long legs twined around each other. He had brought him a stiff drink and they settled down to their presupper ritual of talking over what had happened during the day. Ronnie's day was typical of the pattern that had developed during the summer. He had taken over the management of the apartment, down to the last domestic detail; he was careful with his friend's money, a promising cook who enjoyed experimenting, and meticulously tidy. Little touches—bright cushions, a cheerful potted plant—made the austere flat bloom with color. Ronnie did everything for Humphrey; he reckoned that he owed him so much that nothing was too much trouble. There was no more talk of finding a job. He didn't mention it because it only alarmed and even irritated his friend.

They had spent a ten-day holiday in northern France, and Ronnie couldn't stop talking about the experience. He had no idea what Humphrey's job entailed, but he accepted the explanation about the civil service without having the least idea what it meant.

"Had a bad day today?"

Humphrey shook his head. He didn't want to upset Ronnie. The boy was so sensitive and inclined to think he was the cause if

Humphrey's mood was low. "Not too bad," he said. "What about you?"

Ronnie wasn't to be diverted this time. "Same as usual. What's the matter, aren't you feeling well?"

Humphrey glanced at the anxious young face. He had never confided fully to anyone in his life. He couldn't and wouldn't do so now, but he went a little way, just to stop the boy worrying about him. "Well, I'll tell you," he said. "I've got a new boss. It's rather a blow to me, because I thought I might have got the job. That's all. Nothing to bother about." He smiled and went on, "I'll have another sherry. That'll cheer me up."

Ronnie got up and hurried to get it for him. The worried expression was deeper when he came back. "Humphrey," he said, and went red as he spoke, "it's not because of me, is it? You not getting the job, I mean?"

"Good heavens." Humphrey sat up quickly. "Don't be silly! Of course it's not. Why should it be?"

Ronnie looked down and shuffled awkwardly. "Well, it might be," he insisted. "Me living here. I don't want to cause you any trouble . . . you've been so good to me."

He turned away, and Humphrey saw to his horror that the boy was in tears. He sprang up from the chair. He had come back from his interview with Davina wearing his disappointment and depression like a flag at half-mast. No wonder Ronnie was upset, thinking he was responsible. He put his arm around the boy's shoulders. "Listen to me," he said. "I lost the job to a woman; that's what riled me. I don't like her and I've got to work under her, but I'll get used to it. It was just pride, that's all. Ronnie, I swear to you, your living here has nothing to do with anybody but us. We're friends, and it's nobody else's bloody business. . . . For God's sake, what would I do without you now?"

"Somebody else would look after you," Ronnie said simply.

"Not like you do," replied Humphrey gently. "You mean more to me than any job. Now, go and get yourself a handkerchief and come and we'll have our drink together like we always do. Never mind." He pulled his neatly folded handkerchief out of his breast pocket. "Here, take mine, I haven't used it."

He turned away and picked up his drink. He couldn't bear to see the boy cry. It gave him a physical pain, like a jab in the stomach. He knew that Ronnie was right. He didn't have to know about Humphrey's real work to see the outside world for what it was. A cold, intolerant place, where neither of them was at home.

He said, "There's nothing on earth would make me give you up, so just remember that. And don't let's talk like this again. It upsets me too." He's like a child, he thought, the tears all gone and that cheery grin taking over.

"I'm ever so glad," Ronnie said. "We'll have a cozy evening to make up for it." He raised a glass with a little of the sour sherry he didn't like much, and Humphrey drank a silent toast.

"You'll have to get another flat," Tony Walden said. "I'll find one for you." She turned to him in the bed and nestled into his shoulder. After they made love he liked to talk. He seemed revitalized, his extraordinary energy restored instead of diminished.

"Stop organizing my life," she murmured. "I'll find my own flat. Besides, what's wrong with this one? You haven't complained before." She closed her eyes and drifted hazily; she was tired and deeply happy.

"It's poky," Walden said. "Dull. I'm going to give you a nice apartment to celebrate your exalted status, my darling. And you're going to live in it with me. Don't go to sleep."

She raised her head and smiled. "Why shouldn't I? It's two in the morning."

"A flat near Belgrave Square," he went on. "Close to your office, and not too far from mine. I'll have it decorated for you. Wouldn't that be nice?"

"No," Davina murmured. "I like Marylebone."

"I don't," he said. "It's too full of Colin Lomax."

She came wide-awake at once. "You're not serious? We've been coming here for months, before we went to Florida. You never said anything before." She sat up and stared at him; the bedside light was still on. He refused to make love in the dark.

"I didn't want to rock the boat," he said. "I wanted to make sure of you first. I don't feel at home here; let's find somewhere else, somewhere that begins with us, instead of you and someone else."

"All right," she said. "If that's how you feel, I'll move. You should have told me before. But I'm not taking a flat from you, darling. I'm not taking anything. We'll choose a place together, that's a promise."

"Why won't you let me spoil you?" He tilted her face toward him and kissed her. "I'm making so much money, and you won't let me give you anything."

"Tony darling," she murmured. "I'm not a mink-and-diamond type. Your idea of a nice little flat would make me feel thoroughly uncomfortable. I don't want the millionaire life-style. I just want to be alone with you whenever we can manage it. If you're unhappy here, we'll go somewhere else."

He stroked her hair; he told her how silky it was and how he loved the reddish color. He paid her compliments about her face and body until she felt beautiful because he insisted that she was. He swept her along on his own tide of energy and enthusiasm and he told her over and over again how much he loved her. He discussed everything with her, from disagreements at home to major policy decisions in his flourishing agency. Everything Walden touched was galvanized into success. He had lost one account with an oil sheikhdom, but won another from their oldest rival. He turned disaster into triumph, and the only arguments she had with him were over presents she wouldn't accept, from a diamond ring to a Mercedes car.

"Why aren't you like other women?" he demanded. "Why aren't you just a little bit greedy?"

"I am," Davina said. "As you won't let me go to sleep, here's something you can give me. . . ." She said to him later, when daylight was breaking through the curtains, "I'm frightened of something, Tony."

"You're not frightened of anything," he scoffed at her. "Except spiders—remember the fuss you made when I found that little one on the wall over there? I told you, spiders are lucky, but you made me get rid of it. What are you frightened of, my darling? Tell me, and I'll make it go away."

She raised her arms above her head. The ceiling was smudged in the center where a lamp had been removed. It was a shabby place, and he was right. She'd lain in that bed and seen the same mark with Colin Lomax. "I'm afraid of what this job may do to me," she said suddenly. "I don't want to turn into a female version of James White. You won't let it happen to me, will you?"

"I don't see how it could," he said softly. "But even so, how can I stop it? You have one of the most important jobs in the country. You're the first woman to hold it. This isn't the time for scruples, Davina. You won't be a James White. You'll be Davina Graham."

She didn't accept it; she moved restlessly and sighed. "If you see signs," she said, "for God's sake, tell me, Tony. Whether I like it or not."

"I promise," he said, "if you're serious."

She looked at him and said, "I'm very serious. You mightn't like it if I changed. It won't be easy not to. I can see that, and it worries me. I don't want anyone to hate me as much as I hate James White."

"Still?" he asked her.

"Always," she answered. "Nothing will change that."

"I must get up," Walden announced. "I have an appointment at eight-fifteen." She lay back while he pulled the curtains and the room flooded with daylight. "It's my birthday today," he said. He stretched and flexed his arms. He had a fine muscled body, heavy-chested. "Forty-six. Four years off fifty; do you think I'm too old for you?"

She slipped out of bed and came to him. "Why didn't you tell me? Happy birthday, darling."

He held her close. "I want to spend it with you," he said. "But I can't. There's a family party arranged for tonight. I shall miss you."

He kissed her; she saw the unhappiness in his eyes. It lurked there under the ebullience, the quick wit. She remembered another man whose moods could change as rapidly. That was what made me fall in love with him, that shifting sadness underneath the laughter.

"Tomorrow?" she asked.

He nodded. "Tomorrow. That will be my real birthday."

She stopped on her way to Anne's Yard. He was a difficult person to buy anything for; she wandered through Dunhill's, rejecting the wallets and expensive knickknacks which he already owned in triplicate.

It was a salesman that solved the problem for her. "Birthday," he said. "These are very popular." It was useless, she knew, but beautiful. It gleamed inside a heavy crystal globe. "They make very attractive paperweights," he went on. "October 24. That would be this one. I think it's one of the best." Davina picked it up. The little gold figure glittered inside its crystal prison.

"Scorpio. His zodiac sign," Davina said. "I think my friend would like that." She could afford it on her new salary. She understood why he was always trying to give her things. There was a special pleasure in giving a present to the person you loved.